The Bingo Queens of Paradise

The Bingo Queens of Paradise

JUNE PARK

HarperCollins*Publishers*

HarperCollins_Publishers_

First published in the USA in 1999 by HarperCollins_Publishers_ Inc.
First published in Australia in 1999
by HarperCollins_Publishers_ Pty Ltd
ACN 009 913 517
A member of the HarperCollins_Publishers_ (Australia) Pty Limited Group
http://www.harpercollins.com.au

Text Copyright © June Park 1999
Cover design and illustration © Honi Werner 1999

HarperCollins_Publishers_
25 Ryde Road, Pymble, Sydney NSW 2073, Australia
31 View Road, Glenfield, Auckland 10, New Zealand
77–85 Fulham Palace Road, London W6 8JB, United Kingdom
Hazelton Lanes, 55 Avenue Road, Suite 2900, Toronto, Ontario M5R 3L2
and 1995 Markham Road, Scarborough, Ontario M1B 5M8, Canada
10 East 53rd Street, New York NY 10022, USA

National Library of Australia Cataloguing-in-Publication data:

Park, June, 1934 –
The bingo queens of paradise.
ISBN 0 7322 6540 1
I. Title
813.54

Printed in Australia by Griffin Press Pty Ltd on 70gsm Ensobelle

7 6 5 4 3 2 1
02 01 00 99

Dedicated to my husband, John.
Without you, this wouldn't be possible.
I am blessed.

Acknowledgments

I am eternally grateful to Bonnie Spear and Jack Bickham for fanning the flame.

To Prairie Wind Writers and Central Oklahoma Roundtable of Authors, I owe more than I can ever put into words for their unflagging friendship and support. Many thanks to my wonderful agent, Bob Tabian, for finding me a fantastic publisher. I am forever obliged to Diane Reverand and the staff at Cliff Street Books/HarperCollins.

Once Upon a Time

. . . .

Paradise, Oklahoma. 1976.

It's Friday night, and Momma's going dancing, so I'll be in charge of Rhonda and Granny again. And when the Rialto closes, when Mr. Jarvis has cleaned up the soda fountain and locked up his drugstore, and the traffic light keeps switching from red to green to yellow for whoever the hell happens by, Preacher Maples will wrestle in the dark with Momma.

The sun's gone down, but it went to one hundred and two degrees today so it's still mighty hot up here. The black metal floor lamp is lit, and on the table next to Momma's ashtray are our leftovers: slices of bread, curled at the corners, warm cherry Kool-Aid, and a few Good Time Baked Beans stuck to our plates.

Me and Rhonda just got outa the tub. I was supposed to wash us and dry us top to bottom, but I skipped parts, so our watery footprints, mine first, Rhonda's kinda pigeon-toed, dog each other across the gritty floor. And we still stink. Not of sweat or Ivory soap, 'cause Ivory costs too much, but of Daisy Fresh which Momma says is just as good but ain't 'cause it gets slimy in the water and makes me and Rhonda smell like two rusty skillets.

Her hair is almost dry, my black curls are dripping wet, and our drawers, which ain't seen white in a trillion years, are stuck in the cracks of our butts. We stretch across the back of the orange sofa, Rhonda's sweaty legs curled around mine, and we stare down at Main Street, at two lines of cars and trucks creeping along with their lights on, at folks roaming about in shirts, shorts, and sandals, laughing and smoking.

We live over Macy's Hardware Store. The smell of paint gets into our oatmeal and a fine layer of dust covers our floors, but we can see lots of stuff from up here.

"Close the window," I tell Rhonda, "or them hard little June bugs'll fly in our hair."

"Momma says they send folks crazy, like Granny," she says, scratching the mosquito bite on her butt.

"Granny ain't crazy. Got a lot on her mind, is all."

"What's on at the movies?"

"*Bambi*. See them two girls in line with their mommas? They're in my class. Cindy Harker's the one with white patent leather shoes— Henrietta's are black. Elijah said Henrietta's daddy is rich 'cause he buries all the dead folk 'round here."

"Yuk."

"Momma said if we didn't eat for a month I could have a pair of those shoes. I said that was okay with me, but she must've forgot 'cause we're still eating."

"I want black, too."

"It's agin the law for six-year-olds to wear patent leather. You gotta be eight, like me."

"You lie like a rug, Darla."

I pretend I don't hear her. "Stupid the way Cindy and Henrietta are all doodied up. Them starched dresses'll be creased and ugly when they come back out."

"I wanna see *Bambi*."

"We seen it already."

"That's what you said about *Snow White* and that was a lie."

"Was not, and shut that window." I leave her to the sofa with its torn cushions, her forehead wrinkled, her chin cupped in her hands, the Rialto's lights reflecting in her eyes.

Granny's in bed and her lamp's turned off. She's finished counting her invisible frogs and she's watching Channel 3. There ain't no Channel 3 hereabouts, but the flickering screen and the crackling noises is how The Planet of Headbreakers sends her "Divine messages from God."

See, when Granny got sick after birthing my momma, the doctors in Arkansas drilled holes in her head and shot her into the mind of God, and He made her Keeper of the Frogs, something only me and her understands. And when folks ask, I tell them that's not a wire coat hanger on Granny's head, it's an honest-to-God, planet-to-earth antenna, that every night, sure as the world, she's gotta wrap her legs in newspaper and twine so her red, white, and blue blood cells don't get radiated.

Momma steps outa the tub, hair burning like fire under the glare of the bulb. She runs her fingers across her waist and over her breasts, rakes 'em through her hair, pulls wisps across her forehead and over her pink ears, pats Woolworth's talcum powder into her belly button with a blue fuzzy puff, presses the top of a black, diamond-studded bottle. The smell of the Avon lady's Occur perfume explodes into the steam and heat.

Momma's every step is recorded in the black and white linoleum. Outlined by drifts of talc, her smudged footprints shuffle forward, backward, and side to side as she admires herself in the mirror. Wish she looked more like them church ladies who bring us their kids' worn-out clothes. Their skin's so white they prob'ly sweat milk, but their hips don't wiggle and they don't wear short red dresses on Friday and Saturday night. I love what Momma wears to Bingo, though, them scoop-necked tops and the flowery skirts that dance with her sandals—

but I hate her girlfriends. Loud, they are, with tapping feet, snapping fingers, and eyes like Momma's, the kind that hanker after cold beer, black undies, and fat old uncles.

Momma slides her feet into black stockings, catches the fronts and backs in the tabs of a frilly belt. Black bra, black shoes with high pencil heels come next. She wiggles into a tight red dress with slits up the sides, snaps on a pair of red earrings. Dancing stuff.

"Wash the dishes, Darla," she says, running a comb through her hair," and *don't* go to Elijah for *anything*, understand?"

"But he loves us."

"Love, hell. Don't want him in my business."

"He's my best friend."

"Ain't mine. Go to him again and you're in big trouble."

Heels clicking, curls bouncing, she heads for her bedroom, a dark smoky place with heavy green curtains and a velvet picture of Elvis. Last year, she went some place to hear him sing, but the uncle who babysitted us got drunk and Elijah had to take care of me and Rhonda till Momma got back—a week later.

She grabs her makeup bag and sits on the bed. "Ain't fittin', two little white girls all the time hanging 'round a nappy-headed nigger."

Hate her, hate her, hate her. "He ain't no nigger, Momma. He's a black man. Smart, too. Told me to follow m'heart."

"Shows how stupid he is. Other than pumping blood, the heart's a sorry organ."

"And he believes in angels."

"Angels, shit."

"They don't either. Angels don't do anything people do. Don't even eat or sleep. Elijah says so."

"Elijah says so, Elijah says so."

"Granny loves Elijah."

"Granny don't know dog doo from shark meat."

"She does so."

"We move from Railway Road to better ourselves, and here comes Elijah with his pussy-pink lips, sets himself down not a hundred yards away, like we can't live without him."

"I can't."

Momma curls up her top lip. "Well I can."

"Who's Pussy Pink?"

"Huh?"

"You said Elijah's got Pussy Pink's lips."

"Woman I know."

"And I thought we moved here 'cause we was thrown outa the house on Railway Road."

"Never been thrown outa any place. Leave when I'm ready."

"And if Elijah's stupid, how come we couldn't rent this place 'til he signed the papers?"

"Darla—"

I sit beside her and hug m'knees. She lays a blue towel across her lap, unzips the plastic makeup bag, and looks into the mirror with blue flowers on the back. She spreads cream on her face, makes her cheeks rosy, dabs on powder, brushes her eyelashes with dark brown goo, and smears her eyelids with Vaseline. Now she's stretching her mouth, smearing top and bottom with Coty's Red Satin. She don't smile at her reflection on account she's got two bad teeth up front. They're black near the gum, like mine.

"What if Granny wants outside?"

"She watching Channel 3?"

"Yep."

"She got her legs wrapped?"

"Yep."

"Won't go anyplace then, will she?"

Momma returns everything to the plastic pouch and slides it inside a red shiny handbag with skinny shoulder straps. She fires up a Camel with her Elvis lighter. "Will she, Darla?"

"What if Rhonda throws up?"

"She won't."

"She might, she's allergic."

"To tuna. She had tuna?"

"Nope."

"Then she won't throw up, will she?"

"What if she's allergic to baked beans but we don't know it yet? What if she starts puking all over the place?"

Momma's lips go tight and thin, like sticks of blood. She grabs my arm and shakes it. "Listen to me," she says, "I'm going out and you're in charge, hear?"

"Yes'm."

She lets me go. "Be in bed by ten. I'll be back near twelve."

I could say I saw an old man hiding in the bushes out back, that he's waiting for her to leave so he can break in and kill us, cut us up into iddy biddy pieces and flush us down the toilet. I could say it's scary when the movie house lets out and those rowdy boys race their cars up and down Main Street—how when they're gone, the blacktop turns dark and mean as Rattler's Creek. I could, but she won't listen.

Hips swinging, she heads out the door. "Uncle Maples will be here 'round midnight. Be asleep, y'hear?"

Uncle Maples is the potbellied preacher from Big Bow, Oklahoma, wherever the hell that is. He's the nice old man who helps pay the rent and brings us boxes of oranges when it's not even Christmas, who wrestles in the dark with Momma.

A slap in the face wakes me up. Rhonda's flailing about, her face as shiny and white as candle wax. I'm sweating and I gotta use the bathroom. The attic fan sounds like the midnight freight—like it's running over the same stretch o' track again and again. Black as a gopher hole in here, but I won't bump into anything 'cause every chair leg, every turn and door is listed in my head. I know which knob waits to punish and which knob bears the weight of a man's pants, its pockets heavy with change. Momma's door is open. I know she's asleep 'cause air is whistling outa her nose like wind through a crack.

I flick on the bathroom switch, and there's Preacher Maples, nary a stitch on, not even socks, sitting on our toilet, head thrown back, mouth open, his eyes fixed on the light bulb. His chubby legs are so short his feet don't reach the floor. Not one part of him is moving, so I'm thinking he might not be preaching no more, either.

I smell roses, and the noise behind me is the same one I heard over on Railway Road, the rustling, clicking sound of a million feathers getting ready to fly. Over my shoulder I see Shamir, my guardian angel, wings spread over his head. Part heat, part haze, he's floating two feet off the ground. I turn, and we smile at each other, same way we did the first time we met. He reaches down, takes my hands in his, and *poof!* He's gone.

I yell for Momma. She don't even cry when she sees what's happened to Uncle Maples. She just stands between Granny and Rhonda, bare-ass nekkid, stinking of beer and smoke.

"Poor old thing," she says, her eyes blinking like the light's too bright. "Reckon his fat little heart just plumb gave out, don't you, girls?"

"Reckon so," I say, though I don't know nothing 'bout hearts or how they plumb give out.

Momma lights up a Camel, sucks hard and puffs out a smoke ring. "Darla," she says. "Go get Elijah."

Granny, a box of invisible frogs tucked under her arm, trembles inside her cotton nightie and says, "Well, ain't that a sight," and Rhonda whispers, "I want my Daddy," even though we ain't had one of them in a coon's age. She's scared, I reckon, but I ain't. I snucked into Bolton's Funeral Parlor a while back and got a good look at dead folk—two old ladies, their heads on satin pillows, all fixed up in jewelry and lace like they was off to a wedding. Which makes me think what this uncle'll look like with his eyes closed, wearing his Sunday-Go-To-Meeting suit and tie. Fact is, if Henrietta's daddy can shut that mouth good and paint a nice smile on his face, they could prop him up in the pulpit and no one'd know he'd met his maker till it came time to pray out loud.

Wonder who'll take Preacher Maples's place on Friday nights? Wonder if he'll bring us oranges and pay our rent—and wrestle in the dark with Momma? And when me and Rhonda are all grown up with kids of our own, I wonder if we'll remember standing here in the middle of the night, staring at a nekkid dead man with two blue feet?

Big Bucks Bingo

. . . .

June 1996.

Wednesday night and here we sit, two hundred folks, more or less, our butts glued to gray metal chairs. We're pumped up and ready, armed to the eyeballs with our wages, unemployment money, and workmen's comp benefits, and, I might add, cursed with the primitive intellect of blind rabbits in a sandstorm, 'cause we believe we're here to win a fortune. Failing that, we'll settle for a dinky Tappan microwave, a twelve-inch G.E. black-and-white TV, or a three-speed Sunbeam mixer. Which means, we'll all concentrate on the stakes at hand as if our breathing depends on it. Not a friggin' soul is worried about tomorrow, how they'll buy groceries, how they'll gas up, or how they'll pay the overdue phone bill. Tomorrow is God's problem. If not God's, then unsuspecting friends and relatives, or those uppity, tight-assed welfare folk.

Momma, a purple-and-orange muumuu flouncing around her knees, totters in on high-heeled sandals mumbling under her breath.

"Those crazy Englishwomen will be the death of me," she says. "Freda drives like she's got her tail caught up in a wringer."

An audible hum of expectation merges with the sound of metal chairs being hauled across the sticky floor. The bombing, the drought, and Oprah for President are not on the agenda today; neither is the young Tulsa boy whose stepfather burned him with cigarettes and beat him to death with a tire iron. No sir, no room for politics or other folks' misery when microwaves, TVs, and three-speed mixers are at stake.

Lot of fat people here. At the table to my left sits a three-hundred-pound heart attack. He's stuffing himself with ketchup-drenched French fries while his equally obese wife attacks a foot-long hot dog smothered with chili and cheese. Everyone is smoking or eating. Momma does both with the rhythmic ease of a juggler, but she hasn't ordered yet.

"Makes me madder'n hell," she says, "seeing our table in enemy hands."

She means the four middle-aged women in floral polyester, their pearl necklaces swinging like trapezes. Momma, her graying red hair in a ponytail, her Sally Hansen eyelashes flapping, her Lee Press-On Nails drumming the table, studies the intruders with flinty-eyed suspicion—as if they're about to jerk the pin from a live grenade.

"That's my lucky table," she says. "I always sit there."

"Well, you were late and I was late, so I grabbed the closest one."

"Close won't cut it. Wait till Muff and Freda get here. It's their lucky table too."

"They won't care." The smell of old grease, fried onions, Momma's Jungle Gardenia, and fatty hamburgers, not to mention the smoke, would repel a skunk, and the coffee is foul. Tastes like it was brewed in a barrel.

Momma's right. When Freda and Muff arrive, they look from one table to the other, their mouths hung open.

"Why the hell are you sitting here?" Freda asks. She looks clownish in her baggy plaid shorts and black knee-high socks.

"Darla said ours was already taken," Momma says, "that you wouldn't care."

Freda throws her red-and-white Oklahoma University cap on the floor. "Well, I care one hell of a lot."

"What do you want me to do?" I ask. "Make 'em move?"

Freda nods. "Of course, dear."

"Well, I won't. Folks sit where they want."

"Where they want," Muff echoes in a prim English voice. "Our names aren't on that table."

Freda stares at her. "Who asked you, Miss Nose Ache?"

Muff, equally weird in a pink frilly blouse, a short red flared skirt, and pink ballet slippers, ribbons crisscrossed, ballerina-style, around her chubby calves—replies, "Nobody asked me. I speak when I feel like it."

"Go get your cards and cool it," Momma says, "or you'll jinx us, sure as hell."

They march off, Freda swinging her ornate walking stick back and forth, Muff padding behind her, their spines stiff with irritation.

Momma starts unloading her necessities. "Y'know, I've tried to imagine those two flailing about under the sheets, all sweaty, but the picture just won't come."

"Thank God for small favors." Seeing Momma's big black purse reminds me she made house calls when she was a whore, that she carried a doctorlike bag with thick handles. She'd drive off in some strange man's car, her eyes sparkling and full of dare, waving like the queen of England—like she was on her way to a garden party instead of a quick screw. Her dates, wanting me and Rhonda to think they were mere acquaintances, sat awkward and quiet behind the wheel, staring straight ahead. When they took off, though, they'd slip an arm around Momma's shoulder. Sometimes, as they turned the corner, I'd see Momma's hand pop out the open window, her fingers extended, wiggling, like she was reaching for something beyond her grasp—the brass ring, or a shaft of sunlight, maybe.

Momma, still standing, sips coffee from a tall Styrofoam cup. "They'll kill each other one of these days, and I'll die in the crossfire, you see if I'm not right."

I say, "I doubt it," even though Muff and Freda have been fighting since they arrived here from England fourteen years ago. They call themselves Clairvoyants, Interpreters of Dreams, and Tea Leaf Readers Extraordinaire. When they're not planting, gathering, or mailing off their herbs, they tell fortunes with Ouija boards, tarot cards, and tea leaves—or the crystal ball they ordered from the World of Magic catalog. For twenty-five dollars, they'll hold a recreational séance at their kitchen table. "A bargain, my dear," Freda claims, "seeing as I serve complimentary spiced tea and imported English biscuits."

Momma lights up a Camel. "Wanna know what got 'em started tonight?"

"No."

"Muff said they were eating supper, mushrooms on toast or some godawful thing, when Mrs. Boles pulled up 'round back and asked for a palm reading, so—"

"The undertaker's wife?"

"Only one Mrs. Boles in Paradise, for Christ's sake."

"But she's Pentecostal now. Lamb of God'll run her out of the church for that."

"For what?"

"Dabbling in witchcraft."

"Witchcraft?"

"That's what Pentecostals call what Muff and Freda do."

"So they throw her out the church. Do you wanna hear what happened next or not?"

"Not."

"Well, when Mrs. Boles showed up for a palm reading, Muff and Freda both gave her one. Trouble is, they each came to a different conclusion. Freda started cussing, Muff started cussing, and shoves were exchanged—and Mrs. Boles left in a tizz-wazz. Said she'd never come back."

"Uh-huh."

"That's when Muff poured Lea & Perrin's mint sauce over Freda's new polyester pants."

I ignore her.

"Didn't speak all the way here."

"So leave 'em be."

"Freda was like an insane person. Skidded 'round corners, went over the speed limit. I thought any minute we'd land in a ditch."

Muff returns to the table and settles in her chair. Like a young girl seeking attention, she thrusts her cone-shaped breasts forward and tosses her bleached head with abandon until the short brassy curls bounce and quiver. Freda, a tall, square-shouldered woman with cropped gray hair, scans the crowd with feigned curiosity.

I could play peacemaker, I have many times, but not tonight. "Like those shoes, Freda. They new?"

"No, dear. Had them for years. Muff's the shoe freak. Put a shoe on every foot here, she could—assuming they like big black bows and rhinestones."

I watch a single tear well in Muff's eye and remember my sister— how when she phoned from a neighbor's trailer this morning she sounded weepy.

Think I'm coming down with the flu again, Darla. Got a
miserable headache. Pearl and Jessie missed school. Sump'n
they ate, I reckon.

My mind is awash. I gaze at a bald head across the aisle and wonder if the man ever had hair—if Rhonda really is ailing or if Frank's the problem. I settle for Frank.

"Y'sister's puny and can't afford a doctor," Momma says. "The kids are ailing, too. Frank's been spared, thank God."

"Thank God, my ass," I tell her. "Save your thanks for when he's dead and buried. He's as useless as a glass eye in a keyhole, for Christ's sake."

Momma flops into the empty chair between Muff and Freda. "Don't start, Darla."

The stones in her dangly earrings flash so hard and bright under the fluorescent light they blind me, and the words tumbling from her mouth rattle my head and make my teeth ache. I squeeze my eyes shut and colored sparks fly in all directions. Red. Orange. Purple. Yellow. Green. Blue.

Got a coupla cute little girls there, Roxie. How old?
Too young for you, you miserable sonovabitch.
Says who?
Says the law. You here on business or just wasting m'time, baby?

When Momma stops yakking I open my eyes. To her right, lined up at the one o'clock position, she's placed an open can of Sprite, her brass ashtray, a fresh pack of Camels, and the Elvis cigarette lighter. Her colored markers sit at three o'clock, along with two Moon Pies and Buster, her redheaded troll doll. Muff and Freda's good-luck charms are glass paperweights. Inside Muff's sits an impressive tarantula. A green lizard with startled eyes stares out of Freda's. Poor things. I'd like to smash the glass open and give the critters a decent burial down by Rattler's Creek.

"This here's a miracle," Momma says, and waves a five-dollar bill in the air. "Y'know why?"

Muff and Freda shake their heads.

"I do," I say. "That's my five-dollar bill, and it'll be a miracle if I ever get it back."

Freda slaps the table and laughs out loud. Muff giggles behind her hand.

Momma glares at each of us in turn. "It's a miracle because I'm about to turn this five dollars into at least a hundred. I feel it in my gut."

Unsnapping the waistband of her pants, Freda says, "Feel something in my gut, too. Muff's cooking. Those mushrooms she cooked tasted funny."

Muff grins, all innocence. "They looked odd when I picked them," she offers. "And in case you've forgotten, the Methodist Church serves senior citizen's dinners every day except Sunday, so eat there from now on, ducky—assuming you live through the night."

"I'll do that, deary." Freda's face is livid. "And I'll find someone to keep me company while I'm about it."

"Quiet," Momma hisses, "or we'll never hear the numbers."

The muscle in my left eye starts twitching, and that five-dollar bill starts doing a number on me.

I was almost fifteen, and I was on my way home after swimming in the Rattler with Dale and Millard Hoskins. Momma's car, an old Chevy with mismatched wheels, was gone, but Uncle Dave's car had turned up, and Momma had run him off days ago.

The minute I entered the house I heard a thumping noise. My eyes started adjusting to the light, and I spied movement in the kitchen. I blinked a couple of times, got things in focus, and saw Uncle Dave's back, saw he was bare-assed naked, saw his pants and undershorts gathered in an ugly pile around his ankles. Head thrown back and grunting like a pig, he kept shoving and pushing Rhonda against the fridge, which made it rock back and forth on the linoleum.

That's when I saw Rhonda—part of her, that is, her skinny white legs, bent at the knees, either side of Uncle Dave's rear end—him holding them up. I squeezed my eyes shut, pressed them together so tight I saw stars. I prayed over and over that when I opened my eyes I would see only the fridge door with its big silver handle—the smear of jam from my fingers the night before. Only when I summoned the courage to look again did I see Rhonda's thirteen-year-old face. She looked hot and flushed, her hair was askew and damp, and her eyes glittered with tears. With one finger pressed to her lips, she stared at me over Uncle Dave's shoulder as if to say, "Keep your mouth shut, Darla," and God forgive me, when I saw the five-dollar bill in her other hand, that's exactly what I did.

I ran to Granny's room, shoved cotton balls in my ears so I wouldn't hear the thumping, then, for what seemed like an eternity, I brushed out Granny's hair and hummed the national anthem as loud as I could. Just like that, I erased everything I'd seen from my mind—until now.

"What's gotten into you, girl?" Momma says. "They're about to start, and there you sit like a knot on a log."

I jump to my feet. Sweep the colored daubers into my purse. "Can't stay. Things I gotta do."

Momma glances up. "Like what?"

"Are you poorly, luv?" Muff asks. "Are you?"

"No, I'm fine, honest. Got things to do is all." I shake my purse and listen for keys. Nothing.

Freda rises from her chair and hitches up her pants. "What things, hon?"

"I'll play your cards," Momma says matter-of-factly.

"Use my cards and we split the winnings, or pay me for the cards," I tell her as I get down on my knees. The keys are under the table.

"Where you going?" Freda asks.

"Gonna buy luggage. Here I come New York."

Momma bats her Sally Hansen eyelashes. "Oh, no. Not again."

"Yes, again, Momma. We've got no business here, 'specially you. You draw disability and you're gambling with my money. You're friggin' poor, for Christ's sake. We're all poor. If we'd saved everything we've spent here, we'd have money in the bank."

"Paradise doesn't have a bank."

"Not anymore it doesn't, and it's 'cause of people like you and all these other idiots. The minute you get a dollar in your pocket you march down here and hand it over to the smart bastards who own this place. And y'know what they do with it? They deposit it in their bank accounts. It's a joke, Momma. A goddamned joke."

She looks puzzled. "So?"

"Soon as I've finished one wedding dress, two evening gowns, and a blue wool suit, I'm outa here—and don't forget you owe me five dollars for those cards. See y'later Freda, Muff. Kiss and make up, okay?"

"Five minutes to seven, ladies and gentlemen," someone says over the intercom, and there's a collective stampede for vacant seats. I zigzag in and out of the crowd.

"What in the hell brought this on?" Momma whines, right on my heels. "Something I said? Is it Rhonda? Frank? Are you mad 'cause I borrowed another twenty bucks from you? Is it on account I got a new boyfriend? What the hell's wrong, huh?"

I spin around, stare at her gaudy face—pond-green eyes ringed with kohl, mauve eye shadow, orange lipstick, plum lip liner, shiny earrings, hot swollen flesh ready to explode. "Stuff, Momma. Just stuff."

"Stuff?"

"Nightmare stuff, Momma. Stuff like blue feet, old uncles, and dead babies," I say, and she looks at me like I'm speaking Chinese.

I smile at the Wal-Mart checkout girl. "I'm moving to New York," I tell her.

Bucktoothed, she yawns. "That all for you today?"

"Reckon so."

Her black-varnished nails tap away at the register, and in a slower-than-death drawl she finally says, "Comes to sixty-five dollars and seventeen cents."

I glance at her name tag, count out the bills, and rifle through my change. "Ever been to New York, Reba?"

"Nope, and the thought of getting my throat slit in a drug bust or having my head blown off during a gang fight keeps me from thinking about such a dang fool thing—but to each his own." She yawns again, clearly too tired to cover her mouth, let alone stand unaided.

I slide the money closer. "Yeah, well, some folk aren't cut out for travel, are they? Bet you have a hard time finding your car when you get off work—let alone drive it home."

Within minutes, as me and Miss Ladybug, my polka-dot Volkswagen, advance on Paradise, the press of a button puts me in New York, front row center, Lincoln Center. Pavarotti starts singing Verdi's "Un Di Felice" from *La Traviata* as magnificently as I first heard him on Elijah's radio. I was a scrawny kid then, with no notion of what the words meant, but the powerful voice so overwhelmed me, I fell into Elijah's arms and wept. Listening to Pavarotti now, I am Darla Moon, Sewer of Seams, Dreamer of Dreams; I am Pavarotti's Mimi, his Madame Butterfly—Aïda, queen of his thoughts, light of his life.

Lincoln Center. Befitting the occasion, an exquisite strand of perfectly matched oriental pearls caresses my throat. I'm wearing the Lincoln Center Gown, my top secret Darling Darla Creation. Created from dusty-sapphire Renaissance silk with ruched leg-o'-mutton sleeves and a matching ten-foot stole, this masterpiece is worthy of a Michelangelo madonna.

Luciano is so stunned by the sight of me, so dazzled by my hair, by the unruly mass of Cher-like curls, and the tears in my eyes, he misses a note, God bless him.

I love the sound my tires make on the highway, how one minute they're humming my name, but when I switch to blacktop they start singing "New York, New York." I love the sound of my sandals on the steps leading up to my place over the bakery, the reassuring hum of the air conditioner—the ease with which my key turns in the lock—how, with just the flick of a switch, bolts of luminous silk and taffeta, and wool the color of blue lightning, zap my heart with promise.

I knew I'd leave Paradise someday, just wasn't sure how or when. I dreamed this dream as kids made fun of my secondhand shoes and my black gypsy hair, as night after night Momma came and went with this one or that one and her black leather bag. And as I ironed or fixed sandwiches for Rhonda and Granny, I imagined myself slipping sequined creations over Dolly Parton and Faye Dunaway's heads. While braiding Granny's hair, or changing Momma's sheets, or sweeping out the mud our uncles tracked in, I went onstage amid thunderous applause to receive Oscar after Oscar for my designs.

I put the suitcases on the cutting table, pop the silver locks, and raise the lids, imagine them packed and ready to go as I tear the wrapping from the Passion Red lipstick I bought. Will it look as good on my lips as it does in the tube? And who cares?

Where I'm headed, folks don't sweat the small stuff—they don't wait all year for the annual tractor pull, and they sure as hell don't get excited about Snout, Hoof, and Beak Barbecue Day. No siree. They're movers and shakers. They're out there grabbing life by the tailpipe and rushing headlong into the thick of things.

Our Town

. . . .

When a stranger wanders into Paradise, it's by mistake. No one 'cept transients, amnesiacs, and idiots would enter this hell hole on purpose, and those who say otherwise are cozied up to the Devil himself or his next of kin. It's the Kalahari Desert out there, a chaos of heat, glare, and biting gnats erupting like a boil on Satan's backside. Three in the afternoon, the first Monday in July, 102 in the shade. The sun bores into your skull like a steel spike. The land is so flat words don't echo— they float midair for a second or two then drop like bricks. Red-hot dust devils spin across the blacktop, career over barren fields, and disappear as magically as they arrived. Dogs bite their owners, storekeepers tell customers to go to hell, and if we reach 106 degrees today, as predicted by Gary England, weatherman on channel 9, Paradise could, 'fore sundown, burn to the ground like Sodom and Gomorrah.

The view from Momma's living room window is etched into my brain like a concentration camp number. Every blank-eyed window, every knotted board, every sun-bleached rock and stub of barbed wire grass, even Momma's beat-up old Pontiac, are gouged into my brain's surface with indelible ink.

The sign at the curb says, WELCOME TO PARADISE, POPULATION 927, a doubtful number seeing as it hasn't changed in nineteen years, proving, among other things, that no one around here keeps track of such stuff, or cares. Across the street, the Lamb of God Church sign says, JOIN US EVERY SUNDAY AND WEDNESDAY AND PRAY FOR THE RAPTURE, an invitation Momma sometimes accepts, but I never have, on account they expect a body to hoot and holler and tear about like a mindless lunatic "when the power falls."

Behind the wooden, one-room church, under five rows of chiseled headstones and an ocean of crab grass, lay forty-five dead folk, including seven children, who didn't hang around long enough to witness this rapture—and who can blame them? Paradise is no place to wait for any damn thing, least of all something as vague as a rapture, but wait we do—for everything.

We wait for miserable winters, ice storms, snow storms, and forty-mile-an-hour winds that roar across the plains 'cause there's nothing to stop them. Folks wait for the right time to plant crops. Come spring, when floods come, when row upon row of corn, beans, and tomatoes drown along with the worms, those same folks wait for floods to recede. Come summer, they're on their knees praying like hell for rain.

When it comes to dying, some folk wait on porches, feebly waving at passersby, their dentures slipping, their water-thin blood encouraged to flow by brightly-colored afghans. Those who can walk wait in Possum Perkins's Domino Parlor—dribbling tobacco juice and staring at dots through clouded eyes. Lem Silver, a man with the IQ of a mothball, got so antsy waiting for his Maker, he drove his tractor through a raging thunderstorm on his ninety-second birthday while praying for lightning to strike his ass. To Mrs. Silver's relief, God obliged. In one zillionth of a second, a couple hundred thousand volts transformed Lem into a slab of barbecue that filled every corner of Bolton's Funeral Parlor with the sweet, smoky stench of charred flesh. Mr. Bolton used every skill and trick he'd learned during his ten-year apprenticeship at Gardner's Funeral Home in Kansas City to make the corpse "presentable." He Super Glued the eyelids shut, and covered the crispy-brown scalp with Mrs. Silver's favorite short blond wig which, sad to say, didn't match old Lem's gray moustache.

Women don't wait at home for babies to be born, though. They drive to Layton or Palm Grove where they congregate at the Salvation Army Thrift Store to rifle through size-ten jeans when they know for damn sure they'll never lose down to size sixteen again. Others squeeze into booths at Wal-Mart where they fill up on barbecue sandwiches and thick slices of cherry pie topped with chocolate ice cream. Eatin' for two, they say.

The "Too Late Syndrome," another problem in these parts, more closely resembles an incurable disease than an unexpected happenstance, and is more likely to strike women than men. When it does hit a man, usually as he balances his checkbook or opens his lunch bucket to discover another bologna sandwich staring him in the face, he finds himself yearning for the lips of a childhood sweetheart, or a long red convertible with bucket seats, or a one-way plane ticket to the Bahamas. Anyplace there's sand, boats, and easy ladies. And when his teenage son brings home a girl with satin skin and breasts like oranges, he is filled with envy and his loins stir. And when that same son drives off laughing and hollering, his hair slicked back, his skin glowing with lust and aftershave, this same man might build a fence where none is needed or pick a fight with his wife.

Russell Peach got hit by the Too Late Syndrome in the cold blue heart of December, when the air was thin and the ground was hard. He tiptoed down the unlit stairway, unplugged the Christmas tree lights, drank a cup of hot chocolate laced with marshmallows, put a loaded gun to his head and pulled the trigger.

Women throw open windows and gawk at the moon when the Too Late Syndrome hits. One might take up smoking cigarettes, the long, skinny kind with fancy names, while another might caress her breasts and recall how boys flocked around her like flies on a honey pot, that she invited the best-looking one to join her on the grass and press his lips to hers. The syndrome is doubly hard on obese ladies. It makes them feel light and vulnerable, as if the slightest breeze could knock them down or nudge their indifferent husbands out of the house and into the arms of another.

Dottie Perkins, Possum Perkins's wife, a fine, upstanding Christian woman with nine grown children, seven bibles, three hymnals, and a complete set of Collier's Encyclopedia, was paying her paper boy when she was struck. Distraught by the young man's rejection, Dottie went to the city, where she got a boob job and had her lips plumped. When Possum made the mistake of telling her she looked deformed, she said, "Kiss my ass," thumbed a ride to Idaho, and joined a cult.

Old timers say the Too Late Syndrome is inescapable, that it travels on the wind, lurks in corners where brooms can't reach, and like a dark intricate thread, is woven into the very fabric of this miserable, one traffic light town. One damn thing's for sure. Darla Moon's not staying 'round long enough for it to strike her.

As I see it, Paradise is trapped between memories and progress. We once had a bank, a movie house, a dry cleaners, and a Humpty Dumpty, but they're all boarded up, and the only entertainment is Jed's Dance Barn on Telephone Road, or the Hollywood drive-in movie theater near Layton. Fact is, when Big Bucks Bingo opened west of here umpteen years ago, some said, "Hello, Las Vegas," like that was a real possibility.

The one true thing of beauty hereabouts is Momma's goldenrain tree. Thirty feet high, a mass of glorious yellow blooms in June and July, it puts Paradise to shame. If Momma ever truly loved anything, it's that tree. She cried the entire time she dug the hole and planted it, a fact I recall despite being just nine at the time, and she's watered, pruned, fertilized, and insecticided it with dogged reverence ever since.

It's miserable here in Momma's house. Clammy and tropical, like a hut on the banks of the Amazon. The evaporative cooler in the window is the problem. In one day, it can pump out enough moisture to fill a bathtub. Doors won't shut, not even the bathroom, and Momma's drawers, filled to overflowing with see-thru panties and bras, won't see light till September.

—How old are your kids, Roxie?
—Not old enough. Go on outside, Darla.
—You gonna put 'em out in this heat?
—They like it hot, don'tcha girls?

"Man, it's stifling in here. No wonder Granny's in her slip." She's sitting straddle-legged, fanning herself with a folded newspaper, watching *The Price Is Right*.

Momma kisses Liz T, her apple-head Chihuahua, on the nose. "Got a Mrs. Smith's peach pie in the oven. Heats up the place."

"I'm impressed."

"Meaning?"

"Meaning Mrs. Smith's is an achievement for someone who's never served anything more exciting than a soft drink for dessert."

"You've got a piss-poor memory, Darla."

"Yeah, right. Do I get a slice?"

"I'm saving it."

"For what? Christmas?"

"Someone important might show up."

"Sure as hell leaves me out."

"You said it, I didn't."

An explosion of sunlight glints off the church windows. "Dear God. Show me just one tight-assed hunk of manhood, and I'll show you one reason a hungry woman like m'self would stay in this godawful place."

"That's blasphemy," Momma says. "And move your ass from the window. You're blocking the goddamned cooler."

I stay put. Granny, poor little thing, leans forward, squints at the ceiling, and silently counts her frogs. She's making sure none of them high-tailed it out the door when she wasn't looking.

Bob Barker is interrupted by a cleanser ad. "Pines Three-Way Cleaner," a tinny voice says, "performs like a champ in the bathroom."

"Stupid commercial," Granny mutters. "Don't want nothing performing in the bathroom but me."

Momma's in one of her I'm-still-sexy-and-don't-no-one-forget-it moods, having squeezed all two hundred pounds of herself into one of her Mature Wisdom catalogue favorites—a scoop-necked leopard print top, black spandex tights, and black high-heeled mules with gold pom-poms on the front. My guess is, Dusty Duke, her latest boyfriend, is headed in this direction.

The name Roxie doesn't suit Momma anymore. She more closely resembles a Sylvia or a Gladys with that faded red hair and those flinty green eyes—eyes that had a front row seat to the seedier side of life— eyes with an edge. Not from knowledge, you understand, but from massive doses of nicotine and beer, not to mention a common condition among women like Momma—the pain of an injured soul caused by opening their hearts and bodies to angry men for too many years. The wounds weren't fatal, nor were they intended to be, but they robbed her face of softness and stole the fire from her gait.

She is engrossed in the *Star*, reading about the alien child President and Mrs. Clinton are raising in secret. Blind to the clothes and magazines strewn across the floor, she taps a one-inch tube of ash from her cigarette into an overflowing ashtray before taking another bite of her second Moon Pie. Banana, always banana. Close to two dozen a week if she's not dieting, a dozen a week if she is—at my expense, of course. This is a nondiet week, meaning anything goes, including the one-inch slab of Peter Pan chunky peanut butter she wedged in the middle.

I'm ready to leave, hungry for my place over the bakery where the memories are mine alone, memories made since I moved in, almost ten years ago. I soar like a comet within those walls. I'm a one-man band.

The Ringmaster. David Copperfield. The Good Witch of the East. A god in a two room Garden of Eden who, with a flourish or two, transforms yards of dazzling silks and satins into glittering prom dresses and bridal gowns for the "comfortably well off" in three counties. Dreams are conceived and born there. The Lincoln Center Gown hangs there, locked in a closet, awaiting my needle, biding its time.

The smell of smoke starts me to wondering for the umpteenth time if Momma felt anything when she worked as a whore, if, when she stripped off her undies and abandoned herself to that procession of long-lost uncles who "just happened to drop by," she ever worried about me and Rhonda laying under our candlewick bedspread across the hall, if she cared that we were awake, that we held each other's hands while listening to every grunt and groan, that sometimes we believed the men were torturing her, killing her even, that as we grew older, some of her clients wanted our bodies too, that they snuck into our bedroom, eyes glinting, smelling of Momma, promising kittens, puppies, and chocolate bars—that one succeeded?

I try to restrain these memories that roost under my scalp like bats in a cave, but a rise in temperature or an unexpected breeze can make them shudder to life and flutter about inside my head.

—Where the hell you been, Roxie baby?
—Bathroom.
—Took you long enough.
—Some things can't be rushed, sweet stuff.
—Ain't that the truth? C'mere.

As I peer through the dust-laden miniblind, I feel Momma's eyes drilling one-inch holes into my back and realize for the first time in my life that I am certain of only one thing—that until the day Momma fell off the bed with a customer a year or so ago and hurt her back, she was a whore. As for her "business," she long ago rendered down those endless nights of lust and pleasure into a weak brew of barely remembered blunders. If asked, she says, "I raised my girls by sewing collars to shirts at Harker's Western Shirt Factory in Layton," a job, I recall, she held for less than a year.

Whoring is bad enough, but it's all those times she gave it away that gnaws at my gut. No different than a garbage man enduring a gruelling day of heat, stink, and aggravation, then saying, "Don't pay me today, boss. I had a great time and my kids ain't that hungry."

Momma didn't advertise or anything. What I mean is, she didn't parade up and down Main Street in short shorts winking at farm folk, but men knew. Maybe they spread the news like Masons—with a secret handshake or a password.

Nowadays, Momma's schedule consists mainly of Big Bucks Bingo. Monday night with me, Rhonda, Muff, and Freda, Wednesday night with Rhonda—and again with me, Muff, and Freda on Friday night. God knows what she does the rest of the week. I enjoy bingo, but I can quit any time I like.

A big, white car speeds past, screeches to a halt, backs up, and eases into Lamb of God's parking lot. Even from this distance, I can see it's a '79 Cadillac Sedan DeVille with sliding moon roof and gold hubcaps. Mr. Boles, the undertaker, used to have one just like it.

Granny says, "Frog fifty-two," and Momma parks behind me, breasts to my shoulder. The smell of smoke and fake banana flavoring makes me gag. When the driver steps outside and looks around, the blooms on Momma's rain tree start dancing, as if a puff of wind just got tangled in the branches.

The guy is way taller than me, close to six foot, I'm thinking, and he's dressed in white. White stetson, white suit, and brown western boots, eel most likely. Show up at Jed's Dance Barn dressed like that, sugar, and watch the stampede.

I lift a slat and peer out. "Out-of-towner, that's for damn sure," I say. "Overalls smelling of shit and moth balls are in fashion here."

My mind races, records all the good stuff, takes in the tanned face, the sideburns, the black hair curling against his neck, the intense, dark eyes, but it's his "Who-gives-a-damn" stroll into the church that sends a rush of heat to my belly and makes my knees tremble—a sensation I experienced once before. Different place, different man, different way of walking, though.

No cocky, swaggering uniform here. This one moves with dignity—with the satisfied gait of someone who knows his worth. "If that ain't the purtiest thing I've seen in a coon's age."

"Hands off," Momma says. "That's our revival man, the Reverend Spirit E. Jackson from New Mexico. He's filling in for Preacher Daley while him and his wife do mission work in Panama."

"Panama? Who paid for that?"

"We did."

"We who?"

"We brothers and sisters of Lamb of God."

"You're no Lamb of God sister, Momma. You're a part-timer, a twenty year hanger-on. You show up once a month for potluck supper—and you go empty-handed."

"So? They feed me, I pitch in a dollar for Panama, and everyone's happy."

The preacher's back at his Cadillac, rummaging in the trunk.

Liz T leaps from Momma's lap to the cooler and growls.

"Very nice indeed," I say, admiring his high, tight tush.

"Hush y'mouth. That man's a miracle worker, a Christian fella."

"Well, God bless Momma, God bless Granny, and thank you Jesus for what I'm about to receive."

The car trunk slams. Liz T growls again. Momma bought her for protection, from what I don't know, unless it's ants in the kitchen, 'cause faced with anything larger, she'd pee on the floor. Besides, Momma don't need protection from burglars or rapists. Everything she owns is old, not working, or gathering dust in Joe's Hole-in-the-

Wall Pawn Emporium over in Layton, and a rapist would get one hell of a surprise considering Momma's innate fondness for fornication.

With the guy in white back in the church, the view turns dull and familiar. I am under guard in a deserted outpost on the fringes of the Sahara, a political prisoner awaiting the firing squad. Behind the wooden church, beyond the tick-infested weeds and a carpet of bright-eyed blanket-flowers, the world plummets down to an older-than-dirt black willow named Sage. His trunk rises up and out of the earth like a long crippled arm and a hand with four fingers, having lost his thumb to a tornado in 1983. When me and Elijah put an ear to his spine he speaks—not with words, you understand, but with a low steady hum that, in the past, has calmed nerves and erased headaches. Seeing as no other person has ever mentioned this wonder, me and Elijah have kept this secret for nigh on twenty years. Elijah claims Sage is special, says his roots burrow "deeper than the dead" in search of knowledge, not the Devil's knowledge, but God's—there in the underworld He claims as His own, a place where truth and water flow clear as crystal.

Farther down, through tangled brush, past a worm-riddled pecan tree and a vast carpet of wild strawberries, a stand of pine trees stretches upward. Chattering cardinals, black-capped chickadees, and tufted tit-mice dart like arrows through the sunlit branches. Midsummer, after a seventeen-year hibernation underground, cicada nymphs climb those same pines into the shade, where they trade their ugly carcasses for exquisite, translucent wings, and rattle out their hearts for a mate.

Beyond the trees, down in the holler, below an impervious mat of crisp, brown pine needles, lies the Rattler, a tributary of the South Fork River—a narrow, blackhearted devil. Years ago, me, Rhonda, and some other kids tried to change its nasty color by dumping red, yellow, and blue food dye into it. When nothing much happened, the boys stood on the bank and pissed into it, while us girls waded in and did the same. The Rattler didn't object at the time, but later, on three different occasions, it devoured three small children—sucked them under—

propelled them around Devil's Elbow and, like a cat delivering its finest catch of the day to its astonished master, vomited them up twenty minutes later under the bridge in town.

Come winter, the creek is friendlier. In January and February, when it slows to a dawdle, ice gathers at its edges like salt on a Margarita glass, shadows move among the trees like tall skinny men, and the hesitant step of a deer can make you gasp with surprise. Sometimes, around sunset, bats stream through the air like a giant black brush stroke, making barely a whisper, and the world seems perfect—but I never trust the Rattler—never will.

I've often wondered what I'd do if I happened upon Momma or Granny in the creek, drowning and screaming for help. Without hesitation I'd risk my life for Granny, but Momma? If I felt like I do now, I'd wave till she drifted out of sight and check under the bridge later.

"Whatcha doing?" Momma asks. "Waiting for the preacher to come back out?"

"Hell, no," I lie. "I'd cut m'hair off 'fore I'd wait on another man." I sit at the kitchen table behind Granny and Momma's black recliners. Momma won them at bingo five years ago. "Genuine, honest-to-God Naugahyde, the best money can buy," she said, and six months later, I'm repairing one split seam after another.

"Well, it's hands off, Darla—remember that."

"Don't raise your voice to me. I'm not deaf."

"I ain't worried 'bout y'ears, missy. It's them eyes o' your'n. See a pair of tight pants and you paw the ground."

"Look who's talking."

"I mean it, Darla."

"I swear, I'm back in this house twenty minutes and it's like I never left."

Ten years, and I'm still attached to a chain that begins here and hooks up to my place on Main Street. I've gotta get out of Paradise, gotta see who and what's on the other side of the state line even if it's bad. I've gotta get to New York where someone's looking for a designer with keen eyes, magic fingers, and a knock-'em-dead, bug-their-eyes-out imagination, and that's me, by God.

I'll get me a nice Buick, a two-bedroom apartment with dish-washer, garbage disposer, washer and dryer—and every month or so, I'll treat myself to a fancy dinner and a ticket to Lincoln Center where I'll spend the evening with Pavarotti. I'll buy Job Squad paper towels by the carton, and I'll have at least two dozen pairs of leather pumps in my closet with handbags to match. I'll buy meat.

One thing's for sure, if I'm not out of Paradise by the end of September, they might just as well lock me up in Rose Hill Asylum, where in all likelihood I'll finish myself off by tying one corner of a sheet around my neck, the other over a pipe, and jumping off the toilet.

Momma sits slumped in her chair submerged in smoke and indif-ference, while I remember how, after nights of moans, squeals, and hysterical laughter, our uncles headed out looking ten years younger and five pounds lighter, their lips stained crimson. She showed genuine concern for the mean ones, but the good ones, those gentle souls who gave me and Rhonda candy and let us ride in their cars, she chewed up like Sunday roast, leaving only a cold, hard bone. Memories like that roost in my head, and despite my efforts to restrain them, they often come to life and take flight around sundown.

I remember the parched red clay around the house, how it cracked open every July, how me and Rhonda sat on the porch watching Momma, her red hair blowing in the wind, unwind the long garden hose to water her precious goldenrain tree. Other than me and Rhonda, it's the only thing she's raised to adulthood. Corn, okra, toma-toes, potatoes, periwinkles, you name it, they all paid the supreme sac-rifice for Momma—including a hardy honeysuckle. Momma, believing hungry aphids, white flies, and Japanese beetles watched and waited on the roof till she got something new in the ground, sprayed each new invasion over and over again until the plants, overcome by Malathion and pyrethrins, toppled. The soil round here don't help much, either. Weeds thrive in this red clay—which means I'd better plant myself in some good dirt 'fore it's too late.

As I mull over my departure plans, Momma lets out a big sigh. "Foolin' around with a preacher," she says, "is asking for a big mess o' trouble," and Pastor Albert Meeks, a straw-thin Baptist preacher from Palm Grove, leaps into my head like an old ballerina and wobbles to attention—reminding me that Momma "entertained" at least two publicly devout men during her career—Preacher Maples, the old fart who died for the privilege, and Preacher Meeks.

"Never was a bigger piece o' trouble than Mrs. Meeks, was there, Momma? Must've weighed more'n three hundred pounds, not counting the gunnysack of a purse she clobbered you with."

Momma glances at Granny who's staring wide-eyed at the light fixture, as if Jesus Christ himself is swinging from it. "What I'm trying to get across is," Momma says, "folks love to gossip about us Moons, so don't give 'em the ammunition."

Granny's counting out loud now. Momma tosses the *Enquirer* on the floor and fires up another Camel. "Quit frettin' over them things, Mother. I've done counted 'em already and they're all there. All ninety-one of 'em."

Granny jumps from her chair. "Then one's missing, and you damn well know it." Eyes heavenward, she cocks her head to one side and pads down the hall.

"Hey," Momma yells. "You said ninety-one this morning."

"Ninety-two," Granny says. "A new recruit. Small critter."

She's tugging on drawers, opening the doors to the hall cupboard. Now she's in the bathroom, unscrewing the cap on the toothpaste. "Zebras in the sink," she says. Momma flutters her Sally Hansens and heads for the fridge—leaving behind two large depressions. Moon Pie craters, I call 'em, seeing as she's inhaled them on a regular basis since Wal-Mart started carrying them six years ago.

"You'll get old like her one of these days, m'girl," she says, "so you'd best start worrying about what folks'll say at your funeral."

"Worry about your own cotton pickin' funeral, Mother Teresa."

"What I mean is—"

"Besides, I won't die in Paradise, and seeing as I'll be under six feet o' dirt when I do, I won't give a damn what anyone says, will I?"

She shrugs. "Your life."

"Like hell it is."

Granny's back, her hands gently cupped around some illusionary frog. She tosses it skyward. "Found him."

Here comes the preacher, looking good enough to eat—a five-star meal in eel-skin boots, a walking advertisement for the latest how-to book, *The Thrill of Sex and the Power of Clorox*, a man of endless possibilities. I go to the window and raise the blind, but he drives away with nary a glance.

"Yeah, let 'em talk, Momma. Let 'em say I had skin like marble, that I walked like Marilyn Monroe and was one hell of a lay. Let 'em say I seduced a traveling preacher man, that I made him happier than a toad in a deep pond."

Her cold silence compels me to add, "Let 'em say I taught Preacher Spirit E. Jackson how to cuss and screw like a driller, that he jumped into Hell stark nekkid with a big old smile on his face."

Momma snatches a Coors from the fridge, pops it open. "Wish to God you'd get married."

"Nah, wouldn't work. I go through men like a lawnmower."

"The right one'd straighten you out in a cold-ass minute."

"The right one ain't been born. Men are so riddled with vices, so goddamned unredeemable it's pathetic—and it ain't stupidity that makes women think they can save the bastards, it's arrogance."

"Yeah, yeah, yeah. What happened to that plumber up in the panhandle?"

"Got a hernia."

"And that Greg Something-or-other from Palm Grove?"

"Gave me a hernia."

"What about Billy Joe Comfort? You dated him lotsa times."

"So?"

"And what about Charlie Wainright—that fine-looking fella from Oklahoma City?" she asks, ripping the cellophane from another Moon Pie. "He seemed interesting."

"About as interesting as watching a stump rot. He's a health freak. Fix him pita bread packed with alfalfa sprouts and he glows like neon. Unnatural, if you ask me. Not my type."

"Who is? A fat Italian with a big mouth?"

"Luciano Pavarotti isn't fat, for Christ's sake. Opera singers need extra padding to make their voices resonate."

"Resonate shit. A glutton for lasagna is what he is." She totters outside, slams the door behind her, and sits in the rocker. It groans under her weight.

"If'n you do get hitched," Granny pipes up, "pick y'self a homely man. Good-lookin' ones think they shit milk chocolate bonbons."

"I'll remember that," I tell her, and she adds, "And don't go after a no-good man with y'best skillet. Use a gun."

Granny, who has the attention span of a moth, God bless her, exists in a perpetual state of separation and obscure unreality, unsure for the most part who she is or where she's from. Her input, though, sometimes credible, sometimes not, is never dull and often profound. When I first saw Shamir, over on Railway Road, she told me everyone had an angel, that they stay with us from the moment we're born till the moment we die, that they walk us to "the other side." When I asked her how she knew, she shoved my hand into the saucer-shaped cavity in her skull, and said, "When you return from the Planet of Headbreakers you either know everything or you know nothing, you miserable little piss ant." I believed she knew everything.

She holds my hand to her cheek, and I recall that I've seen Shamir dozens of times, and felt his cool moist breath on my forehead more times than I can count. I've also smelled him, an elusive, airy essence— "a marvel," says Elijah, "seeing as most folks never see one in their whole lifetime, let alone feel, hear, or smell one."

I kiss her head. "Love you, Granny."

"Saddling yourself with the wrong man is worse'n having all your teeth pulled," she says. You hurt all over, you turn ugly as a pig's butt and mean as a snake. Look at that woman out on the porch. That should tell you sump'n."

"Can I get you anything before I go?"

"A dab o' arsenic'd be nice."

"Oh, Granny."

"You'd put a mule with a broken leg outa its mizry, wouldn't you?"

"You're not an old mule and your legs are fine."

"That's what you think."

"I'm going to New York."

"I can spit further'n that."

"Leaving pretty soon."

"You'll be back."

"Only to visit."

"Who'll wash and braid m'hair?"

"Momma."

"My momma?"

"No, my momma. The woman on the porch."

"She gets soap in my eyes."

"Elijah then."

"Don't know him."

"Sure you do. He washes your hair all the time. Does mighty fine braiding too."

"Reckon he'll do." She yawns, revealing smooth shiny gums. When she's wearing her dentures, I see a lot of her in me; the high cheek-bones and the Indian nose—but hair that used to be as black and shiny as mine, and just as heavy, has turned wispy and dull-metal gray.

I often wonder about the inside of her head, if the wheels turn easy or if they get stuck, if she remembers my dad and grandpa, and exactly how many brain cells those specialists short-circuited back in the forties. Maybe they didn't read the instructions. Maybe it was a paint-by-number operation and the chief painter was color blind. Maybe a blade slipped. Maybe an eye blinked. Whatever happened, Momma says the only ones who knew were the ones holding the weapons. The same ones who called the outcome "unfortunate."

No skin off their asses that Granny woke up with no memory of her native language. They didn't care that, for the rest of her life, she would be a permanent citizen of some uncharted planet in the constellation of La-La Land, that for the next fifty-plus years she would protect herself from dangerous night rays by wearing a wire crown and wrapping her legs in newspaper and twine.

When she nods off, I go outside. The wind, out of the south at about twenty miles an hour, teems with dust and is as fierce as a hair dryer. In the bright, dazzling light I see two Liz Ts sitting on two laps. Both mommas stare at the rain tree, smoke seeping from all four nostrils.

I envision Momma in a white glossy casket—a gold-handled, pink-velvet-lined job costing thousands of dollars, like the model in Bolton's Funeral Parlor. She's wearing a sheer red nightgown, nipples and pubic hair visible. Her Sally Hansen eyelashes are lopsided and she's clasping a fresh pack of Camels to her chest. She lights up a cigarette with her favorite lighter, the one with Elvis on the front, and lowers the lid.

—If I'd had a heart attack while we were doing it, Roxie baby, I think I'd die happy.
—Wanna try again and find out for sure?

I blink away the image. "You and Rhonda should quit smoking those filthy things."

"We enjoy 'em."

"And if a cannibal was eating you for dinner, I s'pose you'd offer him a piece of Mrs. Smith's pie right before he chewed y'goddamn lips off."

She shrugs.

"Go ahead and kill y'self then. See you at bingo."

"Which reminds me."

Here it comes.

"Lend me ten dollars. My welfare check's late again."

I locate two crumpled fives in my purse. "You still owe me ten from last week."

She shoves the bills down her front, inside her bra. "I'll ride along with Muff and Freda. Don't see well enough to drive at night no more."

"I said you still owe me ten dollars for last week—and the clinic claims you have the eyes of an eagle."

"I do, in daylight. You ain't never seen an eagle fly at night have you?"

This is Advil territory. "I'm leaving. Rhonda asked me to drop by."

"Sump'n wrong?"

"Who the hell knows?"

"She sick again?"

"She is if she's still living with Frank Slater in that tin box."

"She should be thankful she's got a roof over her head."

"It's not a roof, it's a lid, and if he's beating on her again, I'll whoop his ass."

"A feller twice your size and meaner'n hell? Yeah, right, Darla."

"He's also older than me and blind without his glasses. When I get through with him, he won't have nothing left to piss through."

"Go ahead, blame Frank. Problem with you is, you forget how ornery Rhonda can be."

"You're right, she can."

"Damn right."

"You know what? Maybe Frank should knock her about on a regular basis—say every Monday, Wednesday, and Friday. Sunday, too, if she needs it."

Momma's face twists into an ugly knot. "That's not funny."

"Sure as hell ain't." Lightheaded from heat and mindless conversation, I'm off the porch and down the steps.

"Frank says he's had enough of you nosing in his business."

"Too bad."

"Can't believe he's as bad as Rhonda makes out. Married for years and she still don't know what sets him off."

"Stop while you're ahead, Momma. You're pissing me off."

"What else is new?"

I head for the car, anxious to leave behind the five room frame. When the light's just right, you can see straight through it, front to back, right through its skin to its bones—like an X ray. The porch posts are crumbling, and the add-on, where the washer and dryer sit, gapes where it once joined the house. "I'm outa here. Gotta sew fifteen billion seed pearls and beads on a wedding dress."

"Make your bed, you gotta lay in it."

The sun feels like a blowtorch. "Damned right, Momma, and remember, I'm about ready to take my bed someplace."

"Won't make me no nevermind. And don't forget to take that big mystery you got locked in a cupboard with you."

"New York is where I'm going. America's best designers got their start there, and I'm as good as any of 'em. Maybe better."

"So you say, but I don't think much of them jeans you're wearing. Too baggy. And them sandals make your feet look big."

"Won't be able to pay your light bill, or replace your tires, or stake you at bingo, but make your bed, you gotta lay in it, right?" I forgot to open Miss Ladybug's windows when I got here. "Shit. I could bake bread in there between here and town if I had a mind to."

"What's that?"

"I said shit, Momma. S-H-I-T, shit." The latch burns my fingers. When I open the door, a fist of hot air hits my face. "In case you're interested, the Stop 'N' Go needs help and the nursing home is looking for kitchen help." I take a bath towel from the basket of dirty laundry, throw it across the plastic seat, drape another over the steering wheel, and start the ignition.

"People are gettin' shot in Stop 'N' Go's and I'd never last inside a nursing home on account of my blood pressure," Momma yells.

Engine idling, me and Miss Ladybug sit among the chickweed. "Right."

"Besides, can't leave y'granny all day."

"Elijah can watch her. He'd love it."

"Always gotta have that man in our business, don't ya? Hell, his miserable black ass has followed us from here to yon since the fucking ice age."

"He ain't moved in twenty years."

"Neither have I."

"There you go." Sitting here, facing south, nothing separates me from the horizon 'cept heat, red dirt, and searing sky. A tad east, scrub oaks. Beyond the scrub oaks, more scrub oaks and unforgiving soil. Pickings so poor, buzzards carry their lunch.

Ten, maybe fifteen years ago, Seth Dalton and his sons, Jake, Murphy, and Seth Junior, raised cattle out there, but as each man worked himself to death and succumbed to heart trouble, the barns, storage buildings, and silos crumbled one by one. Now while the Daltons sleep under crabgrass across the street, some rich Japanese fella out in California reaps the tax breaks.

Barreling down the road in his shiny eighteen wheeler comes another problem—Ol' Dusty Duke from Selma, Alabama, his shiny head wrapped in a red bandana. "A staunch Southern Baptist whose wife's a nag," according to Momma. Staunch or not, he'll stop off for a chunk of Mrs. Smith's peach pie, help himself to a thick slice of Roxie Moon, and hit the highway before *60 Minutes* is over. Momma said I'd like him if we got acquainted. I said I preferred his wife even though I don't know either one of 'em.

I look back at Momma, but she's gone. Saw Dusty, I reckon. Went to spray herself with that generic Chanel No. 5 crap. Never latches the screen door. She'll let the damn thing swing and squeak in the wind till Satan throws a party for Jesus.

How Sweet It Is?

. . . .

I drive off pummeling the steering wheel. Don't know why the hell I
bother when it's the same ol' same ol', day in, day out—Momma and
Rhonda competing in the who-can-piss-Darla-off-the-most Olympics.
The drinking, the smoking, the irresponsibility, the helplessness, the
sickness, and their "Just so long as we get by" attitudes curdle my
brain and burn holes the size of quarters in my stomach.

God knows what I'll find at Rhonda's. She's way overdue for a
five-day migraine or some exotic, life-threatening illness like Legion-
naires' disease or Rocky Mountain spotted fever, which, after a
month or two of antibiotics, painkillers, and sedatives from this doctor at this clinic or one at another, none of them knowing what the
other's prescribing, and me worrying myself sick, evaporate like
puffs of smoke and are never mentioned again. A perpetual roller
coaster of highs and lows, of debilitating sickness and unexplained
recovery.

A mile down the road I spy Elijah, heart of my heart, a man with a
secret, I think—a grizzled old wolf enjoying one of his last summers.
Skin shining like a polished eggplant, he sits on the porch of his neat
frame house, fanning himself with a folded newspaper. I beep the horn
and pull in, watch him lumber down the steps into his recently mowed

yard, the evergreen bushes perfectly trimmed, his teeth white as piano keys.

"I swear, I swear, Darla," he says, peering in. "Don'tcha know this world'd be a happy place if ever'one drove a spotted Volkswagen like your'n?"

"Sure would brighten the highway, wouldn't it? Wish it had air conditioning, though."

"Come in a spell and cool off."

"Can't. Gotta go to Rhonda's."

"Sump'n wrong?"

"Who knows?"

"Uh-huh. Who knows? She came by last week with some o' them coconut candies I like. Looked down in the mouth, but couldn't get nothin' outa her. Maybe Frank tying one on the week before had sump'n to do with it—or maybe sump'n else was brewing."

"Reckon I'll find out when I get there."

"You know how I worry about her and them kids, so let me know, y'hear?"

"I will."

"Roxie steady today?" he asks. He sounds concerned, but him and Momma have never been friendly. Never so much as exchanged a smile, yet I can't help but feel they share a secret that binds them together like sticks of dynamite.

"Coupla beers is all."

"Granny okay?"

"Same as usual."

"Roxie let her eat here yesterday. Fixed her favorite, chicken 'n' dumplings. My oh my, did she enjoy it. Made a nice dent in a choco-late cake, too."

"She always does. C'mere, m'sweetheart. Plant them pussy-pink lips on m'cheek 'fore I go."

He sticks his head inside the car. "Hush yo shameful mouth 'fore I slap it."

I give him a kiss. "I'll be back in a day or two. Something I wanna talk to you about."

"Look forward to it, hon. Take care."

I'm doing forty on West Oak. Even though I have the right of way, I slow down before Elm Street intersects on account of the firethorn bushes at the corner. I'm rammed on the passenger side.

Rubber squealing, my '71 Super Beetle slides and spins in a graceful arc toward the ditch until, without even knowing how, I regain control and slow her down to a soft slide before stopping. I'm trembling inside and out. A sharp metallic taste fills my mouth. A semiattached flap of tissue on my tongue tells me I bit it.

I exit the car and stand on legs that feel like Twinkies. For one heart-stopping moment I can't believe what I'm seeing: Leroy Poteet, city marshal of this five-and-dime town, grim-faced, unblinking, sitting in his squad car, crosswise in the middle of the road. I can't abide Leroy—and my bad opinion of him has got nothing to do with the fact that I once dated his nephew, Mike Rollings, who's now serving ten years in the state penitentiary for grand larceny. Leroy's a short old fart with a melon-size paunch and ugly dentures, a man bloated with gas and bad intentions who takes various and sundry bribes for "looking the other way."

Miss Ladybug's door is dented, and a swath of orange paint and a dozen black dots are missing. City marshal or not, I'm tempted to jerk the miserable creep from his seat and clobber him, but I daren't. Word is, he hasn't arrested anyone in ages and the jail's empty, so he fears folks won't vote for him in the next election. This fear, they say, has turned him predatory.

He opens his door and steps out, belly first. Glancing at his lopsided fender, he swaggers toward me, withdraws a ballpoint pen from the breast pocket of his olive-green uniform, and proceeds to scratch on a notepad. He smells of garlic.

"Reckless driving is a high-priced violation, Darla Moon."

"Well, aren't I the stupid one? I thought for a minute this run-in was all *your* fault, Marshal, when I've known for years us women must come to a dead halt right here so you men can speed through the intersection first. Sorry, it just slipped this silly little mind of mine, you know?"

"You bein' your usual smart-assed self, Darla Moon? Thought my nephew cured you o' that bad habit."

"No, he never did, but the bastard sure landed himself in a heap o' trouble, I'm told."

"You drunk?"

"Now, Leroy, if we was better acquainted you'd know that milk straight from the udder is this baby's choice."

He adjusts the wide leather belt supporting his stomach and rubs his stubbled chin. "In my opinion, an orange Volkswagen with black polka dots puts Paradise in a damned poor light and should be put outa its mizry."

Sonovabitch. His tone is decidedly threatening, yet he smiles as if this is one of his better days. "And where exactly in your 'How to Be a Cop' manual is that rule written down, Marshal?"

"Ain't written down anywhere, girly. That rule's filed away up here." Grinning, he taps his forehead with his pen a couple of times.

"Is that right?"

"But for a *small, quick consideration,* I'll see this ugly incident doesn't appear on your nice clean record. Get my drift?" His piggy eyes slither across my breasts and down to my thighs, linger like raw oysters.

"Small? Quick? Not underrating yourself, are you, Leroy?"

The grin enlarges, turns into something only a mother could love. "That's for me to know and you to find out, girly."

Pompous ass. Wonder where he wants to do it? In Miss Ladybug or in the squad car? Either place would require the kind of agility he ain't got. "You must be fond of living on the edge, Marshal."

"Huh?"

"Well, we live in health-conscious times, don't we? They say *casual friendships* are dangerous nowadays. Lethal even."

"Ain't nothing wrong with me."

"Me neither."

"Well then?"

"That I know of."

"What's that mean?"

"Just what I said, nothing wrong with me—that I know of. Which is to say, something might be wrong with me but I don't know it yet. That isn't to say something *is* wrong with me, only that as far as I know—"

"You jerking my chain?"

"Leroy, my great-great-grandma crossed the United States in a covered wagon, put a bullet 'tween the eyes of the Indian who chopped off her husband's leg, and made him one out of a pecan tree. Granny Moon may act weird, but she can shoot the head off a rat in a thick fog without so much as a kiss-my-butt-and-call-me-Tinkerbell. And when a man cheated Momma outa two dollars, she decked him with an electric iron. All of which should tell you I've inherited some powerful genes from some sturdy stock, that I'm a little different—know what I mean?"

He turns red. Hot Melon by Max Factor. "That a threat?"

"Hell, no. I'm saying I like to do things in my own time, Leroy, when I'm at my best, when *I'm* ready, you know?" We stare at each other till he blinks. "And my car's no problem. I'll repaint her. Fact is, I've located some great glow-in-the-dark paint that'd be perfect for a Ninja Turtle motif. Or are they outa style already?"

He stomps off, his rear end bouncing like two sacks of groceries, and starts his car.

"As for Miss Ladybug putting this town in a bad light," I call out, pushing my luck, "Paradise ain't seen light, good or bad, since Bolton's Funeral Home burned to the ground in '84, which is why I'm checking outa here in the very near future."

He guns his engine.

"Say, Leroy?" I yell. "Wanna spring for the fluorescent paint?"

He drives to where I'm standing. "Listen good, Darla Moon, 'cause I'm only gonna say this once. Without a special wildlife permit, it's agin the law for private citizens to confine or possess *any* wild animal. Breaking that law gets you a stiff fine *or* imprisonment."

"Meaning?"

"Meaning, watch your step, girly, or I'll pay a visit to that pretty niece o' your'n and that critter she's so crazy about. Don't want her folks going to jail over a goddamned deer, do you? And if I catch that nigger friend o' your'n going one mile over the speed limit, I'll slap his black ass in the slammer for a week or two, and have him paint it one end t'other."

Rhonda lives four miles east of town, spitting distance from the railway tracks, among eighteen trailers in various stages of decline, on a winding path in a sparse grove of skinny oaks. Rhonda's, the sixth one down, sits blistering under the sun. A week after he moved in, Frank, who can't spread margarine without amputating a finger, "pruned" their only shade tree, a giant maple. That winter, after being chopped and hacked into an uncertain shape, the tree toppled in an ice storm, keeled right over and took the sun awning right along with it—leaving only a swamp cooler like Momma's to battle the heat.

Frank's doing the same thing to Rhonda—chopping her down bit by bit, sapping her strength, intent on destroying all that's good and beautiful in her. Never knew a lazier, more useless man. If he was scheduled for execution on Monday, he'd rest up all weekend for the event.

Frank's dog Bowzer is stretched out under the steps like a shabby old overcoat. He ambles out for a head scratch, takes a long drink from his water bowl, and disappears under the trailer.

Pearl answers the door in the yellow sundress I made for her last spring. Thirteen years old, breasts like strawberries, and bronzed by the sun, she has an undeniable softness about her, as if instead of blood, a warm brew of pollen and honey coursed through her veins. Blessed with the long, graceful legs of a colt and long, straw-colored hair, she's a fresh-air fiend who dances with butterflies, who adores a deer named Archie despite his malformed lip and ear, who's more at home in the woods or up in a tree than she ever will be under a roof— a girl who finds beauty and joy in imperfection.

She looks puzzled. "Did Mom call you?"

"Uh-huh. Last night. Told her I'd drop by."

"Didn't call you this morning?"

"No. Something wrong?"

She brushes her hair from her face and turns away. "Nothing more'n usual."

Sprawled on Rhonda's Salvation Army couch, spooning a soggy yellow gruel from a glass of milk into her mouth, is a huge girl with pale eyes and stringy bleached-blond hair.

I close the door, even though it feels hotter in here than it does outside. "And who are you?"

The girl doesn't answer. She's too wrapped up in what she's eating.

"That's Mardel," Pearl says. "She just moved into number ten with her momma. She's fifteen."

Mardel does not eat like a regular person. She slurps, smacks, and sucks like a sow—as if she hasn't eaten in weeks. "What's that she's got in that glass?"

"Chee-tos and milk," Pearl replies. "She loves the stuff, can you believe it?"

"Where'd she get it?"

"Here. She fixed it herself."

"Where's Jessie?"

"On his bed, drawing storms 'n' stuff."

"Frank?"

"Gone."

"Y'momma?"

"In the bathroom."

"She okay?"

Tight-lipped, Pearl sighs and sits cross-legged in front of their twelve-inch black-and-white TV to watch a documentary on lizards.

"Pearl. Is she okay?"

"Depends on what you mean by okay. She's breathing, if that means anything."

Pearl and I are pros at this. Have been for years. When she's worried about what's going on around here, she can't confide in me all at once, any more than I can hear about it all at once, so we do it bit by bit.

I stroll into the kitchen. "Where'd Frank go?"

"To Grandma's to tell her Momma's a lying bitch."

"Is that right?"

"That's what he said 'fore he tore outa here foamin' at the mouth."

"Whatcha having for supper?"

"No telling."

She gets up, peers down the hall, and sits at the bar. "Don't let on I said so, Aunt Darla," she whispers, "but I think Frank starts the fights just so's he can go to Grandma's and bum free beer and money, or go into Layton and fool around. I mean, he's always broke. When he left here, all he had was time on his hands and a half tank o' gas. No money far as I know."

She sounds like she's twenty-five years old. I scout the fridge and find half a loaf of bread, a tub of margarine, a few slices of bologna, half a carton of milk, two six-packs of Coors beer, and a fresh carton of Salem cigarettes. The trash can is stuffed with empty beer cans, cigarette butts, and newspapers.

As if deep in thought, Pearl traces imaginary lines in the Formica with her forefinger. I open the cupboard doors. Salt, cornmeal, flour, two cans of whole-kernel corn, three cans of turnip greens, and a box of Hamburger Helper. "Didn't Frank's unemployment come in a few days ago?"

"Yeah, but Mrs. Barnes turned up when he came home from cashing it and threatened to evict us if he didn't pay what he owes—but he only gave her twenty dollars. Claims she's gotta give us thirty days' notice."

"That's right, she does."

"I know, Aunt Darla, but she's got four little kids, a husband in the hospital, and we owe her four months rent, so she must need the money real bad."

"Does Frank know her situation?"

"Sure he does, but he told her she can't get blood from a turnip."

"He *knows* he's a turnip? Who told him?"

Pearl doesn't even crack a smile. "And Momma's too scared to argue with him."

"We shouldn't be talking about personal stuff like this, Frank warned us not to."

She returns to her spot in front of the television. "I don't care. If I was old enough to have a job, things'd be different around here."

Mardel's still slurping. Rhonda's got Garth Brooks singing in the bathroom. Drawers are opening and closing, water's running.

"Momma knows how I feel about Frank," Pearl says. "I've told her lots of times."

Wish you'd tell Uncle Bob not to come back. Me and Rhonda
    don't like him.
Well, don't that make me shake in m'shoes.

"What'd she say?"

"Same thing she always says—he's got a lot on his mind."

"He needs more. A freshly honed axe, for example."

"She said he's got a lot on his mind ever since he moved in, and—"

"And—?"

She turns up the volume on the TV. "Don't let's talk about him any more. It makes my stomach hurt, and we're out of Tums."

I join her on the floor and take her in my arms. She holds on tight, squeezes me back. Poor baby. If I had to live in this tin can with Frank Slater day after day, year after year, my brain would unravel like a ball of yarn. Mardel, her eyes glued to the television, licks her lips, oblivious. I massage Pearl's back, neck, and shoulders.

When she tires of it, I check in with Jessie, a frail, quiet kid—a peeled twig with his mother's small mouth and his dead father's gray eyes.

"Hi, Darling Darla," he says, and brushes a shock of hair from his eyes.

"Hi, handsome."

The giant sketch pad I gave him last week for his birthday disappears under the shabby bedspread. I know not to hug him. He prefers a perfunctory kiss on the cheek or forehead, so I greedily baptize him with both.

At birth, he more closely resembled a freshly skinned rabbit than a baby. Delicate as a snowflake, he cried like a kitten and rarely slept— unwilling, it seemed, to accept the crazy family he'd been assigned to, and who could blame him? But he soon gathered strength and filled out his skin, and before long, he smiled easily, as if he knew I loved him.

"You ornery little cuss. You okay?"

"Yep."

"Feel any different now you're eleven?"

"Nope."

"You look different. Too good-looking, in my opinion. Bunch of girls outside, waiting for your autograph. Had to fight 'em off to get in the door."

He turns pink and rolls his eyes. "Yeah, right."

"Whatcha drawing?"

"Clouds. Lightning. Charts. Weather things."

"Gonna be a TV weatherman like Gary England, right?"

"Hope so."

"What did you buy with the twenty dollars I gave you?"

"Nothing, yet."

"How come?"

"My bike needs new inner tubes," he says, rubbing his nose. "Can't get to town."

"I'll take you. Now, if you like."

"Can't."

"How come?"

"Frank's got my money—saving it for me."

"Is that right?" Miserable sonovabitch.

Jessie takes a comic book from the shelf over his bed, flips through the pages. The clang of his drawbridge is loud and clear. He'd rather be alone. Silence is a rare commodity when you live with Frank Slater.

Two baskets of dirty clothes sit on the washing machine. Rhonda's still out of bleach and Tide, and the dryer hasn't worked in months.

I tap on the bathroom door. Rhonda opens it a crack. Her eyes are bloodshot, her left cheek is red and swollen. As I mentally record what I'm seeing, wondering if I'm seeing it at all, she slams the door in my face and locks it.

"Be out in a minute," she says.

"Now, Rhonda."

"In a minute."

"If you don't open it *now*, sis, I'm gonna kick the friggin' thing down."

"Don't blow a fuse, okay?"

"Open this goddamned door."

She's wearing Frank's Roadrunner T-shirt and the green seventy-five-cent shorts from Goodwill—so thin she bends like a hairpin when she brushes her hair. Momma's used to be that same red color, 'cept it had more fire and body.

I squeeze past her, silence Garth Brooks, and sit on the toilet lid. I try my damnedest not to look too close at her for fear I'll see Frank's handiwork. Her purple toenail polish is chipped, and an open packet of Salems is tucked into the pocket of her shorts. "What's going on, sis?"

"I told you on the phone, I don't feel good. Eyes red. Nose runny. Headache. Like I'm coming down with something."

"And?"

"Then me and Frank had this small run-in."

Can't help but look. Saucer-shaped welts and clearly defined fingerprints on her calves and thighs. "Looks like you had a big run-in, with a tractor."

"Don't exaggerate."

"It's amazing."

"What is?" She brushes harder.

"How after your *small run-ins* Frank walks away looking freshly scrubbed, and you resemble roadkill."

"Don't, Darla." She straightens up, gazes into the mirror, and says, "It's not always his fault. I can be testy, 'specially when I feel bad." Her voice is uncertain, her eyes a green mist of bad memories.

"Testy, shit. If Frank shit in your shoes, you'd kiss his feet and say, 'Thanks, hon. They feel so much better.'"

"All I want is for Frank, me, and the kids to be happy. Is that asking too much?"

I shake my head, not because I disagree with her, but because we've had this conversation at least fifty times over some husband or the other, yet here she stands, bruised and battered, telling me all she wants is happiness.

"You know what?" She stares at herself in the mirror. "Life is like clean underwear."

"Clean underwear?"

"Yeah, you know how before you put 'em on you hold 'em up to make sure which is the front and which is the back, but when you get 'em on they're still back-to-front or inside out?"

"Yeah."

"Well, that's my life. I try my damnedest to do things right, but I always manage to screw up."

"So use a laundry marker on y'drawers to remind you how you messed up last time—that way, you won't do it again."

She dabs at her eyes. "Just like that, huh?"

I want to cry too, but I can't, not in front of her, so we stare at each other like two conspirators sharing the same grim secret. "Didn't say it was easy. You feed the goddamned squirrels and they repay you by shitting in your attic. But you don't just sit and ignore the stink day after day, year after year. You fight back. You go after your dreams like a ferret up a drainpipe. You run them squirrels off and reclaim your god-damned life. You shoot for the moon. You tell everyone to go to hell and shoot for the fucking moon, Rhonda." For some crazy reason I flush the toilet.

"Getting ready to take your own advice?"

"Huh?"

"Momma says you bought luggage."

"Wal-Mart had a special."

"So when are you leaving me?"

She always looks like a child with her nose pressed against the window, watching a party on the other side. "Leaving you?"

"When?"

I want to say "In eight weeks," but a specific length of time would terrify her, and because I'm a friggin' coward, I say, "I'm not sure, but if this family thinks I'm gonna hang around Paradise for the rest of my life, they'd better think again."

Now I'm thinking, what if, in eight weeks, she's all battered and bruised again? Will I have the strength to go? Will I?

Rhonda sits on the edge of the tub and gazes off, twisting her wedding band around and around on her finger with that look on her face, a look beyond intensity, haunting—as if we'd been locked out of the house again while one of our uncles puts yet another coat of paint on Momma's bedroom.

How come the walls aren't wet, Momma?
Magic paint, Darla. Just like always.

Magic paint. Always magic paint. And we believed her.
"What the hell went wrong, Darla?"
"Meaning?"
"Meaning, how come we weren't born into a G.E. family?"
"A what?"
She swallows hard. "You know, like on those commercials where everyone hugs and kisses each other and smells the coffee and cuddles the babies and Grandpa and Grandma dance like newlyweds in that sparkling kitchen. How come we didn't get a family like that, huh?"
"Because G.E. didn't bring us Moons all the good things in life, that's why."
"I'm serious, Darla."
"Me too."
"We could've had it all."
"Nah."
"If our daddy hadn't run off all those years ago, if Momma had been different, we could've been a G.E. family."
"Hell, we don't know who our real daddy is, but he did run off, Momma is different, and we'll never be a G.E. family, so we get on with it. Besides, other than Granny, we never had what it takes to make a real family. No aunts, no uncles, not even distant cousins to talk about. For all we know, we hatched from a pod or fell from a spaceship."
"But—"

"I hate to be the one to break the news to you, Rhonda, but the truth of the matter is, a tornado didn't drop you and me in Paradise, Oklahoma. That's Highway Twelve out yonder, not the yellow brick road, and no fairy godmother is gonna bail us out. We make it on our own or we die trying."

Anxious to leave, I open the door. "I'm leaving. If I hang around looking at that face o' your'n much longer, I'll get so mad at Frank—"

"I'll make coffee."

"You're out."

"A beer, then."

"No."

"We'll talk about other stuff."

I spin around. "Are you blind, Rhonda? Are you so goddamned used to being mistreated you don't notice it any more than a fish notices the water it swims in?"

Her stare turns blank. It always does when it comes to Frank's shortcomings—like I'm talking to the dead.

"But I need him, Darla—need him like a pig needs mud, and he's doing better, honest."

My neck feels hot and that weird little eye muscle starts to twitch. I nudge her back into the bathroom so the kids can't hear. "Better than who? Ted Bundy? Jeffrey Dahmer? Well, praise God. Now I can sleep nights."

"You know what I mean."

"No, I don't know what you mean. Frank's a pothole in the road of life, and that," I say, pointing at her face, her arms and her legs, "is physical abuse, not to mention the mental abuse, the drinking and the screwing around with God knows who. He's not a kid, Rhonda. It's not something he'll outgrow like wetting the bed or biting his fingernails."

"He's good underneath."

"Underneath the sheets maybe, but it's what he's like when he comes up for air that counts."

"Don't go, Darla."

"You want me to stay? Okay, I'll stay." I pat the bulge in my purse. "But if Frank shows up I'll blow his goddamned head off his shoulders, then I'll fly all over you for exposing the kids to this mess all these years." I press ten bucks into her hand.

She hugs my neck, her baby breasts pressed to mine, strands of her hair in my eyes. I taste salt. Her tears or mine? She's lighter than air and pale as bread, this girl. "Get some groceries. If you or Frank use it for smokes or beer, I'll report you to welfare."

I head down the hall, Rhonda on my heels. Jessie's door remains closed. Pearl is gone. An empty milk carton sits on the counter. Mardel is sucking up the last drop. I nudge her foot, stare into a moon-shaped face and empty eyes.

"Money's tight in this establishment," I tell her. "From now on solid food ain't on the menu and milk's a dollar a glass. Put your money on the counter as you leave, okay?"

"But I was hungry and—"

"So are the Bosnians. Rhonda can't feed them, either."

Driving off, I look in the rearview mirror. Rhonda's standing by the garden hose in a small scrap of dirt, spindly legs apart. She's hugging herself, mouthing the words *I love you, Darla,* over and over again like a monastic chant.

I back up and get out. We cling to each other, sob on each other's shoulder like those poor folks on *Oprah* who, after endless years of searching, separation, and heart-wrenching misery, are reunited with long-lost kinfolk.

"Please, Rhonda, the kids deserve better. Get strong. Get a job. Go back to school. Learn typing. Something. Anything. Stand on your own two feet. Do it for you, okay?" We both know I've said the exact same things before—that in all probability, I'll say them again.

She nods in earnest, the way she always does, but when Frank comes home smelling of beer or woman and slobbers all over her and calls her his "hungry little love slave," she'll forget every damned thing I've said. And tomorrow night, she and Momma will sit side by side, betting their crazy hearts out at Big Bucks Bingo without even mentioning Rhonda's bruises, like two little girls under the kitchen table playing make-believe.

Rhonda stands in the same spot as I drive off, and that feeling of dread is back, the one I've had dozens of times over the years. Any number of things can trigger it. Evening heat, the incessant whir of katydids, flared cotton skirts, and green garden hoses all summon a cold hand to the middle of my chest—suggesting that something unpleasant lurks right around the corner.

Great swaths of orange, yellow, and purple paint are smeared across the western horizon. Later, somewhere between breathing out and breathing in, night will drop like a veil and the earth will roll over and play possum while I toss and turn and think about Rhonda, Momma, Granny, and the kids—while I wonder what'll become of them when I defect in September.

Then, with more than a twinge of guilt, I realize if I could spend just an hour or two of *quality time* with the Reverend Spirit E. Jackson, I might not give a shit one way or t'other.

Is This a Ghost Town?

On Main Street, near Woody's Bar and Pool Hall, I spy a familiar relic sandwiched between a beat-up El Camino and a Dodge van. Frank's Chevy pickup.

I slam on my brakes. Knowing Jessie's birthday money found its way into Frank's miserable gut ricochets around my skull like a stray bullet. My hands shake, and my heart flogs itself against my ribs. Wish I could bottle what I'm feeling right now, put a match to it, and blow the friggin' bar and Frank Slater straight to Texas.

I take a last look at the truck, a rattling pile of crap, and drive on, past Macy's Hardware and the Dead Bolt Cafe, past Flynn's Jewelry Store with the GOING, GOING, GONE sign in the window—past Jefferson's Shoe Mart with its fancy double doors where, I imagine, Mr. Jefferson stands in the shadows, jaw clamped, fists clenched, listening to his store take its last breath—past the bakery where, in the window, a two-tiered wedding cake, complete with bride and groom, is growing a fine veneer of green mold—a sad reminder that, two weeks ago, Maggie Parks called off her wedding to young Earl Wilks when she caught him in bed with her mother, another victim of the Too Late Syndrome.

Torn between what I know I should do and what I'm aching to do,

I drive to the end of Main Street and park in my usual place behind the bakery. My creative part says, "Go upstairs and finish that wedding dress or work on the Lincoln Center Gown," but my fighting mad part screams, "Go get that sonovabitch," even though I'm not sure what I'll do or say if I find him.

Poor Rhonda. Frank's her third mistake. At sixteen, she married the first paycheck that proposed, Stan Potts, Pearl and Jessie's daddy, and soon learned of his amazing talent. He didn't need a key to open a lock—any lock.

The marriage lasted four years, a nightmare of drugs, cops, and jail time that ended with one abrupt and terrible act of stupidity. While Rhonda fried burgers at Big Bucks Bingo, Stan, at home with little Jessie and Pearl, overdosed on some shit or the other and died on the living-room floor in front of them.

How those precious little things got over it I'll never know. Truth is, on more than one occasion, including today, I've looked into their eyes and been absolutely convinced they haven't recovered at all.

Rhonda's second marriage, to Dan Rogers, a rock-and-roll guitar player, fared no better. His nimble fingers went from picking strings to stealing cars. A five-year stint in the state prison ended that fiasco. I footed the divorce.

As for Frank, he appeared on Rhonda's doorstep like blight on a pear tree, ate two plates of SpaghettiOs, had Rhonda for dessert, and, in as little time as it takes to say "Oops," he'd moved in—along with a sack of dirty laundry, a lifetime of bad habits, and Bowzer the dog. Since then, other than the occasional job at Frick's Welding and Barton's Household Movers, both minimum-wage jobs, Frank's done little more than drink beer and collect unemployment.

The memory of Rhonda's swollen face makes up my mind. I grab my purse and head for Woody's.

★   ★   ★

Main Street, two blocks long, one traffic light, a dozen stores each side—some brick, some wood, many boarded up. A street where the passing of time is measured by the thickness of dirt in the gutters—a stretch of peeling paint, cracked sidewalks, and ragged awnings that prompts strangers to ask, "Is this a ghost town?"

Most folks around here like the place well enough—mainly shuffling old-timers who recall how things were fifty or sixty years ago. According to those familiar with pain and suffering, America was innocent back then, so they reach into their hearts and forgive Paradise for its shortcomings. I'm not so generous. We could have hooked up with the interstate years ago, but those in authority, those who feared progress would rob Paradise of its "charm," declined the offer and scuttled back to Possum Perkins's Domino Parlor.

Standing outside Woody's Bar, I can just make out the thumpety-thump-thump of the jukebox. Tammy Wynette is singing "Stand by Your Man," the biggest piece of male propaganda since God blamed Eve for snatching that friggin' apple. The pearl-handled .32 in my purse offers no sense of security whatsoever. I'd feel a hell of a lot safer if I knew how to load and shoot the damn thing, but I sure as hell wouldn't admit that to the know-it-all jerk who sold it to me. I tuck my shirt deeper into my jeans and tighten my belt a notch. Despite Frank's reputation for being a mean sonova, I'll lay some words of advice on him. That means I've gotta look determined, like I'm capable of inflicting serious pain and injury should he hurt Rhonda again.

Woody's, an awful, dingy old place, is filled with smoke. Unwilling to close the door behind me and shut out what remains of the day, I hold it open as I look inside. Woody, a short, compact man with a receding hairline, is drying glasses while he converses with a couple of guys in white sleeveless tank-tops—John "Red Man" Haney and Mickey Crow. They're welders, big, broad-shouldered guys. A year ahead of me in high school, both married, sometimes unemployed, sometimes flush with money, they greet me with raised hands. No sign of Frank.

"Shut the door, for Christ's sake," Woody yells. "You're ruining the ambiance."

I oblige, and, though I can't see a thing, I'm tempted to scream "SNAKE ALERT!" 'cause even as a kid I could smell 'em. I'd stand on the porch screaming, "Snake alert! Snake alert! It's under the house!" and sure enough, no sooner had Momma got on her knees and turned on her flashlight than we'd see it, head erect, coiled around itself, the tail rattling. Me and Rhonda always screamed like heathens until Granny arrived, shotgun ready, to fire into the crawl space. That's sorta how I feel now. I can't see Frank, but I'd lay money the creep is here somewhere.

A thick slab of yellow smoke undulates midair. I find it amazing that any normal person would choose to pass the time of day in a hell-hole like this.

You and Rhonda wait in the truck.
Where you and Uncle Earl going?
In Woody's, for a glass of lemonade.
But it's dark out here.
Go to sleep and you won't notice.

"Git your ass over here, Darla."
The throaty voice is familiar. "Brandy?"
"Over here, girl."

She's alone at a table, her brassy hair bigger than ever, a tight orange T-shirt stretched across her impressive boobs. She smells of Opium, keeps it in her fridge next to the eggs, in its original box, just as I gave it to her last Christmas.

I pull out a chair. "What you doing here?"
"Waiting."
"For who?"
"A guy who's an hour late."

"Anyone I know?"

"I'll float right out the door if I drink another glass of water."

"Anyone I know?" I ask again.

She smacks her gum. "Brad."

"Who the hell's Brad?"

"The guy we met at the Dance Barn few weeks back. The redhead with the black Firebird."

I take a sip of her water. "You're kidding? The one from Tulsa?"

"Uh-huh."

"You made a date with him? You never said."

"So?"

"So nothing. You never mentioned it is all."

"I own Kayla Mae's Beauty Shop. I work in that goddamned shop six days a week, eight hours a day, dyeing old women's hair blue, waxing their mustaches, and trimming their goddamned nose hairs till I'm sick of it, and you're saying I'm to check with you 'fore I make a date?"

"I didn't say that."

"That's what it sounded like."

"Sorry."

Something about the way she's fumbling in her purse, like she doesn't know what in the hell she's looking for, makes me think she's got something else on her mind. She leans over, as if she's about to divulge a secret, the low neck of her T-shirt exposing more of her breasts. "He slept over, if you must know. I didn't tell you before because—"

"I don't want to hear about it. You know what happens. You tell me something you know will make me mad, then *you* get mad at *me* for being mad at *you*. I hate it. I really hate it."

"Well, it was too late for him to drive back to Tulsa and he seemed okay."

"What if he's a serial killer or a rapist? We met him thirty minutes before the place closed. You only danced with him once."

An artless grin spreads across her face. "Yeah, but one dance can be enough, right, Darla? I mean, look at you and Billy Joe Comfort. The dance floor was still smoking when you two high-tailed it to Tulsa for the weekend. Or was it a week? I don't remember."

"Why do you always bring that up? I was eighteen, for Christ's sake. I didn't have a lick o' sense and my hormones were howling."

"But Billy Joe Comfort? I mean, he's handsome as hell, but he always looks like he's brooding about something—kinda scary."

"I know, but he was a risk I had to take. I thought he was different."

"And?"

"First inert object I ever screwed."

She smacks her gum and gets in my face. "You mean the earth didn't move?"

"Billy Joe's a real sweet guy, but I've had haircuts that were more exciting. The thing is, we were kids then. We thought we were invincible, right?"

"Guess so."

"We're older now. We're supposed to be wiser, cautious."

"I'm as cautious as the next person, and Brad seemed okay."

Brandy believes sexually transmitted diseases only strike bad folks in big cities, not *decent* people in small towns. But it's not all her fault. I mostly blame television and television commercials, and all their advertisements for douches, tampons, and pregnancy tests. The world's become too casual about women's vaginas—about what's put in 'em, how, and why, et cetera, et cetera. Taken away their mystery. Don't see any jock straps on TV. Don't see any guys unwrapping rubbers.

"For all you know, this Brad could be an escaped convict."

"He's a nice guy, Darla."

"Nice guys don't stand you up."

"You're right. He's a no-good shit, just like the rest of 'em. Satisfied?"

She blinks back a tear, stares into nothingness, her profile almost beautiful, a hungry soul who craves warmth and conversation, who willingly spends the night with total strangers while waiting for Mr. Right to knock on her door, who cooks him breakfast for his trouble—who crochets baby bootees for the children she hopes to have.

"I've had it with the beauty shop, Darla. What I'd really like to be is a nurse."

"Since when?"

"Remember when Bubba Jeffries tried to kill himself outside the Dance Barn last year? Remember how I held his wrists to stop him from bleeding to death till the ambulance arrived?"

"Uh-huh."

"That's when I knew."

"So what are you doing about it?"

"Nothing yet. Gotta give it some serious thought. Maybe take evening classes at Layton Votech. By the way, what are you doing here?"

"Hunting Frank."

"Saw him ten minutes ago. Started bothering the hell out of me till John and Mickey stepped in."

"So help me, Brandy, if he doesn't stop messing with Rhonda I'll kill him."

She digs in her purse like a hungry squirrel. "Got a cigarette?"

"You know I don't smoke."

"Just asking. Don't look now, but Frank's just left the men's room."

I'm up in a flash, .32 out of the bag, in my hand, making tracks. "Hey, Frank."

His cheeks are flushed with beer and he looks like a hermit with that scraggly hair—and while he's not a big man, I'm told he's a meaner, more wicked sonovabitch when he's sober.

Like Kramer on *Seinfeld,* his feet get tangled. He stumbles, grabs the cigarette machine for support, looks up, recognizes me, and, grinning like an idiot, stumbles in my general direction with his index fingers crossed—thrusts them at me like he's the priest in *The Exorcist*.

"Whoa, Darla," he says, his voice thick with booze. "You look madder'n hell."

I pocket the .32, step close as I can get, and knee him in the balls. The move is perfection. Frank collapses to the floor, moaning and groaning. I can hardly believe I'm doing this, but I want to hurt him, hurt him so bad he'll never lay a hand on Rhonda again—so bad he'll leave town. That way, I can get on with my life without worrying what he's doing to her.

I straddle his backside, and shove his face to the floor. The bar is quieter than Boles's Funeral Parlor, but when I ram the serious end of my .32 into Frank's right ear, I hear an audible gasp of disbelief. "You no-good bastard."

"Oh, God," Frank moans. "Is that what I think it is?"

"It's exactly what you think, and if you even breathe funny, I'll turn that no-good brain of yours into a lace doily."

"You crazy whore. What the hell's wrong with you?"

I prod his ear with the barrel. "I saw what you did to Rhonda, Frank, that's what's wrong with me."

"Shit, Darla. Get that thing out of my ear. It hurts."

I grab a handful of oily hair, yank it back and slam his face to the floor. "You don't know a thing about pain, you stinking slab of cow shit, and if you lay another finger on Rhonda, I'll do such a job on your privates you'll be singing duets with Pavarotti, understand?"

Folks have gathered round to watch, but I don't give a damn. "This lazy, no-good bastard beats up on my sister," I tell them. "Gives her and her two little kids more heartache than they deserve, and I'm sick of it."

Somewhere nearby an unfamiliar voice says, "In Romans 19, verse 16, the Lord says 'Vengeance is mine, I will repay.' Why not let Him take care of this man?"

I catch a glimpse of eel-skin boots, white pants, and when the man inside them kneels down, I'm staring into eyes of uncertain color. His white Stetson is unblemished, the brim a perfect angle over black brows. Here's a man who doesn't have to do or say anything to work his magic on me. All he has to do is look at me the way he's looking at me right now to make m'tongue sweat. If at this very minute Brandy, Woody, John, Mickey, and Frank Slater fell off the earth, I'd never know it.

Someone grabs my shoulder.

"Give me the gun and put your hands behind your back, Darla," says Leroy Poteet, "and we'll let these nice folks get back to business."

Crazy in Love

. . . .

When someone you're ready for comes into your life, it's not a coincidence. Even if things don't work out the way you want or expect, I'm convinced they happen for a damn good reason. We don't know the reason at first, 'cause it takes a lot of shit and unbearable heartache to figure out the details—a fact I'll take up with God if and when we come face-to-face.

I remember my last time like it's imprinted on my eyeballs, as if that moment in time, and everything about the man in question, including what happened and how, are recorded—as if I mentally taped the entire event, which in a sense I did, so that with a simple press of the button I could sit back and enjoy the show, which is what I'm doing now seeing as the city marshal has seen fit to lock me up in his run-down, two-cell jail on account I shoved an unloaded weapon into Frank Slater's miserable head.

What better feeling than being crazy in love? It's like falling head-first into an enormous banana split and slowly eating your way out, leaving the cherry till the end. Delicious. Last time it happened to me was during a blizzard in December 1988, inside room 24 at the Ponderosa Motel on Highway 9, while I was shacked up with Chris Burton, an Oklahoma Highway Patrol officer. Not that I think about him on a regular basis anymore. He might, on occasion, blow through my mind and stir up the dust a second or two, but that's all.

We'd dated for months, three to be exact, having met when he drove his soon-to-be-married seventeen-year-old niece to my apartment for a fitting. The mutual attraction was instant. It felt like a charge of electricity that bounced off the walls, scorched my fingers, and made me sweat. So much excitement sparking the air, we couldn't keep our eyes off each other.

Angie, blond hair piled on her head, her scrawny arms at her side, stood on the cutting table watching *Wheel of Fortune,* unaware that as I adjusted the hem of her gown, I swapped unspoken messages with her hunky uncle—that if she'd walked between us she'd have suffered third-degree burns.

I can still see him sitting on my couch, sipping a Sprite. His gaze washed down my back and across my hips, penetrated my T-shirt and jeans and blistered my flesh, while I stood cool as a milkshake, wishing I wore nothing at all.

The gold band on Chris's wedding finger bothered me, but by the time they left, thirty minutes later, his velvet voice, and a smile as big as Wyoming, had reduced that concern to the size of a loose thread, a flaw of microscopic proportions on a bolt of lush taffeta. The tan uniform with metal buttons, the sensually snug pants, the badge, even the gold-braided Highway Patrol cap perched on his knee—one gigantic turn-on—everything so handsomely put together, not a crease out of place—and somewhere underneath it all, something I couldn't quite put my finger on. A sense of the forbidden, maybe.

I know about the fine art of seduction. Fact is, I could write a how-to book—having learned the subtleties from television and movie stars. I start by raking back my unruly hair, knowing a piece or two will tumble forward over my eyes. I lick my lips and lower my lashes while my hands graze my jeans. I trace the length of my neck with my fingers, and once I'm close enough, I outline his lips with a fingertip or caress his ear—or whatever else rises to the occasion. To move things along, I use Chanel No. 5. Warm and simmering on my skin, it rises like a cobra to slip into the victim's nose and addle his brain.

Seduction doesn't happen by accident. Oh, no. It's more like a well-defined plan mapped out eons ago by an equally man-hungry woman—Eve. Same then as now, though. The minute Adam tasted her goodies the party ended, and life with all of its burdens and complications began in earnest.

Other than his long hair and sideburns, the Reverend Spirit E. Jackson greatly resembles my married patrolman, especially his walk, the easy loose-limbed stride of a cocky, to-hell-with-the-world adolescent.

My watch says nine-thirty, and I haven't seen a soul since Leroy Poteet put me in this cell over two hours ago. Creep, embarrassing me like that, dragging me out of the bar and into a car with Miss Ladybug's blood still smeared across its face. And I'm so damned tired and hungry I'd give my soul for some of Elijah's fried chicken livers and onions and a good night's sleep, but I'd have to be dead to lay in that cot yonder. A map of yellow stains dots the pillow's striped ticking—the drool and urine of drunks, most likely—and I'm suspicious of all military-type blankets, especially olive-drab ones that look like they came from the Army and Navy Surplus Store in Layton. I mean, who's to say they've been laundered since Desert Storm? Or World War II?

Chris and I used to rendezvous at the Ponderosa Motel. Growing up, I'd driven by the one-level red-brick building hundreds of times without giving it a second thought. Never even wondered what kind of people stayed in it. Nothing. On the other hand, Grady's Armadillo and Gator Farm next door fascinated me, and every other kid in town. We believed thousands of tourists paid their three-dollar fee, went in, but never came out. We believed the owner, Hilda Wharton, an unkempt woman with paranoia glinting like glass in her beady eyes, served unwary folk spiked lemonade and cookies, that when it came time to feed the gators, she tossed the comatose visitors into the gator pool. A grove of scrub oaks along the highway and down the gravel driveway hides the place from the prying eyes of families headed for Texas and Florida beaches, but billboards that read THE ONLY TWO-HEADED ALLIGATOR IN CAPTIVITY, AND YOU JUST MISSED IT suck them in. Vehicles turning around on the highway have worn ruts six feet wide and a foot deep into the dirt.

When I see the Ponderosa Motel nowadays, though, I feel a whole lot different about it. I know it's there, but I keep my eyes on the road and the radio turned high, so high it almost drowns out the memories—the biting smell of disinfectant, cold white tile, the stained ceiling, and a red-hot poker that set my insides on fire.

A girl, Darla, if you're interested.

If you're interested? The wound never healed, and the feelings of loss and guilt never go away. Hard as stones, they lie in the bottom of my uterus where, at the sight of a baby buggy or a Pampers commercial, they rattle and jar, one against the other. It is then that the horror of what I did returns to haunt me. I might be laughing with Elijah, taking a shower, or counting out change when the evil black thing drops from nowhere—slips over my head and shoulders like a muddy cape.

Where, I wonder for the umpteenth time, did little Mandy end up? Flushed down the toilet? In a Chamber of Horrors tent at a county fair? Is the poor little mite, along with her budding arms and legs, condemned to bob about for all eternity in a tall, wide-mouthed jar of formaldehyde? Is she trapped between heaven and hell, waiting for her momma to show her the way home? Had I been strong and brave, would she have grown into a curly-headed angel with Chris's mouth, my hair, and a dimple in both cheeks?

I don't miss Chris anymore, but I do recall the blind, crazy adoration that filled my head and wouldn't let me sleep till I saw him again, and that's what scares me. What if I never have those feelings again?

What if no one ever feels the same way about me? Assuming Chris loved me in the first place.

The last time I was in room 24 of the Ponderosa Motel, nothing else mattered. No deadlines. No place to go. No one waiting for me. Nowhere I belonged 'cept there with Chris. The wind howled like a coyote. Snow drifts tall as me. Temperatures below zero. Freezing rain turned poles and trees into ice sculptures. Each twig and leaf, each unwary bird instantly crystallized in time, while we stayed warm and crazy in love. I worshipped every inch of his flesh, every eyelash, every half moon on every finger, every crease and crevice, every throb of his pulse. Every breath he took, every word he uttered I treasured, and when he said he loved me more than life itself, I believed, to the deepest chambers of my heart, that we'd be together for eternity.

But three days, eight pots of coffee, six ham-and-cheese sandwiches, and two dozen assorted donuts later, the blizzard faded—and so did Chris. The pain in my belly, an ache too big and too awful for aspirin, felt as if a surgeon had carved out a vital organ and neglected to sew me back up. Two months later, after the abortion, with my wounds healed and some common sense restored, I had an inkling of what insanity felt like. I'd ridden that mule to hell and back, and had the calluses to prove it.

The door to the marshal's office springs open, and here comes Leroy Poteet, a wad of tobacco jammed in his jaw, toting a ring of keys.

"If my old lady wasn't pissed 'cause I missed supper, I wouldn't be doing this," he mutters, fumbling with the lock, "and you can thank the party outside for making it worth m'while."

"Who? Brandy?"

"No, some preacher beat her to the gate."

"Oh, God."

"Could be," he says, unlocking the cell door. "He's mighty clean, got a beard, and goes by the name of Spirit. Now, hustle y'tail outa here."

"What about my gun?"

"What about it?"

"When do I get it back?"

"You don't get it back. You committed a crime with it. A serious, punishable-by-jail-time crime."

"Wasn't loaded."

"Your victim didn't know that."

"Victim, hell. Frank Slater's a son of Satan."

"Makes no nevermind. You posed a threat to his health, girly, and that had a negative effect on the man's rectum, which, as you can imagine, mightily embarrassed him in front of his friends."

"He's got no friends."

"Anyways, consider your gun confiscated."

"You're joking. That no-good drunk battered my sister. You should lock *him* up and give Rhonda my gun for protection."

Leroy offers me a sly smile and motions me out. "Best leave while you're ahead, girly. Most folks never see my generous side."

I step past him. "A receipt then?"

He slams the cell door shut and shoves me to the bars, his face inches from mine, his piggy eyes squinted. "Darla, you attacked Frank Slater in front of half a dozen witnesses, and I'd bet money that gun ain't registered. What do you say to that, hmm?"

My mind scrambles around for the right thing to say. Bail or not, like it or not, if I want out of here tonight I'd better act submissive—like he's smarter than anyone gives him credit for. Leroy Poteet has gotta be the spider and I gotta make like a fly. I'll worry about details later.

"Well, Darla Moon?"

The lie slides off my tongue like sauce off ribs. "You're right, Marshal, it ain't registered." Without a word passing between us, he lets me out the back door. What's a body to do if their legally owned weapon falls into another's hands and they can't prove it?

My watch says ten-thirty, yet the air's still so hot and heavy I can hardly breathe. Millions of stars in the sky. The moon is huge. And the world is so clear and bright, I can see Miss Ladybug at the other end of the alley, behind Brown's Bakery.

Main Street is deserted 'cept for a couple of cars outside Woody's Bar, a white Cadillac in front of the jail, and the preacher standing on the corner. Quiet, too. Just the soft buzz of wood rot, the tick of the traffic light as it switches colors, and the lingering smell of barbecue from the Dead Bolt Cafe's smoker.

> I brung them ribs for y'momma and me. Eat all y'want of them
>   beans and bread.
> Me and Rhonda like ribs better.
> Listen to Uncle Will, Darla, 'less you're huntin trouble.

The streetlight lends a soft lemon tinge to the Sedan DeVille and the preacher's Stetson. He's changed clothes. He's wearing a striped shirt, top buttons undone, sleeves rolled up, and jeans. Older than I first thought. Weathered, wrinkled around the eyes. In spite of the facial hair and sideburns, he looks as comfortable as a leather chair. Tanned, like he's spent time under lamps. Not movie star handsome, but awful damn close.

Times like this make me wish I'd planned ahead, that I was psychic like Muff and Freda, that I had just stepped out of a bubble bath with my hair freshly shampooed, that I'd worn my good jeans, that I didn't smell of Leroy Poteet, that I knew exactly what to say to a sexy-looking preacher who'd just sprung me from jail—that I could quote the entire book of Revelations.

He's tall, six feet three at least, and he smiles like a boy, shy and uncertain. My hand rises like a magnet to meet his. He has a strong grip, and he smells fresh—a smell that fills my head with thoughts of warm showers and soapy bodies.

"Thanks, Preacher."

"The name's Spirit, and I'd have had you out sooner, Miss Moon, but the marshal locked you up and took off before I could get here. He only just came back."

He has an accent of sorts. With my hand enclosed in both of his, I experience a sensation I can only describe as electrifying. "The name's Darla," I say. His eyes are lighter than I imagined, the color of pale emeralds or sapphires. "I'm really embarrassed about this. Grateful, but embarrassed. Whatever it cost, I'll pay you back."

"No problem. The important thing is to drive you home."

I withdraw my hand. "I am home, and I have a car. I live down there, just beyond the Dead Bolt Cafe, over the bakery. And Darla Moon always pays her own way. How much?"

"Twenty-five dollars."

"That right? Fellas uglier than you had to cough up a hundred." He looks startled. Aided by the streetlight, I locate two tens and a five and hand it to him. "Just kidding. Where you staying in this big ol' town, stranger?"

"On Sycamore, at Widow Spencer's place."

I can't help but smile. Trudy's one of them high-buttoned, helmet-haired, holy-roller church women who, at the mention of Jesus Christ, go into a trance you'll never forget. Eyes closed, arms raised, swaying back and forth like a grove of trees in a sixty-mile-an-hour wind, they groan and howl like they're having an orgasm. And they speak in tongues, a language no one 'cept another born-again Christian can interpret.

They are scary, these women. They do things no person in their right mind would do, and they do it out in the open where everyone can see. Let them overhear a complete stranger speak of his cancer, or impending blindness, or of the crippling arthritis that keeps him awake nights, and these zealots drop their purses right where they stand, slap their open palms on the victim's forehead, and scream to Jesus for a cure.

The sound of our boots striking the sidewalk echo down Main Street. "Saw you in the church parking lot today."

"Didn't see you."

"I was in my momma's house across the street. Lamb of God adopted her years ago. They love a sinner. Gives them something to focus on, someone to point at and say, 'There but for the grace of God, et cetera, et cetera.'"

No response.

"Why, those ladies have laid hands on Roxie Moon's front door and begged for her salvation so many times the paint's wore off. Sad, really, 'cause all she's interested in is their fried chicken and mustard potato salad."

"The hunger for truth comes in many guises," he says.

"Is that so? What guise lured you into Woody's Bar and Pool Hall, Preacher? Thirst?"

He smiles and shakes his head. "God's love led me to Woody's, Darla. I'm a nondenominational Christian evangelist and I just happened to be walking down Main Street passing out these." He waves a piece of paper in the air. "This tract shows man the way to redemption through Jesus Christ."

"What about women? Doesn't our redemption come from the same place?"

"Of course it does. When I say man, I mean—"

"Does it say man and woman in this tract?"

"No, but—"

"Then you'd best correct it. We're in countdown to the twenty-first century. The days of I Am Woman, Hear Me Roar passed into oblivion years ago along with Helen Reddy. Equal rights, equal pay, and long maternity leaves are here. When it comes to saving souls, I'd lay money the man upstairs expects a preacher to be unbiased."

He slows down, falls behind a step or two. When I glance back over my shoulder, I see his mouth is hanging open. "Liked the outfit you had on earlier. Really impressive."

"Thanks."

"Smart thinking on your part. Folks round here have no use for men in long black robes and white cardboard round their necks. Don't care for fellas in pinstripe suits, either, 'less they're selling insurance or cemetery plots. When it comes to preachers, the frenzied, high-jumpin', laying-on-of-hands, dressed-all-in-white western variety really turns 'em on. They'll drop their last fifty cents in the collection plate for a preacher like that."

He catches up with me. "Hey, hold on. I am not frenzied and I don't want anyone's last fifty cents."

"Don't jump then."

"If you don't mind me saying so," he says, "not only are you a very attractive woman, you're *very* opinionated."

"I know, and I don't mind you saying so at all."

His accent, whatever it is, is a bonus. Lashes lowered, I run my fingers through my hair, rake it off my forehead—and catch myself. Who in the hell do I think I am, flirting with a man of God? Momma?

I sure as hell don't want him to think I'm drawn to him, that beneath this airtight exterior I'm as vulnerable as a friggin' ice cube. I hurry past the appliance store. I'll be damned if I'll let myself get involved with this or any other man. I have plans and dreams, by God, and no one's gonna change them, least of all a hell-and-damnation preacher.

"The guy you had on the floor," he says. "I hear he's your brother-in-law."

"You heard right. He beat up my sister and I was madder'n hell. The gun wasn't loaded. I just wanted to scare the S-H-I-T out of him."

"If my nose is any judge, you succeeded."

"Hopefully, he won't take it out on my sister or her kids. I wasn't thinking straight. Never should have done it."

"Are you engaged? Married?"

"Hell no. The only warm thing in my life is my hair dryer, and it's broke."

"Children?"

I keep walking. "Nope, none of them either," I say, but the lie stabs like a broken rib. "How about you? Married? Kids?"

"No, unfortunately. And if I had, I wouldn't have left them to come to America."

I stop outside the Dead Bolt Cafe and peer into eyes deep as a well. "How old are you?"

"Forty," he says without hesitation.

"Is that right?" He may not be every woman's Three Musketeers, but I'd love a bite.

"And you?"

"Younger. Where 'bouts you from?"

"Portland Bay, Australia—small town on the south coast."

I start off again, imagine him in the dusty outback, his brow beaded with sweat, a wide-brimmed leather hat on his head, turning shrimp on the barbie with one hand and wrestling a twelve-foot croc with the other—not a stitch on. "How long you been over here?"

"Ten years. Decided in my twenties I wanted to preach, heard about the evangelical seminary in New Mexico, and thought, Why not? I have a brother in Houston and my name fit. I've been on the circuit eight years—ever since I graduated. Okay, that's enough of me. Where were you born?"

I stop at the bakery. "Right here in Paradise," and in as little time as it takes to breathe in and breathe out, I see my entire life shackled on all four sides by the airless house on Railway Road where Rhonda was born, our apartment over the hardware store, the acreage where Momma and Granny now live, and my place over the bakery. Crudely stitched together, they bind like a stiff wool uniform—the fabric so tight it chokes me, so coarse it has, over the years, rubbed my skin raw. I run my hands through my hair, try not to look at him too closely, and start toward the steps. "I've gotta go. Been great meeting you."

"Likewise—say, Darla."

"Yes?"

"See you in church Wednesday night?"

I laugh out loud at the thought. "Dream on, Preacher. You've got as much chance of seeing me in Lamb of God as seeing Saddam Hussein direct the choir."

"Dinner Thursday night?"

Aware that madness runs in my family, I say, "Sounds great."

"Eight o'clock?"

"Perfect, but why?"

"Excuse me?"

"Why me? Why not one of those *Christian* ladies at Lamb of God?"

"Why eat toast when you crave cheesecake?" he says, disappearing round the corner. Then he's back. "Say, Darla."

"Yes?"

"Your eyes."

"What about 'em?"

"Exactly what color are they?"

"Brown," I reply. "Dark brown tinged with gold."

"Incredible," he says. "Absolutely incredible."

He's gone. A lump rises in my throat. I wish as hard as I can that he'll come back, but he doesn't. A Bible-thumping Aussie is on the loose in Paradise.

"Girl, you do not need a preacher in your life," I say as I head upstairs. "Don't need one messing up your kitchen, nosing in your business, or heating up your bed." So why does Thursday seem an eternity away—like Christmas is coming and the biggest package under the tree is mine?

Out of nowhere, while stretched out on my double bed, Leroy Poteet, of all people, comes to mind. Knowing he's got my gun really pisses me off. I'm bound to hear more about that. Maybe I should go see Muff and Freda, get them to read my palm or check my tea leaves.

Couldn't tell Elijah I was going. He'd have a blue hissy fit. I switch off the lamp and close my eyes.

As for the Reverend Spirit E. Jackson, he's probably got so many sexual hang-ups he'd be down on his knees praying for forgiveness 'fore I got his shirt off. I feel giddy. Haven't felt so excited about a guy since Chris, and that happened so long ago I barely remember how he smelled or how he combed his hair. Anyway, with New York on the horizon, this will be a very short relationship, if it develops into any relationship at all. So who cares if the preacher's as wild as an Apache or as predictable as a Rolex watch—so long as he is truthful. If not truthful, may his pecker rot off.

Twitching and jerking, I fall into a blood-red sleep, topple off a ledge, and wade knee-deep through fine white sand. A hot wind swirls about my head. Other than Paradise, Oklahoma, how many deserts are there in this world, for heaven's sake? And would someone please direct me to Portland Bay, Australia?

Monday Night Bingo

· ·

Rhonda isn't speaking to me, but as she sucks on her third cigarette, I see her watching me watch Momma—that's because she knows I'm angry as hell. We've been here an hour and Momma's yet to mention the mark on Rhonda's face. Not that I expected her to. She made fifteen dollars on the first game, fifteen on the second, and now she's savoring the thrill—figuring how many six-packs and how many cartons of Camels can be bought with that kind of money.

Momma hardly gets her winnings stashed away before she says, "Hear you got slapped in jail for a few hours, Darla."

"You heard right. Worth every damn minute, believe me."

"Frank's madder'n hell at you," Rhonda says, glaring. "Who in the hell do you think you are messing in our business?"

I'd like to smack her. "That bruise made it my business. If you want me to butt out, don't ask me to come by when he's beat you up, and don't call me when you're outa groceries and gas money, okay?"

As Muff reaches for her purse, her elbow strikes Freda's cup. Coffee spills and runs across the table, into Freda's cards. "Oh dear," Muff says. "Sorry."

"Sorry, shit," Freda yells. "Look at this mess."

Muff starts mopping and dabbing with Kleenex. "I didn't do it on purpose," she whines. "When this lot starts arguing with each other, it ruins my nerves."

"Talk about the pot calling the kettle black," Momma says. "You and Freda don't know what it is to be civil to each other."

"Is that right?" says Freda. "Then I suggest you find someone else to bring you to bingo."

Cleta John Simpson, secondhand car dealer, announces the next game, and an eerie silence descends on our table. It lasts until Rhonda says to Momma, "Pearl came home sick again today. Happens every time she eats hot dogs at school. Free or not, I told her she's a fool to eat 'em."

"Damn right," Momma says as I digest this information. "Not worth the aggravation."

Rhonda snorts through her nose. "I mean, why eat something if it makes you throw up?"

I can't help myself. "Because you're hungry, Rhonda."

She looks up from her card. "I'm not talking to you."

"Because you're hungry," I say again.

Momma cocks her head to one side, fiddles with an earring—snaps it off and on. "What's that supposed to mean?"

"Oh, God," says Muff. "Here we go again."

"It means," I reply, "that once a week, the newspaper publishes the school meals. Tells you what the kids are going to get, and on what days. So, if Pearl had money in her pocket on the days they serve hot dogs, she could get something from the snack machine, and she wouldn't get sick."

Eyebrows raised, Rhonda and Momma look at me as if I'd just told them I had kidney failure and needed one of theirs.

Rhonda fakes a laugh. "If I had the money, she wouldn't need free lunches at all, would she?"

"But she's thirteen and Jessie's eleven," I say, like she doesn't know the age of her own children. "Don't you know they're embarrassed to death standing in the free lunch line? What'll happen when they're in high school?"

"Hey, hey, hey," says Freda. "We can't hear a damn thing with you lot carrying on."

Rhonda shakes her head, looks totally confused. "When they're in high school? What are you talking about?"

"You know damn well what I'm talking about. You haven't forgotten. You remember how it feels."

"Tell you what, Darla," Rhonda says, her face red, "if my kids' lunches are such a problem for you, you pay for them."

"This really is troublesome," Muff says. "My head is spinning."

"Tell you what, Rhonda," I say. "If you'd kept all the money you've gambled on bingo, added it to all the money you've spent on smokes, then added that to all the money Frank's spent on beer, Pearl and Jessie could buy their school lunches till they graduate, and take a trip to Hong Kong."

"Never let up, do you?" Momma says, and I want to deck her.

Folks are shooshing us, and Cleta John Simpson yells out, "Ms. Moon, you and your girls keep your voices down or you'll have to leave. You're distracting the other players."

"About time," Muff and Freda say in unison, and Momma throws them a dirty look.

Minutes later, Momma wins another thirty dollars, and tucks it inside her purse.

"This'd be a good time to give back the fifty dollars you *borrowed* from me over the last month," I tell her.

Momma tears the wrapper from a Butterfinger. "Right, but if I do that," she says, "you'd be stuck with my electric bill."

Before we leave, Rhonda loses all the money she came with, including, I imagine, the ten bucks I gave her. Last damn time I fork over a dime, I tell myself.

"And another thing," I tell Rhonda as she climbs in the back of Freda and Muff's car alongside Momma. "The next time Frank lays a hand on you the gun *will* be loaded."

Railway Road

Elijah claims my father was a tall man with dark hair—said he lived with us at number 727, here on Railway Road—a part of the world where, with no apparent signs of disease or injury, hearts regularly bleed and break apart. Folks in this part of town have only sad tales to tell. No matter how old they are, most can count the good times they've known on one hand.

All I recall of my father is a long shadow in brown laced-up boots—how the small space he occupied squeezed him out like toothpaste until he vanished.

Years later, around Halloween, where Momma lives now, I woke up in the middle of the night to the sounds of fussing, raised voices, and scuffling, nothing unusual in our house, and went right back to sleep. Come morning, it occurred to me that maybe I'd heard my daddy's voice, and Elijah's, but Momma said I'd dreamed it all. Still, I've often wondered if it was my father I heard—if Momma ran him off.

This is where we started, though, on the north side of town, tucked between the railroad tracks and a long defunct pig farm, in this row of cardboard cornflake boxes, where walls are held together by tape and thumbtacks. I don't recall Rhonda coming into the world in the back bedroom of number 727, but she did. I know the roof leaked, that we boiled in summer, and when winter howled through the cracks like an angry ghost, me and Rhonda held each other tight and whimpered under the blanket.

Indifference marched through the front door of 727 Railway Road along with the uncles. I saw it in their eyes, smelled it on their breath between the cigarettes and beer, felt it in every passing pat on the head. At school, kids laughed at our shoddy clothes and secondhand shoes, and when my first-grade teacher jerked her perfectly manicured hand from my grubby one, the look of disgust on her face filled my mouth with the taste of rusty nails. For the most part, folks treated us as if we were less than human, like we were a monkey virus that had dared to cross the species barrier—like we didn't belong in Paradise and never would—like Momma's "business" had anything to do with us.

Poverty, and folks' indifference to it, remains alive and well on Railway Road. If a woman's late for work, or stays home to nurse a sick child, she'll quickly meet indifference at the unemployment office and the welfare department. Neatly wrapped in a tweed skirt, beige blouse, and comfortable leather pumps, it calmly feeds her name into a computer already clogged and overflowing with shattered lives.

"The System," according to Momma, is another threat—a threat as real as landlords. Beady-eyed, sharply tucked into long white envelopes with windows in the front, it hunkers down in mailboxes alongside beetles and spiderwebs, waiting for someone, anyone, to gasp with horror at what's written inside. "You no longer qualify for . . . ," "Legal action will be taken on the date shown below . . . ," or "Electric service will be discontinued if payment is not made by . . ." I remember how the envelopes kept coming, one after the other, until, according to Momma, the house and everyone in it was *under attack*.

Do the sons of bitches think we're made of money? Let 'em throw us out in the street. Feed us to the wolves, why don't they? Let 'em turn off the heat and freeze our asses to death and watch me sue 'em.

A tall can filled with bacon grease always sat on the stove at 727. Momma stirred heaping spoonfuls of the fat into simmering pots of beans and mysterious, fishy-smelling casseroles. Under the sink, traps set with pinches of it snared furry little mice—snapped their heads clean off.

In winter, despite a pale watery sun that streamed through the windows to shine on peeling gray paint, ice formed inside the glass, air turned white, our eyes watered, and our insides ached with the cold. That's when me and Rhonda huddled together under the quilt like two skinny spoons, teeth chattering, shivering in the dark, not daring to move an inch in any direction till we warmed up and fell asleep.

In summer, grass grew around the house—not much, just enough to keep dust from flying through the open windows, and so choked with dandelions in spring and summer, the yard resembled a yellow carpet. And I'll never forget the stench—a great hot slab of hog manure that wafted in and out of the cracks, took root on the walls, and stole our appetites. The smell gave me headaches, made me so mad I tipped sacks of sugar and flour onto the kitchen floor and played with matches till the couch caught fire. A man called Uncle Phil pointed a garden hose through the living-room window and extinguished the flames. He then hauled what remained of the couch into the yard, removed his belt, snapped it like a whip, and delivered a whipping to my rear end while Momma watched.

Me and Rhonda knew we were poor long 'fore we started school. Everything about us, the ramshackle house, the street we lived on, the truck we rode in, testified to this dismal fact just as surely as our run-down shoes and our moth-eaten coats from Goodwill. We even smelled poor, that unwashed, uncared-for stink that comes from too little soap, too much cigarette smoke, and no affection.

Elijah lived close by even then. Fact is, he drove Momma to the hospital in his truck after she birthed me in the abandoned car her, m'daddy, and Granny were living in. Two days later, Elijah says, he delivered all of us to 727—just down the street from his place.

I park the car and get out. It's a furnace out here. The simple act of breathing in and out takes effort. Elijah once lived yonder, in that sun-bleached, neglected three-room shanty. I remember the sloped floors, the roof patched with tar paper, and an assortment of strategically placed buckets catching the rain. Out front, near the door, sunflowers grew six feet high, yellowjackets disappeared into cracks under the eaves, and when the sun went down, fireflies danced and winked among the weeds near the railway lines.

Elijah made a living buying, repairing, and reselling vacuum clean-ers. Lawn mowers, too. He spent hours on his knees in the front yard, an old straw hat pulled down over his eyes, taking things apart and putting them back together again, fussing with them till they worked like new. And, over the years, he fixed and painted his little home till it shone.

Granny, me, and Rhonda spent many hours in that little house, 'specially after school when Momma played bingo or went for a ride with "friends." We sat on Elijah's couch and listened to the radio while we ate corn on the cob, field peas, and buttermilk biscuits. We felt safe with him. He made our life of "making do," "eking out," and "minor setbacks" (all of which meant doing without) tolerable.

And the boys who chased us home yelling "Railroad trash" wet their pants when Elijah took after them rattling a gourd in each hand, screaming in an unknown tongue—proving, the boys said, that he was a demon, the Devil's disciple doing the Devil's work.

We were cross-eyed stupid, the boys insisted, for even setting foot in "that black bastard's house," 'cause when we disappeared off the face of the earth, as we most certainly would, the police would find our bones floating in Elijah's cook pots, along with lizards, toads, and new-born babies—but we never believed them.

Miss Cissy Lee, a tall, rawboned spinster lady who, in her prime, baked for profit and recreation, appears on her porch and waves. She once was beautiful. Her graceful neck, well-defined cheekbones, and the shapely ankles beneath her long skirt tell the story. "Well, looky here," she says. "If it ain't Darla Moon. Ain't seen you in a coon's age, girl. Come sit a spell 'fore this heat scrambles y'brain."

She has lived in this narrow-windowed, whitewashed house for as long as I can remember and, I'm told, always enjoyed cooking, especially for good-looking men—regardless of age, color, or religious persuasion. Elijah says he grew fat to the point of having a stroke on Miss Cissy's brown sugar candied yams, crispy-fried chicken, and berry pies, while politely resisting every invitation to cross her threshold to eat a meal at her table—a feat rarely achieved by others.

Avoiding a bed of hot-pink periwinkles, I pick my way across her yard, join her on the porch, and ease myself into a wicker rocker. "You look well, Miss Cissy. Thanks for the invitation."

Between us, on an old oak table, sit two tall glasses packed with ice cubes. The pitcher of tea has sprigs of mint and slices of lemon floating on top.

"Saw you pull up," she says as she pours, "so this is strong and sweet. Just like you and Rhonda like it."

"You remember, after all this time?"

Frowning, she takes a glass between her hot swollen fingers and sips, rocks back and forth. "Ain't been that long, has it?"

"Haven't tasted your tea in more'n twenty years."

"Hell, that's just a hiccup in the scheme of things." She stares into oblivion, smiles at Railway Road, like it's a parade ground, as if all the men in her life, the tall ones, the short ones, the skinny ones and plump ones, their mouths dusted with confectioner's sugar and puff pastry, their stomachs bulging with juicy pork chops and apple dumplings, are marching past in single file, their hands raised in a salute in honor of her culinary skills. "So what brings you down here, Darla?"

"Got to thinking about the old neighborhood. Thought I'd look around."

"What's Elijah up to nowadays?"

"Taking it easy mostly." As we rock in unison, tea trickling down my throat, I mentally separate the sugar and mint from the tartness of the lemon, savor each and every drop.

"Nice man. Can you imagine him showing up here in Paradise same time as your family—and from the same county in Arkansas? Didn't even know each other. Ain't that somethin'?"

"That is something," I say as if I knew all along, as if I'm not amazed by this scrap of history.

"How's Rhonda?"

"Always coming down with something or other."

"Worst thing she ever came down with is Frank Slater. Ain't worth rat shit. Older than her, too, ain't he?"

"By twenty years."

"Should've left him where he belongs, at the bottom of the food chain. Billy Joe Comfort replaced my fuel pump last week. Talked about you. Said he thought you'd be long gone by now, seeking your fame and fortune, as they say."

My new suitcases and the Lincoln Center Gown flash through my mind. "I'm working on it."

"Y'granny still ate up with the goofies and counting her frogs?"

"Yes'm."

"Outlive all of us, I bet."

"Maybe," I reply, but Granny's slipping ever deeper into her fantasy world. Some days, she circles the house laughing, singing, and dancing as she follows a piper no one but her can see or hear.

"Roxie slowed down, has she?"

"Had to. Fell out of bed and hurt her back."

Miss Cissy slaps her knee and laughs. "Mayor get carried away again?"

"Something like that."

"Don't hate her, y'hear."

"I don't." Or do I? I'm not sure what I'm supposed to feel for a woman who derived no pleasure from her kids but found bliss 'neath the sheets, screwing a stranger. Even then, her attention span was short. As soon as he'd "delivered the mail" and paid the fee, she hustled him outside into his vehicle and told him to hit the road.

"Ain't right," Miss Cissy says, "to judge someone by the worst thing they ever did. Besides, when y'momma started school, she left a playmate behind, not a mother. And some women aren't cut out to have kids. They think 'cause they got breasts they gotta put 'em to use. Being the oldest sister of twelve brothers, I soon learned I wanted no part of all that noise and tomfoolery—that I enjoyed cooking for a man, but nothing else."

"Momma tried," I say, but she didn't. She ignored our every whine and whimper while she *entertained*. Sometimes, just for fun, me and Rhonda would stand at the back door screaming, "Daddy's coming! Daddy's coming!" just so's we could watch a naked man clamber out Momma's bedroom window. Barefooted, toting a bundle of clothes under his arm, he'd leap like someone possessed through snow, rain, or stickers, clamber in his truck, and peel off down the road like the Devil had hold of his tail. Hell, we had more escape ruts in our backyard than blades of grass.

I glance at my watch. It's five o'clock, and the thermometer on Miss Cissy's shady porch registers 96 degrees. Sweat slides between my breasts onto my belly. My shirt is drenched, my jeans feel tight. Chunks of ice pop and crack inside the tea glasses. Purple martins soar overhead, delicate V shapes gliding in a brilliant blue sky, hunting mosquitos. The aroma of pineapple mint rises from a wooden planter. From inside the house comes the loud tick of a clock and the sweet, gooey smell of something wonderful baking in the oven, a hint of cinnamon and nutmeg. Across the street, squat and smug, sits 727 Railway Road. The sight of it raises goosebumps on my neck.

"How about a cinnamon roll?" Miss Cissy asks.

"Can't, Miss Cissy. Stayed too long already. Thanks again for the iced tea. You make the best."

Before I can step off the porch she wraps her arms around me and squeezes.

"Hurry on outa Paradise 'fore you forget why you wanted to go in the first place," she whispers, but there's no chance of that.

My heart flipflops knowing the preacher will pick me up in three hours, yet I ignore Miss Cissy's advice and knock on the door of 727. No answer. I stroll round back and find a worm-riddled peach tree, a kiddie's play set with two swings, a slide, a broken seesaw, and three rusty lawn chairs, the webbing in strings. Small handprints on the inside of the windows. Threadbare curtains. Dirty blinds. Did me and Rhonda ever laugh and dance or jump for joy in there? Did we chase each other? Did we play hide-and-seek or blow out birthday candles? Did we ever put a tooth under our pillow and find a dime in the morning? No, I can't recall doing any of those things, and a sense of loss—a cold ache big as a fist—fills my chest and throat.

Something else, too. Other than Elijah and Granny, the adults in our life rarely called us by name. Didn't even glance in our direction when they spoke.

Get out.
Stay out.
You can't come in.
Go piss in the weeds.
Empty the trash.
Go to bed.

They never sat with us, never ate with us, never looked us in the eye or talked to us. Never asked how we felt or asked us what we liked to eat, never asked what we wanted to be when we grew up—like we didn't matter, like we were an inconvenience, nuisances who made the mistake of catching colds or running fevers.

> Sick or not, me and your pretty momma is going dancing
>   tonight.
> Swallow a spoon of sugar for that cough. We can't hear the TV.
> How we s'posed to sleep with you upchucking all night?

As if determined to whip us into shape and prepare us for a higher, more permanent authority, our uncles displayed an uncomplicated desire to punish what wasn't theirs. Belts, switches, rolled-up newspapers, all were swung with equal vigor—usually if Elijah's truck was gone and Momma wasn't home. If she was, they asked permission, and invariably she gave it.

As young as we were, and even later, when we moved to Main Street, and ultimately to where Momma lives now, I sensed that me and Rhonda were in the midst of a struggle, that we were looking—looking for order in the midst of chaos, for warmth in the center of biting cold, for hope where there was despair—for acceptance and love. Thank God for Elijah.

So why, I wonder, when me and Rhonda were hungry, sick, or lonesome, did we always cry out for the one person who was never there—our momma?

Beginnings and Ends

Somewhere, in this world or another, our names are written side by side in the Book of Fates and Certainties, or in ancient dust, because, I believe, Preacher Spirit E. Jackson and I were bound to end up like this, out on the town together.

The fifteen-minute drive into Palm Grove begins as a sunset the color of orange juice spills across the horizon, while the sun hangs on for dear life to an endless length of mauve ribbon. White farmhouses, assorted red barns, and black-and-white cows dot the landscape like so many toys, and the flashing neon sign outside Grady's Armadillo and Gator Farm can be seen from half a mile away: CLOSED. COME BACK TOMORROW IF YOU AIN'T TOO SCARED.

I give Spirit directions as his strong hands guide the steering wheel, and his scent, an ebbing, flowing tide of body heat and cologne, torments the hell out of me. As he drives, I watch him from the corner of my eye, envision his calf muscles tightening, his biceps flexing—imagine, with remarkable clarity, how those arms might feel around me.

"I feel you giving me the once-over, Darla Moon," he says. "Do I pass inspection?"

"Too early to say, but the Australian accent gets a gold star."

"Thanks, and just in case you didn't notice, I polished m'boots and combed m'hair."

"I noticed."

"Washed m'face and dusted m'hat, too."

"Noticed."

"Had you on my mind ever since we met."

"Really?"

"Really."

At the first stop light in Palm Grove he looks directly at me. "You're a stunner. You know that?"

A primeval tail wraps itself around my thighs and nuzzles my belly.

"You know that?" he asks again, but I can't even open my mouth, let alone speak. Me, Darla Moon, dumbstruck.

"Forgive me if I ask stupid questions," he says, "but you make me feel like a sixteen-year-old who's forgotten how to tie his shoelaces."

A cry bubbles up inside my chest. I feel young, too—a shy, inexperienced girl playing in the Rattler with the Hoskin boys, climbing an apple tree, the boys hooting and hollering below, giggling at the sight of my underwear.

I like this man. I like him a whole lot.

Marshall's Steak House isn't crowded, thank goodness. A young waiter with a prominent Adam's apple seats us in a candlelit corner near a window. On the table, a single rose in a crystal vase—white napkins that smell of starch—spotless silverware. The Dead Bolt Cafe it isn't. Spirit's face glows in the dim light, the gray in his sideburns shines like silver, and the meal passes in a blur of light conversation. When we finish eating, he drinks half a cup of coffee, leans back, and studies me intently—smiles—says, "Bet every man in this room wishes he was me."

I pretend I don't hear. "So tell me more about Australia and your folks."

His expression turns serious. "I miss my parents, especially on birthdays and holidays. When they celebrate, they have a real knees-up."

"Knees-up?"

"A party. Lots of people, all our relatives, dancing, tables loaded with food and drink. I used to drink, but not anymore."

"And Australia."

"Ah, words can't describe it, Darla. You'd have to see for yourself. White beaches stretching for miles, coral reefs made by God's own hands, sunsets that make you cry. Friendliest place on earth."

"Sounds wonderful."

He reaches across the table, lifts the hair from my forehead, and says, "You're wonderful. You take my breath away."

My heart somersaults. Tongue-tied again.

He smiles at the waiter and orders more coffee, and adds, "Why don't we top it all off with cheesecake. I'm a pig for the stuff."

More chitchat, and clumsy silences. I've never been at a loss for words like this, but between bites of dessert, I tell him about Granny, Momma, Rhonda, and the kids. None of the crazy stuff, of course. Who wants to hear that? Who'd believe it?

As he speaks of his firefighter brother in Houston, I detect a spiritual, almost Christ-like quality about him. The beard, the mustache, the dark complexion, and the black wavy hair don't enter into it. No, it's more elusive than that.

I note the casual cotton jacket, the hard body under the tan, open-necked shirt, the smattering of hairs on the back of his hands—and wonder why, at his age, he's never married. I also find it hard to believe he's a hell-and-damnation preacher, that he stands in a pulpit pounding the Bible while begging lost souls to seek salvation and return to the fold before it's too late.

He slips his arm round my waist as we leave the restaurant, holds the door, and guides me through.

"Thanks for a lovely dinner."

"Thanks for your company," he replies, his voice reminiscent of warm brandy on a starlit night, of moonlight, of touching and whispering and flickering candles, of Pavarotti's phantomlike voice echoing in the darkness, of that hazy period between passion and sleep when flesh is moist and lips are spent, when your lover is everything you ever wanted and the end of love is a million light years away—but I'm not thinking straight. This is our first date.

It's after ten o'clock and still hot. Close to 90 degrees. The humidity is unbearable. High enough for orchids to root on telephone poles.

"Wait here, Darla," Spirit says, starting across the street. "I'll make a U-turn and pick you up."

Desperate to see what Spirit sees, I look at my reflection in the restaurant window. Staring back at me, dressed in a white peasant blouse and a long, melon-colored skirt, is Roxie Moon's daughter. Roxie's eyes, Roxie's not-too-narrow waist, Roxie's breasts riding high and full on the rib cage. We walk alike, too—a swinging, sashaying stride that makes men and boys whistle. And look at all that hair. It flies like a horse's mane and can scare kids at Halloween, but when I'm wearing nothing at all, it says everything I can't. Too sexy to be cut, that's for damn sure.

I believe Momma's bright makeup and false eyelashes and the red and black undies she hung outside to dry made folks unfriendly—not to mention the way she paraded down Main Street every Saturday morning, smiling like a cat full of cream, to get her hair washed and set at Kayla Mae's Beauty Salon.

As she passed, she exuded the pride of a general inspecting his troops, his chest ablaze with medals, and at least twenty-four eyes would stare and marvel at her swinging rear end. Twenty-five if you count Fess Cobb, the butcher, who got his left eye shot out in a hunting accident. Even Ratchethead, the butcher's dog who slept in the middle of the road, raised his head for a peek at Momma when she walked by.

The men looked sad, too, as if they believed nothing of conse-

quence happened in Clevedale County 'cept between Momma's
milky-white thighs—that like a poultice on a boil, her sorcery alone
could suck the ache from their bones and the misery from their hearts.
A sad realization if they couldn't afford her prices. A romp in that
Garden of Eden cost money, anything from the cost of a carton of
Camels all the way up to that of a keen-nosed coon dog, depending, I
imagine, on Momma's mood and inclination and the persistence of bill
collectors. Price also depended on the frillies her clients chose from
that black bag she carried. For the most part, only funeral directors,
factory owners, and oilfield workers flush with newly cashed paychecks could explain away money like that to a sharp-eyed wife, 'specially if that wife could add and subtract. One thing's for sure, even
though money slipped through Momma's fingers like butter, she
always had enough left over to get her hair fixed.

I recall her coming home from Kayla Mae's, her wavy hair glowing
like polished copper, how she sank into a chair at the kitchen table and
let out a huge sigh, as if all that pumping up and stepping out along
Main Street had been a strain, which it was, especially as she grew
older. Even when we moved to the acreage and she bought the beat-up
old Pontiac, she wouldn't park anywhere close to that beauty shop. No
sir. Unless it rained, or more than an inch of snow lay on the ground,
she walked that pockmarked sidewalk from one end to the other every
Saturday—no matter that her feet hurt, no matter that her calves
cramped, no matter that her back felt like it might break in two. She'd
just smile and say, "Turning a head or two makes the agony worth-
while."

I relax on the ride home. We laugh about the young waiter, how he
fumbled with our empty plates and dropped the dirty silverware. We
discuss favorite books. He likes a series written by an English veteri-
narian. I recommend a collection of short stories by Joyce Carol Oates.
He asks if he may borrow my copy, and I'm amazed that he's interested, that he really listens to what I say and takes me seriously.

"What's the name of that delicious aftershave you're wearing, Spirit?"

"Paradise."

"Really?"

"No, it's Safari. My brother gave it me for my fortieth birthday last year. When's your birthday?"

"Turned twenty-eight back in March."

"Faith?"

"Bunches."

"In whom?"

"In me, of course."

"What about God?"

"Got faith in him too. I'm a member of Fountain Baptist Church. Just don't make it over there very often."

"You should. God's word works miracles on the heart."

"So does nitroglycerin, but I don't need that either."

He looks shocked.

"Tell you what, Preacher, I won't trouble you with selvedge edges, double pleats, and blind stitching if you won't bother me with the Father, the Son, and the Holy Ghost."

He looks surprised, hurt even. "Agreed," he says, "for the time being. And that ring on your wedding finger. What is it?"

"Turquoise."

"I recognize the stone, I just wondered if it had any significance."

"No significance," I lie. *I'll replace it with an engagement ring before spring, Darla—I promise,* Chris said.

Spirit steps into the apartment and removes his Stetson, hangs it on the nearest chair. "This is what I call a king-size room."

I switch on the stereo. Pavarotti begins to sing "Che Gelida Manina" from *La Bohème*.

"Do you ever listen to KTOR out of Tulsa?" he asks.

"No, I haven't."

"It's a Christian radio station. Widow Trudy listens to it all the time."

I act like I don't hear him.

He appraises the fabric screens at the far end, inspects the suspended canopy draped with muslin behind them and, I imagine, rightly concludes my bed is back there, somewhere. He stops at my cutting table, studies my sketch pad—the torsolettes and bustieres teamed with short-short flirty skirts, long slinky knit dresses topped by full-sleeved, brushed angora cardigans—strokes the bolts of tulle, taffeta, and silk with tanned hands.

"What's this, leopard?"

"Fake leopard."

"You're kidding."

"The best fake leopard money can buy."

He runs his fingers through the black chiffon before turning his attention to the red Thai silk. He's engrossed in it, watches it tumble through his hands like a bloody waterfall.

"Incredible."

"Sixty dollars a yard incredible. Belongs to an Oklahoma City client. I'm making her a Darling Darla Creation for Christmas."

"Darling Darla Creation?"

I hand him a business card. "My niece's idea."

"Smart kid."

"Beautiful, too, and seeing as the bulk of my business comes from my own designs, she picked the perfect name." The look of amazement in his eyes when I open the bridal closet delivers a resounding kick to my heart. "This wedding gown, for example."

"Hey, that's gorgeous."

"Enough seed pearls on the bodice and sleeves to choke a goat—and that's a ten-foot train draped over those dowels. The bride and groom live in Dallas."

He stands before the closet where I keep the Lincoln Center Gown.

"And in here?"

"My secret," and to my relief, instead of pursuing the matter, he continues to stroll around.

"Everything here is exactly like you, Darla Moon. Colorful. Incredibly smart, rare, and uncommonly beautiful."

How can a woman ignore comments like that, said like that? Does he think I can just brush my teeth and fall asleep without once imagining what those muscles feel like, what he looks like under those clothes?

He of all people should know that when a godly man fancies a woman with my history, God puts up one hell of a fight. On the other hand, maybe Spirit sees me as a sinner, one worth sampling, even if he ends up stoking the coals. Well, unlike Momma, I won't be a party to this preacher's undoing.

I move toward the kitchen and make a feeble attempt to look busy. I fill the kettle, set it on the lighted stove, and fiddle with the sugar bowl—as if he had already agreed to a cup of coffee I can't make because I don't have any.

"If you want a drink when the water boils," I say, my back to him, "I'll fix you some hot tea—if I have tea bags. If I don't, I'll fix hot chocolate. I have instant. I think I have instant. If not, I can fix the regular kind with cocoa. I have that." I locate two cups. One is chipped. I put it back and find another. "Though I can't imagine why I'm offering you hot tea or hot chocolate in the middle of a heat wave. Did you know that parts of Oklahoma haven't seen a drop of rain in five years—that farmers are going belly-up for want of water—that crops are burning up, that entire herds of cattle are dying? Can you imagine? It's another Dust Bowl. Only thing that could make it worse would be a plague of locusts or a river of blood—like in the Bible."

I sense Spirit behind me—the way I feel someone watching me across a busy room—like hearing the phone before it rings—or knowing what a lover's about to say before his mouth opens. A stirring of sorts. I know what comes next. One dance finished, another begun: a tango of moves and countermoves, heat and desire.

He turns me around. One arm circles my waist, a hand cradles my head. Eyes open, he bends down and touches his lips to mine, brushes them ever so gently, back and forth, back and forth, back and forth until I'm dizzy. Kisses my neck, my ear, my cheek, reclaims my lips, and presses deeply. My ear, my cheek, my lips again. I want this man, crave him like a wild animal might long to devour a flower, driven not so much by hunger, but by the overwhelming need to absorb its beauty, its color—the very essence of its life. At this very moment, I want to make love to the Reverend Spirit E. Jackson.

As I'm about to lead him to my bed and surrender myself, the midnight freight howls through town and splits the night in two. Windows rattle, pebbles fly, broomsedge and Indian grass bend. Once it's gone, the night comes back together, melts into itself, like hands in prayer. 727 Railway Road will tremble in its wake. Rhonda's trailer will shake and rouse the kids from sleep—a cruel reminder that the day ahead will be no better than the one they just left behind.

Spirit whispers into my hair, says my name again and again, blurs its edges, spins it into honey as the aroma of Safari and warm flesh rises thick and heavy as incense from his open shirt.

I am transformed—a cobweb blowing through trees—a stone washed smooth by ocean waves. I come up for air, and there, at the far end of the room, beyond the screens, back in the shadows, stands Shamir.

"I first saw him when I was seven," I say. "He is tall, part haze, part substance, and I have no idea how I came to know his name, only that I knew we'd met before—before I was born, in another, less painful place."

Spirit tightens his grip, but says nothing.

"A place where time isn't measured by the hands of clocks as they sweep across numbers, but by the size of comets, by the dark fathom-less distance that separates one star from another. I know that sounds crazy—but that's what I believe."

Spirit peers into my eyes and asks, "Who are you talking about?"

Shamir dissolves like a cloud in a wind-tossed sky until he's a mist, a tuft of vapor floating six feet off the floor—then he's gone.

"My guardian angel. I just saw my guardian angel again."

Spirit runs his fingers through my hair, strokes it, admires it. "Why did that sound like the most natural thing in the world coming from you?"

"Because you recognize truth," I reply, but I'm desperate for dis-tance, for time to think things through. I ease from his grasp, go to the window, and open the blind to a full moon. Brilliant. Incandescent. The kind wolves howl at. The kind men and women fall in lover under. Main Street is deserted, covered from one end to the other, it seems, in a thin sheet of blue ice. The rooftops look frozen. Smack dab in the heat of summer they glisten with a mysterious frost, as if with the tap of a little hammer they would crack like an eggshell. Desolate outside, as desolate as this room will be when Spirit leaves it.

"Any Indian blood in you, Darla?"

He knows. Someone told him. "A little Cherokee on my momma's side. Why?"

"I've done a lot of traveling the past twelve years. Arizona. New Mexico. Texas. Florida. Met all kinds of Indians. Apache, Cherokee, Crow, Seminole, Navaho, Yuma, you name it. Some full-blood, some not. For the most part, the women are highly spiritual. Like you, they've had many visions and visitations. Some under the influence, others not. I've always found their stories fascinating. Never dreamed I'd come this close to an actual event."

"You do believe me, then?"

"Absolutely. As for ancestry, mine were British explorers who sailed to the South Pacific and landed on the Cook Islands. They found beautiful brown women living there, and the rest is history, as they say."

Reckon his fat little heart just plumb gave out, don't you, girls?
Reckon so, Momma.
Go get Elijah.

I close the blind, blot out the night. Me, Darla Moon, about to hit the sack with a man of God. Total insanity. "This isn't a good idea."
"What isn't?"
"Me and you, together."
"You mean I'm a bad date?"
I daren't look at him.
"I improve with time," he says. "Might even grow on you."
"Uh-huh."
"Make great spaghetti."
"Not hungry."
"Iron like a pro."
"Is that so?"
"Not too bad in the romance department, either."
The muscle in my left eye starts twitching. "So what's first on your agenda, Preacher? Eating, ironing, or falling on your knees and praying for forgiveness?"
"I wasn't suggesting—"
"It's late. You'd better go."
"I thought we had something special, Darla."
"Me too."
"I felt it when we walked down Main Street the other night. This may sound strange, but I felt you, some part of you, that is, curl up inside of me as we spoke. Still feel it. Never known anything like it before."
"Me either, but reality set in."

"Reality?"

I hear him start toward me. "Please don't come any closer, Spirit. We're oil and water, you and me. Let's finish things now 'fore the new-car smell wears off."

"Who are you scared of, me or you?"

"Not scared of anyone. Just don't want this to go any further." I turn to face him, ready to offer up some cockeyed reason, but he doesn't wait. He retrieves his Stetson, opens the door, stands in a slice of moonlight for a second or two, and leaves.

Friday Night Bingo

Momma claims she's broke, and I'm inclined to believe her, but like Muff and Freda, I ignore her fidgety hands, the wide-eyed looks of nervous desperation.

Thirty minutes later she's got money—enough for a hefty supply of bingo cards, a double cheeseburger, a large order of fries, and a maxi root beer.

"I followed you out back, Momma," I tell her. "Saw you behind the Dumpsters. Made me wanna vomit."

Hearing this, Muff and Freda's ears perk up. They stop fiddling with their cards and crane their necks to listen.

"That's what you get for being so goddamn nosey, Darla," Momma hisses in my ear. "And keep your voice down."

"Never knew you were so partial to flies and Rooster Burgess." Just saying his name turns my stomach. Like Leroy Poteet, Rooster has no redeeming qualities. The pock-faced lowlife stays on alert for the law. And so he should. He wheels and deals in food stamps and every illegal drug imaginable. Devious little creep. He'll shake a man's hand one minute and smack him up the side of the head with a two-by-four the next. And no one meets in private with Rooster Burgess 'less they've got something he wants.

"Hell," says Momma, "I wasn't screwing him."

"Might as well have. Sold him your food stamps, right?"

"None of your goddamn business."

"Seeing as some of them were Granny's, I'm making it my business."

"Is that right? Don't see you watching her or cooking for her."

"If I had my way, she'd live with me, and you know it."

"Why start this trash every Monday and Friday night when all I'm doing is trying to have a little fun, Darla? Coupla weeks back, you stormed outa here like Miss Fucking-High-and-Mighty, like we're all beneath you. You buy y'self luggage, say you're off to New York 'cause you're tired of playing bingo with all us losers—yet here you are, still pestering the hell outa me."

"What's the going rate for food stamps now, Momma? Thirty dollars for a hundred dollars worth of stamps?"

"Hush your goddamn voice. You want everyone in Paradise to know my business?"

"Hell, everyone knows your business, and until you fell out of bed it had nothing to do with food stamps."

"Listen, you two," Freda says. "Take your shit outside or me and Muff'll move to another table."

"Move to another table," Muff echoes.

Momma sits down and spreads out her cards. Lights up a Camel. "Fuck you," she tells them. "Usually it's you two scrapping like dogs."

Like trained chickens at the county fair, we respond to Cleta John Simpson's voice for the next four hours. Instead of scratching and ringing bells, we listen closely, our glassy eyes fixed on the lighted board, our hands rarely moving to mark out numbers. Mostly we groan in unison as others yell, "Bingo."

Between us, we put away eight cheeseburgers, six extralarge fries, and six extralarge soft drinks, ingesting, I imagine, five thousand grams of saturated fat apiece, and upping our cholesterol count to stroke level. Combined investment for the evening close to eighty bucks, maybe more, and not one of us wins.

"Oh, well," Momma says. "Better luck next time."

Enemies

. . . .

Given enough time, even an idiot's plan of action can prove deadly, so it's foolish to predict what Frank Slater will do once he's licked his wounds and chewed on the situation. One thing's for sure—he views himself as the victim, which is why he hates every boss who ever fired him for not showing up, coming in late, or stealing.

Momma phoned me from Muff and Freda's this morning to say that Frank, the nearsighted cretin, is truly pissed at me, like it's news. If it wasn't for Rhonda and the kids I wouldn't give a flying cuss. I'd confront him again, say, "So what? Next time I'll have your balls for breakfast," but I'll lay low awhile.

That I haven't seen or heard from Spirit hasn't helped my disposition, but it's for the best, I've told myself over and over while checking for a white 1979 Cadillac Sedan DeVille as I drive down Sycamore Street or past Lamb of God, slowing down outside the church in the hopes that I'd see that white suit and Stetson—that above "What a Friend We Have in Jesus," or "Sweet Hour of Prayer," I'd hear the heartbroken voice of Crocodile Dundee. I didn't quit until, in the frozen food section of Jed's Food Mart, I stumbled upon Spirit's Lamb of God landlady, Trudy Spencer—a thirty-year-old prune in a lime-green polyester jumpsuit.

"Darla," she cooed, her ratted beehive aquiver, "was I seeing things, or did you drive past my place a couple of times last week, early morning?"

"Not me."

"I could have sworn that funny polka-dot car of yours rushed by, even though Spirit insisted I was mistaken. I know you two got acquainted, that you took him out for a sandwich or something, so when I saw your car drive past the church—"

"I was visiting Momma."

She flicked a speck of something from her cuff. "Well, it occurred to me you might be checking up on Spirit. You're not doing that, are you, Darla? After all, he's such a precious man with the highest of principles and—"

"And what, Trudy?" I asked, my temper rising. "A precious man with the highest of principles and what?"

"A bright future, Darla. He's an attractive single man. Any healthy woman would have a hard time ignoring him, so he has to be careful who he—"

"Yes, Trudy?"

She plunged a pristine hand into the freezer and retrieved a box of peas. "Well, Darla, honey—"

"Don't Darla honey me. We go back too far for that. Besides, you're a *widder* woman and the man's sleeping under your roof every night of the world, not mine."

"I beg your pardon?"

"Pardon accepted. Hell, I remember you before you was married, long 'fore that sorry Ronny Spencer insisted you get yourself saved and dunked at Lamb of God 'fore he'd set a wedding date. We were in high school together, remember? I was in the bleachers when the Paradise Bulldogs, God bless 'em, toasted you with Gatorade and swore you were the best thing to come along since Red Man chewing tobacco."

She looked aghast, a germ confronted by Lysol. Seeing as half a dozen folks heard me, I wasn't surprised when Trudy hightailed it outa the store leaving her cart crosswise in the aisle.

This evening, in all probability, while turning buttermilk pancakes or putting together a pan of those frosted blueberry muffins Momma's so fond of, Trudy will relate her version of our meeting to her house-guest—embellish it with tales of Momma and Granny as Spirit directs one of her best silver-plated forks into the icing. Wouldn't surprise me if she raised the incident again just before they pray together—or after she dutifully turns down his bedcovers, damn her soul. And will Spirit believe her? Will she convince him I'm the no-good daughter of the town whore, the infamous "girl gone bad"? Will he accept the picture she paints and be repulsed by it? While on his knees with those gorgeous eyes closed, will he thank God for delivering him from evil? And do I give a crap one way or the other what he believes, or what he prays for? Yes, I do, dammit.

At night, my head buried in a pillow, I have imagined the Reverend Spirit E. Jackson heartbroken, flying to Australia, vowing never to return to the pulpit until I agree to marry him. I've also seen him driving that white Cadillac across the United States searching for me, a bearded nomad—Howard Hughes in a grungy white suit, his dust-laden Stetson bent out of shape with heat and depression.

But it's over, so stop dwelling on it, I tell myself as I hang another Darling Darla Creation on a hanger. Cindy Harker's above-the-knee cocktail dress is red as a fire hydrant. Held together by an invisible zipper and the finest of seams, it's one of many I've made for her over the years. The woman's always showing up—a regular whose fine Italian leather shoes mark up the floor, whose fine-boned fingers hover above every surface as if my tables and countertops harbored a lethal virus, whose eyes search and probe, who wants every stitch perfect, who wants this made, then that—so many clothes I can't imagine where she finds the time to wear them.

Blond hair in a pageboy, wearing an immaculate suit, she arrived at my apartment one evening about a month ago, carrying some fine red jersey wrapped in pink tissue paper. Chin stiff as cardboard, she stepped inside with the familiar I-know-all-about-you glaze in her eyes and held it fast as I showed off my new designs.

After making her selection, she said, "No need to measure me again, Darla, I'm still size six. Harker women always have been blessed with near-perfect figures."

I ignored the comment, ignored the contempt on her face as she appraised my apartment for the umpteenth time, ignored the bag of revulsion she hauled in and spilled on the floor—as if she knew—as if a sparrow had flown straight from those oak trees to her ear with the news.

Her father, Earl Harker, was CEO of Harker's Western Shirt Factory in Layton. Me and Brandy started working there right after graduation. Brandy needed tuition money for Miss Nancy's School of Hair Design in Palm Grove. I needed 250 business cards and a reliable sewing machine.

From the road, the plant looked inviting with its trimmed evergreens and vast windows, not to mention the larger-than-life bronze cowboy roping a steer out front, but the minute I laid eyes on the building's insides, on its high-gloss gray walls and row upon row of grim faces, I knew I'd never care for the place. Everything, from the tinny music piped through the PA system to the smelly, paper-strewn toilets and grubby lunchroom lined with fast-food machines, depressed me. The real misery began that first morning, eight o'clock sharp, when Doris Bumgartner, a frazzled woman with bowed legs and a black mustache, sat Brandy at machine number 4, me at machine number 5, and taught us how to stitch collars to shirts. We soon got the hang of it, but when, as if remarking on the weather, she said, "The minimum quota is two hundred and forty collars a day," an emotional numbness set in, for it was a hot place where fat women who didn't own razors idly scratched their crotches and underarms—then ate a sandwich without washing their hands.

Worse still, out front, away from the employees' parking lot, beneath a nonbearing mulberry tree, sat something I recognized—a black and shiny 1984 Lincoln Town Car with darkened windows that had, on numerous occasions, come by the house for Momma and brought her back an hour or so later.

"Shitty Harker's car," whispered Doris Bumgartner. "Watch out for the bastard or he'll eat you alive."

Shitty Harker, roughly sixty years old, a bald, hard-bodied man with a spiteful mouth and an abrasive attitude, wore $500 suits and Aramis cologne, which did nothing for his hateful nature and razor-sharp tongue. Greed strained at his belt buckle and was etched on his face like a scar. On the rare occasion he strolled around the workshop, hands behind his back, his thick ruddy neck jutting out, he resembled an obese vulture circling a carcass. One sniff, one glance into those hooded gray eyes, and you knew to be careful.

He ate me alive July 16, 1985. Waited for me, waited for Brandy to drive off with her new boyfriend, waited till the parking lot emptied and the front doors were locked, watched and waited from his plush, air-conditioned office, I imagine, till I'd worn myself ragged fiddling with one connection after another under the rusty hood of Momma's Pontiac—waited till the backs of my legs blistered, till I felt sick and dizzy from the heat, before slithering up behind me like the no-good, slime-sucking serpent he was to offer me a paper cup filled with luke-warm water and a ride home. In a moment of weakness, grateful to the depths of my heart that someone, even Shitty Harker, had seen my predicament and taken pity on me, I accepted.

"We'll take a shortcut," he said, and five minutes later we're on a dead-end road parked between two oak trees at the edge of a field ripe with corn, and I'm being raped—hammered into the leather uphol-stery, drowning in a sea of sweat, spit, and Aramis cologne, brawling with my employer, who not only won the battle, but clearly enjoyed the viciousness of it—screams and scratches included. Fact is, soon as I realized the hollering turned him on, I quit.

Strangely enough, what filled me with revulsion had more to do with what Mr. Harker's body wasn't than what it was. It wasn't the fast, wiry body of Millard Hoskins, a boy I'd played with in the cold waters of the Rattler, and it bore no resemblance to the lean-limbed body of Lennie Butcher, a high school sweetheart, nor did it possess the powerful, well-defined shape of Billy Joe Comfort, then a lifeguard at the Layton Community Swimming Pool. Mr. Harker was bull-necked and hairy; his flesh hung in layers.

"God almighty," he muttered when he was done, "you're a scrapper, Darla Moon. Your momma should be proud of you."

The second he lifted himself up I bent down and bit his belly, clenched my jaws tight as I could, dug in, punctured the doughy flesh, and held on like a Doberman while he yanked my hair and howled like a madman. I let go only after he begged and wept like a child. Then, as if he feared I might attack again, he scrambled into the backseat.

"You no-good, motherfucking whore," he wailed. "What the hell d'ya do that for? I'd have paid you twice what I pay your mother."

In an instant, I was out the door and running, Shamir leading the way. He floated tall above the corn, four or five feet off the ground, and I was mad as a hornet that he'd let it happen at all.

"One word about this, Darla Moon," Shitty Harker yelled out, "and I'll make life miserable for you, y'hear? I'll run you and that loose-assed momma of yours outa town."

I never went back to the shirt factory—and that long black car never came back for Momma. A week later, though, I heard Shitty Harker had been hospitalized with a "dangerous, mysterious, skin infection," which didn't bother me none. My only regret was that I'd missed my target by inches—that his weapon still was attached to his body.

Until now, I'd shoved that desolate, dead-end road to the back of my mind, but looking back, I'm convinced it wasn't the first time Mr. Harker had parked there. His Lincoln Town Car zeroed in on those two oak trees like a guided missile—so I'm thinking that's where he and Momma took care of business.

Shitty Harker left more than sperm behind. He left a cold, inert, mud-colored knot inside me. When I mentally tried to examine its shape, its eyes and webbed feet, the odorous, toadlike beast hid. The loathsome thing survived the winter, its soft dark weight shifting slightly as it stole my appetite and the color from my eyes. Only after a sea of crocuses heralded spring, and Mr. Harker's obituary appeared in the *Sunday Herald,* did the creature fall apart bit by bit, scale by scale. A week later, all that remained was the shoveled-out hollow where it once slept. The hollow remains—'longside Mandy.

I encase Cindy Harker's sleeve-of-a-dress in a plastic cocoon, content that, hidden in a seam at the waistline, the infinitesimal tip of a stainless steel pin lies in wait. Sooner or later, as she turns this way or that, at some celebration or another, just before she says, "Why, thank you," in the syrupy voice of a transplanted northerner, it will prick her, remind her that, instead of her strawlike figure and *Vogue* features, I'm the one responsible for all the oohs and aahs she receives—me and my Darling Darla Creation. The jab will inform her that those I'm-better-than-you looks aren't welcome—that my cold silences should not be confused with guilt or remorse—that I am not a whore—that her daddy wrapped his fat legs round my momma more times than he ever did around me, praise God—that I wish she'd take her business elsewhere.

All in the Family

. . . .

On a November day two years ago, when snow was plentiful and men
weren't, I pulled into Elijah's yard and saw Frank Slater's truck parked
ahead of mine, same as now, so I drove off. I'd had a miserable year,
Rhonda puny all the time, Momma at war with the welfare department,
not to mention hordes of pasty-faced girls clad in stockings so white
their legs looked too weak to stand parading through my apartment,
their hearts on fire for the latest craze—anemic print dresses with lace-
trimmed Puritan collars.

But today feels different—nothing like a Monday. The moment I
woke up, I rushed headlong into the day, sewing and pressing, relentlessly
pushing entire blocks of time behind me as fast as I could so I wouldn't
think of Spirit—until I decided a visit to Elijah's was in order. So I don't
give a damn if Frank or Rhonda are here, or if both are here; I'm going in.

I make it all the way to the kitchen before Rhonda and Elijah
notice me.

"For mercy's sake, girl," Elijah exclaims. "You gave me a fright."

"Sorry. Hi, Rhonda."

She turns her back on me and looks out the window, as if I'm the
last person in the world she wants to see, which is probably true, and
says, "Time for me to leave."

"Suit yourself," I reply.

"Now I won't have you girls fussin' with each other in my kitchen, y'hear?" says Elijah. "Sit down and have a cup of decaf, Darla. You too, Rhonda. It'll smooth out y'wrinkles."

He goes about his business in denim overalls, a man heavy with love and time, back slightly bent, the keys at his waist jangling against each other. He has dozens of keys—keys that fit his truck, shed, doors, toolboxes, and trunks. Keys all dressed up with no place to go and nothing to do but jingle, whose only attribute is that they look pretty, that their shape, color, or brightness caught Elijah's eye at a flea market or a garage sale.

He moves with ease, his slippers shuffling across the floor. His hands, which coax miracles from fresh vegetables and herbs at the height of their scent and flavor, rattle cups and dig out spoons. The kitchen embraces him, glows with pleasure as the rest of the house falls quiet. Each tidy room waits for him, every overstuffed chair, every patchwork quilt and rag carpet, hums low, waits in silence for Elijah to grace them with his presence—to settle in one cozy spot with his ragtag Bible and linger a spell. And he will linger. Once he begins a chapter, his radio quietly transmitting sermons and hymns, his lovely lips silently mouthing each word, he will not move till that chapter's finished, at which time he'll lean back, close his eyes, and say, "Nothing so good for a man's soul as pondering on the word of God, 'cept understanding and obeying it."

Rhonda most likely interrupted him as he washed dishes. Half are still soaking, the other half are stacked on the draining board, slick and shiny. I love this kitchen. Pots of every size, shape, age, and color, blue, yellow, silver, and black, hang on the walls, their lids in racks below. Ancient tea towels stacked and folded in drawers; so dazzling white, so often bleached they're feather soft. Knives, forks, and spoons so old, so often handled, so often plunged into steaming pots and eager mouths, their patterns live only in memory. I can almost taste the ham, grits, and redeye gravy on Sunday mornings, the muffins stuffed with raisins and orange marmalade, coconut pies, barbecued ribs so sweet and juicy you'd swear they'd simmered in heaven—and even now, two days past wash day, the smells of Tide and Pine Sol hang in the air just as surely as the cinnamon he sprinkled on his toast for breakfast this morning.

Rhonda turns round and glares at me. "Why did you do it, Darla?"

"Do what?"

"Humiliate Frank like that."

"Hell, you can't humiliate what's already small and insignificant."

"You really don't care, do you?" she says. "Do you have any idea how hard it's been on me and the kids since you decided to act like an idiot?"

"You're right. If I'd had m'smarts about me the gun would've been loaded and I'd have blown his brains all over Woody's floor."

"My God, listen to you, Darla. Have you lost your mind?"

"No, you have. Only a lunatic would live with a man like that."

"Now you listen to me—"

"No, you listen to me, ladies," Elijah says, rapping a wooden spoon on the counter. "I ain't forgotten how to use this, and you're not too old to feel it, so take your trash outside. I won't have you taking the Lawd's name in vain in my house."

"Elijah, if you knew what this is all about," I say, "you'd know why I went looking for the bastard—excuse my language. He climbs into bed with anything of childbearing age, he knocks Rhonda around whenever the fancy takes him, and I'm tired of hearing her gripe about him all the time. You can barely tell now, but last time I went over to the trailer, her face was black and blue—so were her arms and legs."

"That's a lie," says Rhonda.

"That's why I went looking for him, Elijah. Found him at Woody's drinking on Jessie's birthday money, so I knocked him down, threatened him, and got thrown in jail. First time in my life, and believe me, Leroy Poteet got a real charge out of that."

Toting two cups of decaf, Elijah steps into a shaft of sunlight streaming through the kitchen window. "That true, Rhonda?"

Her face is a blank page. "Is what true?"

He sets the cups on the table. "Look me in the eye and tell me Darla's lying."

She glances out the window. "She's lying."

"I said look me in the eye, girl."

"Okay, okay, so she's not lying, but it's none of her business. She had no right to embarrass Frank like that, in front of everyone. No right."

"No, she didn't," Elijah says, "but can you understand why she did? You're always crying on her shoulders and you can't or won't handle your own problems. What she's saying is, it breaks our hearts when you're mistreated."

"And I'm telling you it's awful hard living with Frank since Darla made a fool of him."

"He was a fool long 'fore I brought it to anyone's attention."

Rhonda's eyes blaze with fire. "Butt out my business, Darla."

"So don't drag me into your business. Don't ask for money when Frank won't work. You called me every time your first and second husband knocked you around. Every time you get sick or hurt, it's me who takes you to the doctor, pays the doctor, and buys your damn prescriptions. And every time I think about getting on with my career and leaving behind this godforsaken hellhole, you beg me to stay. None of my business, hell! You've made your life my business ever since you were a kid."

Elijah shakes his head, opens his mouth to say something, but thinks better of it.

"Well, I hope all your generosity makes you feel better," Rhonda says. "More angelic."

"Angelic, hell. All I feel is tired to m'bones. Even my brain's exhausted."

"Hadn't stopped you messing with a hell-and-damnation preacher, though, has it, Darla? Angelic probably don't come close. What you aimin' for, sainthood?"

"Watch your mouth," I tell her. "You're starting to sound like Momma."

"Leave Momma out of it, okay?"

"Oh, what's this? Be Kind to Roxie Week?"

"You find fault with her all the time. Our dad's the one who ran out on us, not her."

"I don't believe you, Rhonda, honest to God I don't."

"I know what's wrong with you," she says. "Preacher Spirit E. Jackson probably did more than bail you outa jail. I reckon he did some laying-on of hands and you assumed he'd wiped your soul clean."

"I'm leaving 'fore you say something else to confirm your ignorance, Rhonda. I'll come back for coffee later, Elijah."

"Wait a minute," he says, "I've got something to say—to both of you. Sit down, Darla."

"I'd rather not."

"Do as I say, this minute. You can't have the window seat all the time."

I oblige, with reluctance.

"When you two were not much bigger than a gallon o' milk," he says, "all of us, y'granny included, got on our knees over on Railway Road and asked God a favor. We asked him to bless you, to fill you with love, strength, and determination—enough to overcome what you so sorely lacked in upbringing, that in return you'd be kind to folks, that you'd tell the truth, that you'd watch out for each other and keep an eye on Granny—"

"And I've tried, Elijah," I say. "Honest."

"—and without even blinking an eye," Elijah continues, his voice echoing off the walls of our past like an old bell, "the Lawd obliged. Didn't matter to Him that Sophie was two cards short of a deck, that I was black, that Rhonda wouldn't close her eyes, that you fidgeted and giggled as we prayed, He come through like the wonder He is. You grew up loving each other, taking care of each other, bein' generous to others—a mite too generous with the men folks, I'm thinking—and you forgave each other just like the Bible tells us to do. You got scratched up a little, lost some shine, missed some sleep and a couple o' meals in the process, but you survived, despite the odds against it. Thing is, you ain't little kids no more. You grown women, and like it or not, the time for watching out for each other is gone—and the time for moving on and standing on your own two feet has arrived. You still gotta love each other, but no one here is obligated to the other, you understand? Ain't no marriage vows passed between you two. Ain't no *in sickness and in health till death do us part* stuff been promised. Rhonda, your first responsibility is to yourself, your children and husband. Darla, you're only responsible for yourself. It's that simple."

"I know, but more than one person in my family relies on me, Elijah, and you know it."

"Some folks create their own burdens, Darla," he says. "They think the world's a big scary place and *choose* to let it remain a mystery."

"You suggesting I'm afraid to leave Paradise?"

"I'm saying there's a time to stay and a time to go. Knowing one from the other is a tricky matter—and if you're waiting for permission to leave, you'll die here. Now, if you'll excuse me," he says, making tracks, "I gotta go to the little boys' room. Make y'self comfy, ladies, and watch your language."

The minute he's gone Rhonda starts in again. "Have you any idea what you've put me through?"

"I'm sorry, but—"

"Have you any idea how fighting mad Frank is at you? If Pearl and Jessie hadn't siphoned most of the gas outa the truck, he'd have gone looking for you the minute he sobered up."

"Bless their hearts. They did that for me?"

"No, they did it for me, Darla. Frank swore he'd run over me with the truck after he'd had a nap, but when he woke up, the one thing he had on his mind was hunting you down."

"And you're sticking by him? Well, praised be thee, Saint Rhonda."

"I gotta hold on to him, Darla. He's my rock."

"He's a stone around your neck. Be your own rock."

"Yeah, yeah. You sound like a broken record."

"Lawd, Lawd," Elijah• exclaims from the living room. "Darla. Rhonda. Come here, quick."

We rush to the front door and look where he's pointing—toward Momma's place, at a small, lopsided figure skipping down the middle of the blacktop.

"Tell me I'm seeing things," Elijah says with a catch in his voice. "Tell me that's not Sophie out in this heat without nary a stitch on."

But it is Granny. She's headed this way, laughing and dancing and kicking up her heels, oblivious to her stunned audience—a dozen or more "sisters," gathered in Lamb of God's parking lot.

Love Is . . .

· ·

"That's right. Everyone blame me," says Momma. "You forget she's supposed to tell me 'fore she goes outside."

"But you was gonna set off a bomb," Granny says, her eyes raised heavenward. "You was gonna blow m'troops to hell."

Momma throws up her hands in defeat. "I wasn't gonna do no such thing, Mother. I'd already herded 'em out."

We stand around Momma's living room staring at Granny. She's wrapped up in one of Elijah's white bedsheets. Given a beard and leather sandals, she could pass for an East Indian guru. While deciding if I should laugh or cry at this fiasco, Elijah's straight face makes up my mind. "Roach bombs don't explode, Granny. They just spray chemicals into the air. They kill bugs, not people."

"A bomb's a bomb," she says. "Who the hell knows what one'll do once the pin's pulled."

Elijah shifts from foot to foot, his hands worrying each other behind his back. "You know, Roxie," he says, "it might be too hot a day for exterminating. I mean, once you set that thingamajig off, you have to leave and stay gone a few hours, don't you?"

"Hell no. I hang around and sniff the fumes 'cause it makes m'hair curly," Momma says, her voice thick with sarcasm. "Of course we leave. Had the woman dressed and ready—or so I thought."

"Where were you going, Roxie?" he asks. "Your car wasn't running yesterday."

"Got it started," she replies. "Was gonna go by the filling station to see if they knew what was wrong with it."

Elijah shakes his head. "I told you I'd come by this afternoon and look at it. It's a coupla miles between here and the gas station. What if you'd broken down in between?"

"We'd have walked."

"In this weather? Sophie nevuh would've made it."

"How come you took your clothes off, Granny?" I ask.

"Because it's damned hot out there," she replies. "Needed shoes, though."

"Don't ever go outside undressed again, Sophie, y'hear?" says Elijah. "You'll get sunstroke."

"I'll do as I damn well please," she says, and drapes part of the sheet over her head and throws the loose end round her neck. "I've got responsibilities. M'frogs needed airin'."

"That's it in a nutshell," Momma says, hauling a beer from the fridge. "Y'all plan on hangin' 'round here all day like a goddamn jury, or what?"

"She's mighty pink," Elijah remarks as we leave, "so be sure and smear that aloe vera I gave you all over her."

"I'll do that, doc," Momma says, her voice mocking. "And I'll leave her with you when I go to bingo. We still on for tonight, Rhonda?"

Rhonda's eyes meet mine and dart away. "You bet. I'll pick you up around six."

"That'd be nice," Momma says.

"What'd be nice," I say, to no one in particular, "is for me to get paid what I'm owed before we play."

Rhonda curls her lip into a sneer. "Oh, you're going?"

"I go every Monday night."

"I know, but I thought you were too good for bingo now. Thought you had more important things to do. Like pack suitcases and leave town."

"And is that all you think about, Darla?" Momma says. "What folks owe you?"

"No, it's not, but if you two thought about it more often, I wouldn't have to think about it near as much. Fact is, I'd be a rich person."

Elijah's gone, in his truck and almost home. Rhonda takes off ahead of me, her skinny legs plowing through the brush and weeds, her neck stiff, her shoulders squared, not saying a word. I keep calling her name, but she ignores me, and before I realize it, she's driven off—a sort of déjà vu thing, seeing as I'm the one standing in dirt waving goodbye, mouthing the words *I love you* over and over again. Elijah stands on his porch watching her go. Even when Rhonda's out of sight he doesn't move. Jaw set, hands buried in his overall pockets, he rocks on his heels, willing her, I imagine, to turn around and come back so he can kiss her and hug her goodbye.

"Let's get out of the heat, Elijah. Nothing we can do, is there?"

He strolls inside shaking his head, the depth of his hurt and frustration showing in the lines of his face and the slant of his shoulders. His slippers sound different against the kitchen's hardwood floor—a tired, whispering noise like shallow breathing.

Heavy-hearted, we hunker over crackling glasses of A & W root beer and wait for the other to speak. I'm thinking Elijah probably wants to scream as bad as I do—that he's as frustrated as I am. I hear the radio playing in his bedroom. Preacher saying something about the kingdom of God being closer at hand than anyone can imagine.

"That's not exactly true," he mutters, "what you said 'bout nothin' we can do. We can pray 'bout *both situations* every opp'tunity we get."

"I'm guessing that both situations means Rhonda's problem and the one we just left at Momma's?"

"Right. Give them ugly messes to God. Put 'em in His hands. Who you think you are trying to fix things all by y'self, Darla Moon? You think all you got to do is stick a gun to a man's head to get your way? Can't change nothing like that, 'cause it's wrong, that's why. Only one person got the right and the power to judge and take revenge, girl, and that's Jesus Christ Hisself."

"I know."

"Where'd you get a gun, anyways?"

"Bought it in Layton—legal."

"What for?"

"I live alone, the world's full of crazies, and Frank Slater's my brother-in-law."

"Where's it now?"

"Leroy Poteet confiscated it—sorta."

"Sorta?"

"He assumed it wasn't legal, and seeing as it was late at night and I wanted to go home, I didn't say otherwise."

"No receipt?"

"No receipt."

"Mmmm, that ain't good."

"I know. I'll figure something out, though. C'mon now. I wanna see them pretty pink lips smiling."

He's not amused. "You drove by here t'other day, said you wanted to talk about something or other."

"Reckon I did." I raise my eyes to meet his and am reminded of a winter's day when a pack of foul-mouthed, snake-eyed boys wearing pants with odd-colored knee patches and thick-soled boots chased me down Railway Road. They tore after me, their breath shooting out like vents of steam. Huffing and puffing, they kept yelling, "White trash! White trash!"—sucking in and blowing out so much cold air I felt the chill on my neck—coming so close I smelled the cigarette smoke in their hair and the stink in their socks. Then Elijah appeared, which I thought was only right, seeing as it was his job to shield me and

Rhonda from the perils of Railway Road, to hide reality, to protect us from every bad thing that walked, crawled, or drove down that ugly stretch of dirt.

Like Moses brandishing his staff, Elijah waved a tire iron in the air and set himself between me and the oncoming army, who immediately retreated amidst a cloud of pebbles. I can't recall how long I lay sobbing in Elijah's arms—only that I felt very small and very safe.

"You did a good job, Elijah, you know that, don't you?"

"Best I knew how," he says, understanding me.

"I used to worry," I say, "worry what it was about me that folks in Paradise disapproved of. Was it my address? Momma? This crazy hair of mine? The touch of red in my skin, hinting, maybe, that I'm related to the blood-hungry Apaches who sliced off their kinfolk's scalps? What?"

"Worrying's useless," he says. "Sump'n real bad happen and you done used all y'worry up. Staying on y'feet is what counts. Walter Cronkite once said, 'When a lion wakes up of a morning he knows he's gotta outrun the fastest gazelle, and the gazelle wakes up knowing he's gotta outrun the fastest lion or he'll die.'"

"Meaning?"

"Meaning, when you wake up of a morning you'd better be running."

We both laugh. "Went by 727 the other day. Visited with Miss Cissy a spell. Got a special place in her heart for you, she has, Elijah."

"That a fact?"

"That's a fact."

"So how was 727?"

"Same as always. An old paper sack, memories flying out its windows like dust motes."

"Uh-huh. Railway Road's a heavy place. Always saggin' 'neath the weight of worry and some government program or 'nother."

"Sun didn't help."

"Worse in winter, baby girl. Folks get sick, cars won't start, and gardens mourn the death o' hollyhocks and daisies."

"That a fact?"

"It's a fact," he says with conviction. "Had lotsa good times, though, like rocking on the porch watching you girls make mud cakes and drag each other around in cardboard boxes—and me wonderin' how long 'fore Miss Cissy Lee makes it by bearin' a cherry cobbler or a peach pie—any excuse, y'know, to show me a stretch of ankle." He slaps the table and roars with laughter, knowing he's revealed something I might not have guessed at.

"You old dog. You knew all the time."

"Knew what? That she was soft on me? Sure I knew, but Lawd have mercy, some folks round here would have come with a rope if they thought for one cross-eyed minute a Nigrah man was messin' with her."

"Who for example?"

"Y'momma."

"You think?"

He laughs. "Sure. Why, she won't hardly deliver or pick up y'granny if'n it's broad daylight—'specially not while Lamb o' God's in session. Besides, I couldn't get too friendly with Miss Cissy on account o' m'lady friends."

"What lady friends?"

"I had a couple."

"Like who? Tressie Dove?"

He shakes both hands like they've gone to sleep. "Oh, don't mention that one, child," he says. "That woman so ugly she hurt m'feelings."

Then I recall Miss Jula Brown, the lady he took to the movies once or twice, how she came to his house all dressed up in hat and heels, like a big city woman. "How about Miss Brown—lady who took in ironing over on Elm?"

He sighs kinda easy. "Oh, yes. Pretty little Nigrah, wadn't she?

Like a dog I once had, though. Always taking off with whoever had the biggest biscuit."

He laughs and I laugh with him.

"Was Granny pretty when she was young?"

"You can't imagine. Cheeks like apples. Braids as black and thick as m'arm," he says, gazing off. "Ever'one said she was the purtiest girl in Fairfield County."

"Fairfield County, Arkansas? You saying you knew her before you all met up here in Paradise?"

He folds his arms, squirms in the chair and sets his chin. "Ain't saying no more 'bout it."

"Miss Cissy says you all arrived here 'bout the same time."

"Is that so? Well, Miss Cissy knows about as much as them two heathen ladies down the road with their crystal ball—which is nothin' at all."

"And m'daddy. How well did you know him?"

"I already told you, not much."

"Did you like him?"

"Nevuh knew him good."

"Why'd he leave us?"

"Ask y'momma."

"I have, dozens of times."

"Ask her again then."

"I'm pretty sure he came back once, on Halloween. I told you, remember? Momma said he was drunk and she run him off, that he was sick, that he most likely died soon after—denied over and over again that he'd turned up. Said I'd eaten too much trick-or-treat candy, that I'd dreamed she and him were fighting in the kitchen. I never believed a word of it."

"Uh-huh."

"I saw a difference in her after that, though—a firmness on her mouth, lines under her eyes."

"That right?"

Fearing I'll cry, I stare at the ceiling as a tall shadow in leather boots marches through my field of vision. "Just once, just once I'd like to hold him—no matter why he left."

Elijah pats my hand. "I know, baby girl, I know."

"He still loves me, I'm sure of it."

"Sure he does."

I refocus, force a smile. "Momma once said my grandpa, Granny's husband, died in a cornfield. You know anything about that?"

"Let's talk about sump'n else, baby girl. I ain't nevuh been at ease with any of these subjects."

He means it too. He looks firmer and larger, a part of the chair.

"I'm thinking we're gonna see a hard winter, Darla."

"How come?"

"Wooly caterpillars got a thick coat and spiderwebs are extra strong."

"That so? Wanna go see a movie? *Independence Day* is showing in Palm Grove."

"Ain't got no use for movies, you know that. Saw one once. This woman takes a roast chicken from the oven—looks like it's crisp with oil and herbs—served it with a salad, she did—elegant, you know? But I didn't see another meal for the entire movie. So I'm thinking, what does she do for dinner the other six days of the week? Pork chops? Meat loaf? What? Really left me hanging, you know?"

I want to laugh out loud but I daren't. "Saw Shamir again."

He grins big, stretches them pussy-pink lips and shows his lovely teeth. "Lucky girl. How many times is that now?"

"I've lost count. Saw him first on Railway Road—saw him again when the preacher died on the toilet—once in the alley behind Bolton's Funeral Parlor—and many's the time when, with a moon in the sky and dew on the ground, I've seen him near Momma's goldenrain tree." I keep the other two times, after the rape and during the abortion, dangling in my head where Elijah can't get at them.

Elijah's eyes sparkle. "Ain't that a perfectly wonderful miracle, Darla—you seeing him like that? Here to comfort your soul, I reckon."

"Maybe so."

Equally hard for me to imagine that Shamir wanted me to see what I saw late that Sunday in '82 when Bolton's Funeral Parlor burned to the ground. I was fourteen and dating Jeff Donahoo, a sacker at Jed's Food Mart. As I recollect, the redhaired senior with long sideburns was my one bright spot in an otherwise difficult summer. Momma was forever taking off for days on end with some uncle or the other and Rhonda was sick with a stubborn ear infection, which left me and Elijah holding things together.

On this particular Sunday, around midnight, me and Jeff were parked in his daddy's truck in the alley behind the stores on Main Street, close to the funeral parlor. We were kissing, cuddling, and whispering and stuff, nothing heavy—when two figures entered Bolton's back door. Minutes later, a glow appeared in a narrow rear window eight feet off the ground. Curious, me and Jeff quietly unloaded a couple of ladders from the back of the truck and went for a look. I made it to the window first, and peeked under the curtains. There, surrounded by lighted candles set in jars on the floor, amid caskets of every shape and size, some on trestles, some not, lay Momma and Mr. Bolton, the funeral director. Bare-ass naked, they were having sex on red shag carpet.

Terrified Jeff would see, I hissed, "Let's get outa here, they've got guns." We climbed down, threw the ladders in the truck, and were about to drive away when the glow in the funeral parlor window grew bigger and brighter. I knew right away the place was on fire. I saw Shamir then, near the truck, floating just inches off the ground, but he disappeared when two people, Momma and Mr. Bolton, rushed out of the back door.

Unable to save Bolton's, the volunteer fire department aimed their hoses at Woody's Bar—and old Mrs. Flood, a large woman by any standards, due for burial the following day, was so burned up her remains fit in one of them under-the-bed storage boxes.

"As a kid, I wanted to go looking for my father," I tell Elijah.

"Ain't surprised," he says, grinning. "Feisty little tyke, you were. Always looking for trouble—always finding it."

"Haven't changed much, have I, 'cept back then I thrived on possibilities. For the longest time I thought I could turn away, look back, and see my daddy standing in the doorway—that he'd know me and I'd know him. Never tried it though. Scared it wouldn't work, I reckon."

"And now?"

"Mostly I want freedom."

"Price of freedom's mighty high. Hope you can afford it." He finishes his root beer.

"I'm leaving soon," I blurt out. "Made up m'mind."

Eyes narrowed, he leans back in his chair. "When?"

"Soon as I can. September."

"Well, that sure is fine. I'm happy for you."

"Thing is, I worry about—"

"Don't fret 'bout y'Granny. Not while I'm breathing, anyway. As for Rhonda, you staying or going ain't gonna make no nevuhmind to how she lives her life."

"Wish I believed that."

"Wish you did, too."

"I keep Granny stocked with newspapers and string and—"

"I'll handle it."

"I'll send you money now and then—for whatever she needs."

"She'll be fine. I'll watch her."

"And Rhonda—well, she needs someone to talk to now and then—to tell her she can make it—to keep her focused—a shoulder to cry on, you know?"

"I know."

"Thinks she can't make it without Frank, that she's not worth much on her own—yet she's scared of him. Deep down, maybe I am, too."

"He bears watching."

"Rhonda's so fragile—like one of them little gnats you sometimes see in the bathroom. Put 'em in a single drop of water and they drown in it. Some of us can handle anything, while others die from what they fear the most."

"I've heard that too, hon."

"She's so damn puny, Elijah. Makes me wonder if she's got something serious wrong with her—some sickness that's been overlooked. I keep her supplied with One-A-Day vitamins and I remind her to take 'em whenever I think of it, but—"

"I'll take care of it."

"Same with Pearl and Jessie, 'cept I buy them kiddie multivitamins."

"I know the kind," he says. "Been with you when you bought 'em."

"And once a year, I put together an emergency box—children's Tylenol, a few bottles of good cough syrup, Pepto Bismol, Kaopectate—so Rhonda's always got it on hand."

He shrugs. "No problem."

"I'll send money for all this stuff, Elijah, it's just that—"

"Not to worry."

"I'm not worried, it's just that—"

"What?"

Back in Elijah's bedroom, a woman is belting out hosannas of praise, singing "Rock of Ages" as only a black woman can, full and strong, as if she were a mighty pipe organ—as if Jesus Christ Himself was pounding the pedals and keys. I am transported to Fountain Baptist, Elijah's church, me and Rhonda and Granny's church, where deep-bellied, black-as-molasses voices roll like thunder and uproot trees, where big ladies sitting on hard wooden benches, their upper lips beaded with sweat, sway back and forth flapping fans imprinted with the words MEET THE LORD IN STYLE. PREPAY AT BOLTON'S FUNERAL HOME, and Willadene Potts, a full-breasted, caramel-skinned girl, blessed at birth with the voice of an angel, releases from her throat a series of high-pitched notes that rise like fingers of smoke and drift to the rafters, where they linger and stir up the cobwebs.

My throat tightens. Tears well in my eyes. An ache the size of an orange forms in my chest. "All m'life I've been told this world is round, Elijah, so tell me, why do I always feel as if I'm hanging onto its edges by my fingernails?"

"Mebbe you care too much."

"I'm so filled up with everyone's troubles, so filled up and over-flowing there's no room for anything or anyone else."

He comes and holds me, and I remember him in his little parlor on Railway Road, rolling Rhonda's hair up in rags on Saturday night so we can go to church with him Sunday morning. I recall us on his porch late at night, holding a jar of fireflies—waving sparklers on July 4th—blowing out candles on Jesus's birthday cake. Back then, Elijah lit up our world. Still does.

I inhale the scent of his skin, the African mink oil in his hair, the Downy in his shirt, the mint on his breath, a dab of salt, a touch of lemon, and without even looking or being told, I can tell by the way he's breathing that he's verging on tears, and I want to scream "To hell with it all, I'll stay right here in Paradise and take my chances," 'cause what I fear the most is leaving Elijah.

"I'm gonna ask God to shore you up and light your way," he says, his voice breaking. "I'm gonna pray He'll give you the courage to leave Paradise 'fore you change y'mind. But I'll be honest with you, baby girl—there ain't a soul livin' gonna feel the mizry of you going more'n this old black man."

Monday Night Bingo

I buy a medium Diet Pepsi and a small bag of M&M's at the concession stand. I usually get a Milky Way for Rhonda, 'cause it's her favorite, but I'm not so inclined today.

The enemy has struck again. They've commandeered the lucky table, and they've got reinforcements. The original four ladies in polyester and pearls are accompanied by two elderly men decked out in Hawaiian-print shirts and bifocals. Huddled at a nearby table, Momma, Rhonda, Freda, and Muff, heads almost touching, hands animated, are whispering among themselves.

"So what's the plan?" I ask. "Guns or grenades?"

"It's not funny," Momma says. "When Muff and Freda came with me and Rhonda last Wednesday, and Freda asked 'em to move—"

"Freda asked them to move?"

"Damn right, and the old lady on the end told her to go fuck herself."

"That's hard to believe," I reply. "She looks exactly like Barbara Bush," but when I glance at the woman she sneers at me, and I can tell she doesn't even come close to being friendly.

"Don't know who the hell you bunch think you are," Mrs. Bush says. "I really don't."

"Well, I'm Darla," I explain, "this is my sister Rhonda, this is my mother Roxie, and these two ladies—"

"We don't give a damn who any of you are," she says. "Couldn't care less."

The nearest Hawaiian shirt stands up and jabs his finger in Muff and Freda's direction. "And those two aren't ladies," he says, "they're a disgrace to the human race, is what they are. Truth is, you're all a bunch of sicko bingo queens. Keep your distance from Christian folk, y'hear?"

Momma gives them the finger. Surprisingly, Muff and Freda are silent, their eyes downcast—as if they've had the stuffing knocked out of them.

During intermission, while the polyester dresses and Hawaiian shirts are in the rest rooms powdering their ignorant noses and relieving themselves, I pour Sprite on their chairs.

Summoning Spirits

. . . .

Drastic times call for drastic measures. I've barely slept for a week. Can't concentrate on my work, my head is constantly bombarded with thoughts of Spirit, and I can't stop wondering what he's doing—how he feels—if he's thinking about me.

I take the long way around, take Miss Ladybug down three dirt roads and over the railway crossing in order to bypass Elijah's house, Momma's house, and Lamb of God Church.

The rose mallow bushes and the beds of purple periwinkles flanking Muff and Freda Bottrell's front door are dead. "Makes me heartsick," Muff says over herbal tea and cookies. Long, lace-trimmed sleeves hide her chubby arms, and blue and pink bunny rabbits decorate her cotton housecoat. "And I followed your mother's instructions. Sprayed them with everything she suggested. Malathion. Pyrethrins. Soapy water."

"That's why they're dead," I tell her. "Momma's an expert when it comes to putting plants outa their misery."

Muff looks surprised. "So explain that goldenrain tree in her front yard. Raised it from scratch, she said."

"Don't see nothing else growing over there, do you?"

Freda shoves her shirt ever deeper into her pants. "Muff's the real culprit. Drowns 'em, she does. Drowns 'em, drowns 'em, drowns 'em till they're dead, dead, dead."

Muff shakes her blond head. "Did not, did not, did not."

"Did, did, did," Freda insists. "You're a fiend when it comes to water. The only reason our herbs thrive is because I won't let you near them till harvest. When they see you coming with a hose they collapse with shock."

"And you can't boil water without burning it. Doesn't make you a bad person, does it?"

"Of course not."

"And I don't intentionally *harm* anything. So where's the difference?"

"The differences are too broad to elaborate on," Freda replies. "Let it suffice to say that you're careless, that you haphazardly drown living, breathing entities created by a supreme being."

Cheeks rouged, lips aflame, Muff shudders at this portrayal. "So stab me to death with your pruning shears, for God's sake, and have done with it."

"Can I get my fortune told today?" I ask, which works like a rifle shot. In the time it takes to light a match, Muff has cleared the kitchen table of cups, plates, and crumbs and drawn the curtains. Freda lights seven candles. She rams one into a candlestick on the table and sets the other six in saucers on the dusty mantel. Above us, tied to hooks in the ceiling, hang every herb known to mankind. Peppermint, lemon mint, pineapple mint, oregano, thyme, and turmeric, et cetera, et cetera. Muff and Freda's home business extends into an enclosed back porch—an odd little room with uneven floors and a table piled high with small jars and mailing boxes.

Muff fluffs her hair. "Tarot cards?"

"Or our new crystal ball?" asks Freda.

"Or tea leaves?" says Muff, skipping to the sink. "I know which cup is yours."

"Same price whichever you choose," Freda adds, flicking a black cloth over the table. "Ten minutes for ten dollars, or twenty minutes for eighteen."

"Leaves for ten," I reply.

Muff giggles with delight and rummages in the pile of dishes. "I guessed as much. Now, who will do the honors, my dear? Me or Freda?"

"Freda," I say, knowing Muff handles disappointment with British grace. "You do it next time, okay?"

"Very well, Darla." Muff ignores Freda's look of triumph and hands her my cup. "Though it's doubtful you'll have it done again. In all the years we've known you, more years than I care to count, you've never had a reading."

"I know. Don't know why I am having one now except someone came into my life and I've got changes ahead, so—"

"Say no more," Freda snaps, "or a certain person in this room will say you gave me clues. Now, let's take a peek."

Drawing the candle closer, she tilts the cup toward the light and gazes inside. I lean forward, study her eyes, watch the flickering flame dance like a firefly in her yellow-flecked corneas. She frowns, curls her upper lip, and clears her throat, squeezes her eyes shut, then rapidly blinks them, as if she can't believe what she's seeing. I feel uncomfortable—maybe because I know Elijah would have a stroke if he knew why I was here, but seeing as my money's on the table, it's too late to change my mind. The quiet is deafening.

Freda squints into the cup. "Did you say you were going on holiday or was that your mother?"

"Wasn't me."

"Mmmm, must've been Roxie."

"Freda, dear," Muff interrupts timidly. "You'd best not—"

"Momma's going on holiday?"

"Hush, Darla," Muff says, "or you'll break Freda's concentration."

Freda sets the cup down with a bang. "Open the curtains, Muff. Got a bad set of leaves here."

"Wait a minute, wait a minute. What was that about Momma?"

"You deaf, Muff?" Freda snaps. "I said open the curtains."

For a second I think she's joking, but her face tells me otherwise. "What in the hell is a bad set of leaves?"

Muff nudges Freda aside and sits in her chair. "You're always so hasty, Freda. Let me have a go." She turns the cup this way and that, her carmine lips uttering a litany of strange clicks, clucks, and squeaks, somewhat like a dolphin. "Oh, yes," she finally says. "Awful set."

"You messed them up when you cleared the table," Freda says.

"Did not."

"Did."

"Did not."

"Saw you."

"Liar, liar, pants on fire."

Freda clenches her fists. Her face turns a brilliant red. "Who are you calling a liar?"

"Me, me, me," says Muff. She promptly sticks an index finger in each ear and starts marching around the table singing "God Save Our Gracious Queen" at top of her lungs.

Freda grabs my cup and hurls it into the sink. "Jesus God," she wails. "What did I do to deserve such a life?"

I am suddenly filled with admiration for the doctors and nurses who, every day, report for work at the county asylum. I know exactly how they must feel, as if the slightest shift in wind or temperature or a single drop of water falling from the faucet, a hiccup even, could start a landslide. Even so, I open my mouth and say, "You two screwing me around, or what?" and one would think I'd just materialized in a blue puff of smoke the way Freda and Muff look at me.

"Screwing you around?" they ask in unison.

"What I mean is—"

"I know what you mean, Darla," Freda says with a sneer, "and I'm shocked that you of all people would even suggest such a thing."

"Yes, shocked," Muff says.

"We take our calling very seriously," Freda adds.

"Very seriously," Muff echoes.

Reminded that I regularly eat their homemade jams and pickled beets, I say, "I'm sorry, I didn't mean it the way it sounded. Why don't we try the cards, or your new crystal ball?"

Freda shakes her head vigorously. "Cards, ball, makes no difference, I'm pissed. God knows when the mood'll come back."

A sharp knock at the front door sends Muff scurrying down the hall. Seconds later, in a singsongy voice, she calls out, "Darla, dear— you have a gentleman caller."

I am shocked to see Spirit on the porch. His bulk shields me from the heat pouring in. I'm shaking, my hands are sweating, and the world is so still I can hear my heart beat. His too, I think.

His blue-plaid shirt is neatly pressed, stiff with Trudy Spencer's starch, most likely. He's holding his Stetson to his chest. "Drove by your place a couple of times, Darla, but you weren't home, so when I passed by here and saw your car, I thought, well, I wondered if it would be all right to—"

Whatever he wants to do is fine with me. He could run stark naked up and down Main Street blowing a trumpet for all I care. Shave his head. Eat spaghetti with his hands. Suck soup through a straw. No matter what he did, I think I'd remain totally captivated, eternally smitten by this hat-in-hand, soft-spoken Aussie. "All right to what, Spirit?"

"Well, I hope the ladies here don't—"

"It's fine, really." He looks tired, yet those eyes are just as I remember, intense and piercing—and he smells wonderful. "Come in out of the heat for a minute. Muff and Freda won't mind."

"No, no," he says, shifting from foot to foot, "but if you could—"

"Yes?"

"Well, it's like this, Darla," he whispers. "I'm having a bloody awful time. Can't get you out of my mind. Can't concentrate. Can't write my sermons. Thinking about you is driving me crazy, so I wondered—are you busy?"

I feel like kissing him on the mouth till he begs for mercy. Who cares if he's a preacher? When a woman feels like this about a man, and he feels the same way about her, they can work things out—right here in Paradise or anyplace else, come to that. And as I stand on Muff and Freda's front porch, I can't imagine myself going anywhere in this world without the Reverend Spirit E. Jackson.

I try my damnedest not to look excited. "No, I'm not busy, why?"

His face lights up, his smile lines deepen, dimples materialize in his cheeks. He takes my face between his hands, traces the curves of my cheeks with his thumbs, slips both arms around my waist and pulls me close—and when his lips brush against mine, when they move against mine, I'm suddenly terrified that some idiot in mainland China will misdial and break the spell—that I'll wake up in bed with the telephone ringing.

"In that case," he whispers into my ear, "I'd be truly grateful if we could go somewhere and talk right now—"

"My place?"

"—sort of talk it out a bit, not for long, of course, I don't want to intrude on your work, but just give me five minutes to tell you how I—"

I throw my arms around his neck and realize immediately that he fills my arms perfectly—the space created for him. "Five minutes?" I whisper back. "For mercy's sake, it's barely noon. Put that hat back on y'head, hold y'mouth just right, and I'll give you the whole damned day."

When I first wake up, I believe for a minute that I'm stretched out in long green grass 'neath a black willow, that the cool spring breeze dancing across my body is perfumed—like it met up with Elijah's well-tended bed of winter daffodils before finding its way to me. Then, little by little, I become aware of Spirit. I can feel the entire length of his strong body curled against mine, his left arm draped across the pillow, over my head—his fingers in my hair—his right arm curled right around my ribs, hand cupping my right breast. His right knee is bent, the thigh gently pressed against my butt. His chest rises and falls against my back. His beard is soft, and his breath flows across my neck.

Twice he made love to me—twice he brought me to orgasm—twice he took me to heights of passion I'd never before known—all the time whispering in my ear, telling me how much he wanted me, how huge and hot his penis felt inside of me, how he loved me, how he didn't want to hurt me—that he felt like a wild animal. He did. He felt like a lithe, sleek panther as he moved again and again over my swollen breasts, over my belly, and between my wet thighs, oh, so slowly at first—endless, delirious, tantalizing, teasing thrusts that left me begging for more—then fast, infinite pumping movements that blurred reality and made the world spin—until, moaning with unrestrained lust and pleasure, we cried out and climaxed together.

I am overwhelmed, bursting with love for him. Surely, no other woman on earth has ever felt like this. Please, God. Make time stand still.

"So what are you thinking about, Darling Darla?" His voice is still husky from lovemaking—still heavy with desire.

"Wishing time would stand still."

"Don't do that, luv," he says, lifting the hair from my face and brushing my cheek. "This is just the beginning of you and me."

New York turns fuzzy at the edges, and just across the room, beyond the afternoon shadows, inside its dark closet, the Lincoln Center Gown fades a shade or two. "Just the beginning?"

"You bet. And what's all this about? You're crying."

"No I'm not."

"Yes, you are. Turn over and look at me, all right?"

I wipe my face on the pillow and turn over, wrap my arms around his neck, look straight into those marvelous eyes, and blink a few times. "See? Nothing."

He kisses both eyelids, then my lips. "You were crying, Darla. Why?"

"Because. Because I felt so close to you—so unbelievably satisfied and happy, I got carried away. I've never felt this way about anyone before."

"No one?"

I shake my head no.

"Never been in love?"

"Once, maybe."

"And?"

"Didn't work out. And you?"

"Twice. Once, in junior high, my English teacher—but she didn't know—and once when I was eighteen. Maureen died in a car accident on holiday in Melbourne, along with her parents."

"I'm sorry."

He sighs and kisses me again, squeezes me hard, but not too hard. "I'm head-over-heels crazy about you, lady."

"Crazy about you, too."

"What do you think we ought to do?"

"Do?"

"Yes, do. I feel like telling the whole world that I'm in love with Darla Moon, that—"

"You'd best not do that. Wouldn't be right, under the circum-stances. I mean, you're here in Paradise preaching at Lamb of God Church and—"

"You're right," he says, burying his face in my hair. "But that's what I'd bloody well like to do. I'm a mere man, plain and simple. I love you—that's all there is to it."

"And I love you, but that's not all there is to it. If word of this gets out—"

"We love each other, Darla. That's the only thing that matters. Before we landed in bed, you said you knew exactly what you were doing."

"And I meant it. But like you said a while ago, this is just the beginning of you and me. We've got lots of time to figure things out and make plans, right?"

I snuggle closer and marvel at the deliciousness of his silky hair, his neck, and his wide shoulders. I rub my tingling nipples against his chest hair—and remember that, under the bed, a new set of luggage waits to be packed.

With a groan, Spirit slips one hand between my legs, grasps my buttocks with the other, and the only thing under the bed is a big blue ocean that sweeps us up and carries us away.

The Morning News

. . . .

In the flickering predawn hours, before sated cats headed home and
lazy yard dogs stretched and shook themselves awake, long before
straw-colored lights appeared in farmhouse windows and all-night
truckers stopped for coffee, Momma showed up at Elijah's front door
with Granny and a canvas tote bag. He phoned me around nine to say
Momma climbed into Dusty Duke's gleaming eighteen-wheeler with
barely a dozen words of explanation, and left for parts unknown. Now,
'midst the ugly scent of bad news and no solutions, Rhonda, a sliver of
cream cheese, her face white and empty as a clean sheet, is telling me
her sad story. Like I didn't see it coming.

She rubs her forehead. "If it's not one thing it's another. Like they
say, no rest for the wicked."

I turn off the sewing machine, cut the thread, drop the half-finished
bodice of an evening gown into my lap and stare across rooftops, beyond
Bolton's Funeral Home, into a cluster of lofty clouds. Yellow and boastful
and tinged with gray, they appeared in the western sky around eight-
fifteen this morning. Since then, according to young Jessie's idol, Gary
England on channel 9, farmers in three counties, some with perfect
vision, others with telescopes and binoculars, have stood in the 102-
degree heat, their eyes honed in on them, praying under their breath.

"Did you hear me, Rhonda?" Darla says.

I wish a storm would roar into Paradise and split the sky open, that rain'd wash everything clean—sweep through gullies and culverts—surge down Rattler's Creek and scrub away the dust. The miserable stuff is everywhere. Storefronts are rosy with it. It's piled up on windowsills, mantels, and bookshelves. It sneaks into gas tanks and the pointed toes of high-heeled shoes. Folks find it between their sheets, in bathtubs, toilets, and washing machines, where it tears up bearings. Red and gritty, it creeps into coffee cups when your back is turned, and into the mouths of sleeping babies, not to mention my new bikini briefs—fresh from a packet this morning.

"Weatherman says grass fires are raging in Tate and Garland counties and only a sprinkle is possible," I say aloud. "Hell, might as well give ice cream to a man dyin' of thirst. Make him crave water even more."

"Did you hear me?" Rhonda asks again.

"A gullywasher would be worse, though. Strip Paradise down to the gray slate and red rock under it, lay it open like a wound."

"Darla?"

"Heard every word, sis. Frank's in jail over in Palm Grove, lewd liberties with a minor, et cetera, et cetera, you're broke, truck's not running, you're sick at heart, sick of trying, and there was one other sick, but I forget what kind."

"Sick inside," Brandy says, from somewhere behind me. "Isn't that what you said, Rhonda? Headaches?"

With the voice of a twelve-year-old, Rhonda says, "It's like a bad dream," and I can't help but marvel at her gullibility.

"Like a nightmare playing over and over in my head," she rattles on. "I mean, who knew? I treated Mardel like one of my own, let her baby-sit, let her eat me out of house and home. Remember when you were there, Darla? She was downing them Chee-tos in milk like she hadn't eaten in a month?"

"Yes, I remember." Mardel's full-moon face and empty eyes flood me with guilt.

"See, Brandy? I told you. And the girl repays me by—well, it's unbelievable."

The clouds above the rooftops resemble a watercolor hanging on the south wall of the high school library. In my estimation, they haven't moved a hair in any direction for hours. "Sixteen years old"—Brandy's voice is high-pitched with disbelief—"and carrying on like that—but girls mature early nowadays, don't they?"

Her memory is flawed and I'd like to tell her so, but time is precious and I prefer to relish the scent of Spirit on my skin, a mysterious cocktail of Safari and orange juice at the tips of my fingers, in the bend of my elbow. He left late last night, and though I washed my hair and showered this morning, his aroma remains, caught in the folds of my pillow, trapped in the weave of my summer blanket, held in memory as words of love rain down like confetti. I want him here, now. I want everything and everyone else, including Rhonda, to go away—to leave me alone with my thoughts.

"I wouldn't be here burdening you like this," Rhonda says, "'specially with Momma taking off like that, but Brandy insisted, didn't you, Brandy?"

Brandy nods. "Picked her up at her trailer. Told her you'd want to know what a mess she was in."

I spin around. Rhonda resembles a pale martyr who's spent a lifetime waiting for her savior to put in a personal appearance, but has now given up hope. Her eyes shine out of her head like chips of glass. Her T-shirt and shorts need a wash. Her toenails need cutting and her bare feet are as dry and dusty as the time she sprawled across Granny's bed clutching the five-dollar bill Uncle Dave gave her for having sex with him in the kitchen.

Uncle Dave loves me like he loves no one else, Darla, honest he does. He promised he'd come back for me. Gonna live with him in a big house.

But he never came back, and his promises faded into the walls. Maybe that's why I find it so hard to look at Rhonda now, sitting there chewing her nails. Why didn't I realize what she was going through back then? Did it ever occur to me to tell a teacher, the school nurse? Lord, no. They would have looked at us as like we were grease spots on a white silk blouse, and God forbid I should tell Elijah. Admit to someone you love, who loves you, that you and your sister were dirtied by another's hands? Merciful God, no. Even if Elijah had guessed, could he confess to those he cherished, who loved him with the bursting heart of a child, that he knew what their downcast eyes told him? Impossible.

"Brandy came for me before I had a chance to clean up," Rhonda says, seeing me stare at her feet.

I recall the color of her skin when Jessie was born. Seeing his little mouth clasped on her breast, I worried he might suck the last drop of sap out of her. "You look like you're fleeing Rwanda."

"Who's Rwanda?"

"It's not a person, sis. It's a place in Africa."

"Where d'ya learn all this stuff?"

"The Learning Channel. The Discovery Channel."

Rhonda gasps. "You've got cable?"

"I work damned hard for it."

She shrugs, frowns. "So what made you ask if I was fleeing that place?"

"Because you look like a starving refugee. Hope Pearl and Jessie are in better shape."

"They're okay," she says, wrapping a length of Kleenex around two fingers.

"What does okay mean? Do they look like you, or are they *really* okay?"

"They're not sick, they're in school. It's just that—"

"What?"

"Well, they're kinda worried and upset that—"

"Like I told her on the way over here, Darla," Brandy says, "just 'cause you two had a falling-out is no reason for you to shut her and the kids outa your life, right?"

I gawk at Rhonda in amazement. "*I* shut you and the kids out of *my* life?"

Rhonda ducks her head. "I didn't say it exactly like that, Darla."

"You sure as hell did," Brandy says, her nostrils flaring. "Exactly like that."

"But what I meant was—"

"Doesn't matter what you meant," I tell her. "Let's focus on what we've gotta do right now, okay?"

"I want Frank out of jail," she says. "But they tell me he's been bound over, so—"

"Which means," Brandy says, her eyebrows raised like commas, "they've got proof."

"He didn't touch her, Darla." Rhonda's cheeks flush slightly. "He swears he didn't, and I believe him."

"I'm not bailing him out."

"It wouldn't be that much, and if you'd just—"

"Won't do it, Rhonda. For all I care, he can stay where he is till his pecker rots off, and if you ask me again, I'll make you leave. What else?"

Rhonda's lips tremble and her eyes fill with tears. "It'll take two hundred and eighty dollars to fix the truck," she mumbles.

"Who said?"

"Duggan's Garage."

"I'll call Billy Joe's Auto Repair."

"Billy Joe Comfort?" Rhonda asks, frowning. "That old boyfriend of yours?"

"First inert object she ever screwed," Brandy says, taking a fresh pack of Marlboros from her purse. "That's what you said, right, Darla?"

I want to strangle her. "How come you're not at the beauty shop?"

"'Cause I don't have a customer till noon, and I promised Rhonda I'd drive her home when we leave here."

"Well, keep your remarks to yourself."

Brandy blinks like I'm broad daylight and offers Rhonda the entire pack of cigarettes.

"She just quit smoking," I tell Brandy, "and the reason I prefer Billy Joe is that he'll tow the truck *and* fix it for less."

Brandy returns the cigarettes to her purse and grimaces. "Sure he can handle it?"

"He makes engines purr like bobcats. What else, Rhonda?"

"Coupla bucks for groceries, gas, and dog food. Enough to tide me over till I sign on at welfare."

"You'll sign on tomorrow. Pick you up at seven."

"Seven?"

"Seven, on the dot."

I dread it. We'll wait for hours in that barren office, its floors tacky with spilled coffee and Coke. Babies crying, smelly diapers, Rhonda wilting under the cold gaze of women with twice-yearly perms and weekly sets, women who gorge on cinnamon rolls at break time and wear high-priced foundation garments—big women who swear by NutraSweet and weigh in private, their lashes wet with tears.

I spent a fair chunk of my childhood in that place, watching Granny and consoling Rhonda while Momma paced up and down and puffed on Camels—smoke pouring from her nose like a bad exhaust. When me and Rhonda get there, men and women of every size, shape, and color, good folks trapped in bad situations, will gripe about their health, their bosses, and their lost jobs. They'll complain about husbands and boyfriends who show up the day the checks arrive and leave when the money's gone—and I'll nod and tell them to *hang in* 'cause that's what folks told Momma back then.

"She really is sick," Brandy says, her palm on Rhonda's forehead. "No fever, but look at her color, her eyes, Darla."

"Frank Slater disease," I say. "Turns skin gray, puts lines in fore-heads, and breaks the spirit in two. It's what he does for a living. It's his job."

Rhonda's lips quiver, her eyes sink deeper into her skull. "Don't, Darla. I don't feel good."

The cords in my neck tighten and my left eye starts twitching. I wish to God I was an orphan, that like the comet Hyakutake, I need only drop by Paradise every twenty thousand years to pick up fresh laundry.

Rhonda rakes her hair from her eyes and adds with a grimace, "Not felt good in a month."

"You've been sick for years." I know I shouldn't elaborate, but my mouth won't stop moving. "Bacterial meningitis. Swollen ovaries. Prolapsed uterus. Inflamed nodes. Arthritis. Influenza. Pneumonia. If you and all your no-account doctors are to be believed, you've had every disease known to man at one time or another."

She sniffs and coughs, like she's coming down with another chest cold. "I know, I know."

"I'll make you an appointment over in Palm Grove."

"What's wrong with old Doc Hartley?"

Brandy gasps. "You let that old quack on the highway touch you?"

"Lots of times," Rhonda says. "Always been nice to me."

"He's given you prescriptions for every damned pill you ever asked for," I tell her. "God knows you've spent half your life sleeping with Prince Valium or Queen Quaalude."

"He does abortions," Brandy whispers, like it's a secret. "Uses his garbage disposal to make sausage outa fresh-born babies."

My stomach shrinks around the toast I had for breakfast. The room twists and turns as my brain frantically struggles to remember if it saw a disposal all those years ago, but draws a blank. I rush to the sink, let cold water run over my wrists. "That's uncalled-for, Brandy."

"Hey," she says with a wave of the hand. "Don't get upset."

"Don't get upset? We've got a crisis here, in case you hadn't noticed. And guess who in this family straightens them out? Me, right?"

"Sorry," Brandy says. "Didn't mean anything by it."

"Feels like I'm walking a tightrope at times—feel it under the soles of my feet, for Christ's sake. One wrong step, and I'll fall on my ass and break my neck. I don't need all this."

"I said I was sorry."

Rhonda and Brandy exchange glances, as if the only real problem here is me. Maybe they're right. I'm being selfish. Poor Rhonda's in a mess of trouble, and here I am, hungering after Spirit. "Like I said, sis, I'll make you an appointment."

"Thanks, Darla."

"And let's get something straight. If either of you ever says another word against that poor young girl Frank's *supposedly* been messing with, I'll rip y'tongues out."

Rhonda makes an odd, squeaking sound and goes rigid. Her left leg stiffens and quivers. Her head falls against the back of my recliner. Her jaws clench. By the time me and Brandy get to her, her eyes have rolled up and out of sight—disappeared inside her head.

Elijah can't keep his eyes off Spirit. Between trips to the kitchen for more coffee and plates of cake, he sits across the room next to Granny and studies him—watches intently as he dials one number after another—listens closely as he asks one question after another—offers a quick smile when their eyes meet by accident.

Spirit finally hangs up the phone. "Some chap at Southwestern Freight in Oklahoma City," he says in a voice that smacks of dingoes and billabongs, "says Dusty Duke's headed for California with a full load of patio bricks."

"And Momma," I say, wishing Spirit wasn't here—that he hadn't insisted on coming along to help. Lord knows what he's thinking.

"I'm tempted to turn her in," says Elijah, "but she'd only lie. Welfare would end up mailing her a check for out-of-pocket expenses."

"That's true," I say, embarrassed by his frankness. "This is one hell of a situation."

Spirit clears his throat.

"Swear again," Elijah says, "and I'll be all over you like a fly on meat."

"Sorry," I mumble. "Rushing Rhonda to the emergency room curdled my disposition."

Elijah hands me a thick slice of fruitcake on one of his best yellow plates. "Eat this with a strong cup of coffee and you'll feel better."

I wave it away. "Not for me, thanks, it's too hot to drink coffee. Hard to believe that out of the blue she'd have a seizure. Wasn't much—just lasted a second or two."

"Terrifying," Elijah says. "Mebbe it's stress or sump'n like that."

Visibly curious, Elijah sees Spirit take my hand and raises one eyebrow at me, as if to say "What's going on here, Darla?" so I just keep talking. "And she won't let me or Brandy stay home with her. Pearl and Jessie are there. They know how to get hold of me if—"

"You're taking her to another doctor tomorrow, you say?"

"Yes, in Layton—and what about you, Granny? You doing okay?"

She answers my question with a quick smile. A fuzzy-headed wren in a cotton housecoat, she squeezes herself between me and Spirit, slips a frail, mottled hand between his two strong ones, and gazes into his beard, up into his lovely eyes as if, with His forehead healed, Christ's one purpose for being in Elijah's parlor is to fly her home.

Spirit smiles lovingly at her, then glances toward Momma's place. He's probably thinking I have a screwed-up family, that in their brains, mine included, most likely, lurks a crazy virus, something akin to Mad Cow Disease, which, with the twist of a head or the turn of an eye, can, in seconds, turn a smoldering cinder into a full-fledged forest fire, creating the kind of mental devastation one must see to believe. He may be right.

"And what exactly did Momma say, Elijah?" I ask for the umpteenth time.

Hands spread over his knees, fingertips resting like pink rosebuds against the washed-out blue denim, he says, "She said, 'Would you watch Mother for me?' and I told her I'd love to have her, 'cause Sophie's got everything she needs here—her own room, newspaper, twine, nine-inch black-and-white tuned to channel three—everything."

"I know."

"But 'fore I can get my bearings or ask anything else, Sophie's coming in the door and Roxie's jumping in an eighteen-wheeler parked on the side of the house, then it's backing out, the radio blaring. Fact is, that Elvis fella was screaming *I ain't nothin' but a hound dog* so loud you'd have thought he was right here in m'yard, and there's your momma sitting up front in the cab with Liz T on her lap, happy as a canary—like she's on a tour bus headed for Hot Springs, Arkansas."

"How did Granny get here? No way she could have climbed in or out of a rig like that."

"Roxie walked her, I reckon."

"And Momma didn't say when she'd be back?"

"Not a word. Soon as I saw Liz T was with her, I knew she wadn't off to Wal-Mart."

"No telling then. Think I'll check myself into the crazy farm."

"Eat sump'n first," Elijah says, and grins like he's a kid in Dairy Queen with ten bucks in his pocket.

And why not? After all these years he's got Granny all to himself for who knows how long. What a pair they make. One black, one half-breed. One sharp as a blade, the other adrift on a nameless sea, ignorant of age and experience. Yet together they're like a clock and a pendulum, each dependent on the other for a smooth, quiet operation.

"What got into her?" I ask, hoping Spirit will believe this is the first time it's happened. "She knows folks can up and disappear. FBI man on TV said they find the remains of men, women, and children every day of the year in forest reserves. Don't take an Einstein to figure all them folks didn't drop dead while hiking. If Dusty Duke claims he dropped her off in Oklahoma City, who could dispute him?"

"Mercy," Elijah says, and gives Spirit a slice of cake. "Don't bear thinking about, does it?"

But he is thinking about it—and if that scenario did come about, he wouldn't be bothered at all.

He passes a fork to Spirit. "She shut the house up tight, too. No cooler going. Nobody got a key."

"This looks delicious," Spirit says, taking a bite. "How about you, Sophie? Care to join me?"

Eyes wide and innocent, she offers him a front-row view of her gums and says, "Oh no, honey. That stuff'll rot m'teeth plumb outa m'head."

Spirit, God bless him, gives her a piece anyway.

"She ate three slices hot from the oven for breakfast this morning," Elijah says with pride. "Fond of the rum in it, ain't that right, Sophie?"

Spirit swallows this news with a loud gulp and returns the plate to the coffee table. "My mother bakes one that's *almost* this good every Christmas."

"That a fact?" says Elijah. "Well, I reckon I'd like your momma. Keep in touch with her reg'lar, do you?"

"Phone her every month, without fail."

Elijah leans back and folds his arms, squints one eye, nods a bit. "That's nice," he says. "Must say, though, I nevuh thought I'd live to see this."

"What's that, sir?"

"Well, I don't mind telling you I was a mite taken aback when Darla showed up with you in tow, and says you're dating—you being a Pentecostal preacher and all."

"Excuse me?"

"Fact of the matter is, in case she didn't mention it, I raised her and Rhonda strict Southern Baptist and got 'em both baptized early."

Spirit looks at me then back to Elijah, a tad confused. "Good for you, sir."

"And Darla was a reg'lar churchgoer till she could buy them tight Lizzie Borden jeans with her own money. Oughta be a law agin wearin' such things, but who listens to me?"

"I understand, sir," Spirit says, "but—"

"Fact is," Elijah goes on, a determined expression on his face, "couldn't be any more surprised if you were that Polish pope."

"But I'm neither Catholic nor Pentecostal, sir. I'm what you'd call a nondenominational Christian evangelist."

"I wouldn't call you nothin', Reverend, 'less I knew I could pronounce it. I ain't got nothin' in partic'lar against any religion, you understand, but seeing as you're filling in over at Lamb of God, I reckoned you was Pentecostal. That, or Assembly o' God."

"Well, I'm not, sir, and when it comes to Darla, I'm as surprised as anyone. I've traveled around the States for over ten years, yet right here in Paradise, I find someone who's down to earth, honest, and beautiful. Who'd believe it?"

"Me," says Elijah, "but then I'm partial. Darla and Rhonda are the kids I nevuh had. Rhonda's kids are my grandbabies. And I know better than anyone that they all got hearts of gold. That's the most important thing, son—what's in the heart."

Spirit's smile reminds me of a boy unwrapping his first football. "Won't argue with that, sir."

"Why would you? It's the truth."

Jaw firm, Elijah turns his attention to me. Glares, squints his eyes. This humble man has no desire to offend, only to sort things out in his head and make his point clear—and I can tell by that empty feeling in the pit of my stomach that he's about to start on me.

"So tell me something, Miss Darling Darla Creations," Elijah says. "The new life, the career in New York City you was so intent on start-

ing not too long ago—whereabouts is that on y'priority list nowadays?"

The house falls silent and chilly, the way it does right before an
arctic wind blows a virgin snowfall all to hell.

Glancing at Spirit, I see bewilderment stamped on his face, but I
can't dwell on that. I matter-of-factly grab my purse, like I'm ready to
leave. "It's still up top, Elijah, same place it's always been," I reply, but
I'm lying. Rhonda's number one now—and Spirit's the only man on
earth who can make me forget it.

We are back in the apartment as the sun reaches its highest point in a
white-hot sky. I have gowns to finish, Spirit has a sermon to prepare,
but without voicing what's weighing on our hearts, I think we both
know unfinished business, my priority list, as Elijah calls it, is wedged
between us.

From the moment we left Elijah and Granny waving on the porch,
I've expected Spirit to ask me about New York. His mouth is primed.
The words are on his lips as he stands looking out the window. He just
can't bring himself to let them go.

I start my cassette player. Luciano starts singing "Celeste Aïda"—
begins right where he left off last night. I place two cans of diet Coke
on the table, and with a satin smile, slide one in his direction. "C'mon,
sweet thing," I say in my sexiest voice. "Sit y'self down and relax a
spell."

He removes his coffee-colored jacket, hangs it on the kitchen chair
and sits across from me—his butter-yellow shirt almost dazzling.

"Your granny's a sweetheart."

"I know.

"Elijah adores you."

"He worries too much."

"Think your mother will come back soon?"

"Hard to tell."

"I'll drive you and your sister to Layton tomorrow."

"I'd rather you didn't."

"Oh?"

"Not sure she'd like to meet someone new right now—not when she's feeling poorly."

"You're probably right. Glad you asked me to go to Elijah's with you, though."

"Did the widow ask you where you was going?"

He smiles. "Trudy? She may have—but I don't hear very well."

Tufts of dark hair peek from the V of his shirt collar. I kick off my leather thongs and cross my legs, and when I hitch the hem of my red cotton skirt to the knee, he sips the Coke and raises one black eyebrow. The look in his eye, a hypnotized "I know the path to every nook and cranny, to every hidden spot in your garden," tells me what I want to know. I can delay the showdown right here and now if I have a mind to. All I've gotta do is rake back this tangle of hair, lick my lips, lower the lashes, drop the chin, reveal a shoulder, a stretch of thigh, hitch the hem high as it'll go if necessary—and before we know it, we'll be smack dab in the middle of a fine hallelujah time.

I'm still deciding what to do when Spirit comes and stands behind me, buries his face in my hair, and with a moan of pleasure, eases his arms under mine and takes my breasts in his hands—weighs them. I cradle the back of his head with one hand, trace the shape of his mouth with the index finger of the other. His lips are wet outside and inside. Smooth teeth—perfectly aligned. He nibbles my fingers, caresses each one with his soft warm tongue.

"Dear God, Darla," he whispers. "Dear God."

A flurry of activity begins. Buttons unfastened. Zippers undone. Fabric whispers, slides to the floor—skirt, pants, shirt, blouse, bra, panties, jockey shorts. Strong hands envelop my buttocks. Rock-hard passion presses against my belly—a sleeping volcano is now wide awake. My head spins. Spirit lifts me, carries me to the bed, and takes his time, nibbling and tasting, working his way up and down the length of my body, stopping only to whisper, "Love me as you've never loved anyone, Darla."

I hear voices; ancient cries riding the beat of Indian drums, feathered dancers chanting. Faces aflame, they shuffle around the campfire in the dark of night—voices that spark in burning logs, that sob in the rain, voices part earth, part wind and fire, voices older than time itself that say, "Open your eyes, Darla Moon, open the door to your soul, the dance of love has begun," and a window flies open—I am sucked through it, caught up in the cyclone's eye, spun around and around, a scrap of paper whirling alongside meteors and stars, spinning around Jupiter and Mars in swirling clouds of dust.

My breasts are on fire, and that deep, fervent place between my thighs, that aching place where he's gone so gently before, now begs him to seek the prize again, to explore the harvest and feast on it, to burst in unrestrained—to turn me inside out.

Our mouths open, our hips glued together, he is wild, my beautiful lover. All power and animal strength, he is above me, inside me, hard, probing, his eyes fixed on mine. With the wind at his back, my brave rides me as he would ride a wild horse. We thunder across the barren plains toward a raging forest fire, and seconds before I am consumed in flames, my warrior is still. Eyes closed, nostrils flared, he utters a faint, guttural sound as we hover on the brink, ecstasy extended. He lowers his mouth to my breasts. I arch my back, raise my lips to kiss his cheeks, to gently bite, to claim his full, ripe lips. He rides again—again and again and again—so fast and furious I can't remember our names or where we are, and when at last we cry out with adoration, I am miraculously sucked into the bowels of the earth and burned to a cinder.

He waits until he's soft before rolling away—even then, he holds my hand. Is anything on earth more wonderful than this feeling of complete love, knowing I'm exactly where I belong, now and always? As for the tears in Spirit's eyes, I don't know why they're there, don't want to know—not now, anyway.

I descend into a cool, shadowed garden, and Spirit enters my dream fresh as lime, soft as new grass, smelling clean, his skin smooth, his lips sweeter than orange blossom honey and more potent than wine. Naked, we stroll hand in hand across a bed of leaves, down into a gentle stream, and submerge ourselves. The water instantly turns dark and rises fast, churns like it's boiling. Bodies rush by, legs and arms bumping against mine, and Spirit is gone.

I wake with a start, sweating. Heaven, a white glare of stainless steel, stares in over the rooftops. Only two in the afternoon and the window thermometer registers 102 degrees.

Spirit kisses my eyelashes, my eyebrows, my nose, and my lips, studies me with rapt intent, as if trying his damnedest to memorize what I look like. Then, misty-eyed, he rolls over to gaze at the ceiling. "How is it possible," he asks, "to be smack dab in the middle of original sin yet feel as if I'm in what can only be described as a perfect state of grace?"

You Sure You Can Swim?

Decked out in red, white, and blue paper banners, Paradise's only fire truck, a throwback to the fifties, along with a troop of Boy Scouts on decorated bicycles, a couple of trumpet players from the high school, and a flatbed truck with a papier-mâché Statue of Liberty in the back (sponsored by Bolton's Funeral Home), will meander down Main Street on Monday. At sundown, a small crowd will gather in the parking lot of the VFW Hall and watch $200 worth of fireworks go off, but what's to celebrate?

Dr. Jon Manson says something is growing in Rhonda's head. It's wedged into a space only surgeons see, on the left side of her forehead. Lit up on a screen, it resembles a misshapen rat sitting on its hindquarters, paws up, mouth open.

I'm hoping the doctor will tell us the rat, the *thing* that has taken three days and two exhausting trips to Oklahoma City to find, the *thing* he is pointing at with one perfectly manicured, antiseptic forefinger, is merely some organ of the body I have never heard of—a useless gland, an insignificant whatchamacallit too trivial for my Time-Life medical books to even mention—but he leaves us at the viewers, sits at his desk, flips through Rhonda's file, and says, "That is your problem, young lady. The last MRI clinched it. Shows us approximately how big it is, et cetera, et cetera—shows us what we're dealing with."

His voice is surprisingly casual—the soft ring of a bell that opens a front door—suggesting he's found a cavity in one of Rhonda's molars, that by using a local anesthetic and a simple filling, it can be corrected. I slip my arm around Rhonda's insignificant waist. She's trembling, and I'm tempted to say, "Don't jump to conclusions, Rhonda, think positive, you've never been as sick as you thought you were," but say instead, "Will it dissolve by itself, Doctor?" and fear the answer.

Elbows on the desk, hands clasped beneath his square chin, the doctor stiffens inside his stark white coat and smiles. "No, I'm afraid not."

Truth arrives with knifelike precision, and I sense someone shining a flashlight on a mortal wound, that faith, no matter how deep, is useless against certain things, that even Pavarotti won't take my mind off this, that every minute of the day, another life slips away as Dr. Manson steers a shiny BMW into a three-car garage—as me and Spirit make love, probably. I feel doubt, too. The kind that erodes courage, the very same variety that, when you leap into a murky pond, whispers, "You sure you can swim?"

We are asked to sit, motioned to furniture that looks and feels expensive—smooth blond wood combined with a knobby mauve fabric. At first glance, the office, with its plum-colored carpet, framed landscapes, coiffed, gold-trimmed receptionist, and fleet of smartly attired, smiling assistants, suggested steadfastness and permanence, that the specialists here are familiar with marvels, but I wasn't fooled.

The dank smell of fear, uncertainty, and brief lives rushed up my nostrils and swirled around my head like a windstorm, and I knew at once the tall, sunny nurses weren't smiling because they were glad to see us or because they'd been told they must. They are so damned grateful they're healthy, that every organ they left their mother's womb with is still attached, their joy comes natural. They are cool, comfortable, and educated, these women. They step out and move along with the well-tuned precision of a Lincoln Continental, and their brick homes, I imagine, mirror the neighborhoods they were raised in. Their men, I think, are as smooth and shiny as the *Southern Living* magazines delivered to their doors each month. If pressed, I bet they can talk for hours on gubernatorial candidates and Japanese cuisine—but time and experience have toughened their hides, immunized them against the truth, which is that only the strong, only those fat with love and power, survive the horrors treated here. Women like Rhonda, puny ones sucked dry as a straw, have about as much chance as a lame deer on the African plains—instant breakfast for the first hungry lion.

That's why, I think, when Rhonda's tests were complete and the verdict ready, when we looked to these narrow-ankled, stiffly starched, sweet-smelling creatures for signs of reassurance, their pastel eyelids dropped like guillotines and their eyes slid away. My guess is, when their husbands come home bearing the funky scent of a strange woman, these same women whip up a carrot cake or rush outside to water begonias.

"Mrs. Slater," says Dr. Manson, "you have a touch of pneumonia, you're anemic, and your blood work requires additional scrutiny—as does the mass."

The mass? It's as if someone struck a tuning fork in the center of my brain. I melt into the chair. The city whirls around me in slow motion. Stone and steel and bronzed roofs crash into each other and explode. Rhonda, however, a sickly flamingo in an old pink blouse and a Goodwill skirt, appears unmoved. Only the rapid rise and fall of her chest and her blinking eyes tell me she heard the ugly word and is mentally processing the information. That, and the way she's twisting her wedding band around and around that skinny finger.

"We're going to admit your sister to our hospital for further tests," Dr. Manson adds.

"Why not a hospital near home?"

"The specialist she needs is here."

"I've got nothing against this hospital, you understand, but it takes an hour and a half to drive here, and my transportation isn't air-conditioned."

"She'll undergo a battery of tests for the next twenty-four to forty-eight hours," he continues. "Monday's a holiday, and test results will be slow, so you could conceivably wait till Tuesday before coming back. I imagine you'll want to get her children settled, won't you?"

"She's got no insurance."

"This isn't the time to worry about insurance."

"Sure as hell is if you ain't got it."

"She's eligible for Medicaid."

"She is?"

"SoonerCare will step in. Leave the details to my staff."

"What sort of tests are you talking about?"

"The neurosurgeon will decide."

"Neurosurgeon?"

"Brain surgeon. Dr. Jeffers is the finest," he says with confidence. "He'll evaluate the tumor."

So now we have a brain surgeon and a tumor. But, the word cancer or malignant hasn't been uttered, thank God. "Can't you treat it with medicine?"

He hesitates. "If it's what I think it is, medicine is not an option."

I glance at Rhonda's forehead, looking for a bulge. There isn't one. "And what do you think it is?"

"A glioma."

"What's that, exactly?"

"A potentially dangerous growth. It's not uncommon."

"So if it's what you think it is and medicine's not an option—"

"Yes?"

"Well, is there any reason the neurosurgeon *wouldn't* remove it?"

"Size and location are always a factor."

"So—?"

"I hesitate to speculate."

"How sure are you that it's a glioma?"

"Fairly sure."

"I'm having trouble absorbing all of this, aren't you, Rhonda?"

She nods.

Dr. Manson says nothing. I have no idea how Rhonda feels, but something close to panic climbs up my back. "Like I told you, Doctor, Rhonda's been sick with one thing or another for years, but nothing to indicate—well, just that one little seizure at my place, and that only seconds, so I'm wondering, could Dr. Jeffers look at the MRIs and reach a different conclusion?"

"Absolutely."

Thank you, Jesus. "When will we know? We want to know as soon as possible, don't we, Rhonda?" but Rhonda stares into space and says, "I'm allergic to tuna."

"Dr. Jeffers will examine her and look at her lab work and scans right after lunch," Dr. Manson says. "He'll see you in his office around two, second floor of E wing."

We sit quietly, me chewing on my lip, Rhonda gazing at a vapid sky, while Dr. Manson, his every move graceful yet businesslike, massages his immaculate hands. Unmarred cuticles, nails white as soap, nothing out of place, a flawless Windsor knot in his striped gray tie. On the wall, perfectly aligned, a gallery of impressive diplomas. On his desk, lined up like a regiment of soldiers, dozens of freshly sharpened yellow pencils—yet the electric pencil sharpener's plastic belly is cleaner than a newly washed window. No cracker crumbs between this man's sheets, no reheated leftovers or plastic forks. Bet he could say "Fuck you" and make it sound like a compliment.

"Any questions, Rhonda?" he says, raising an eyebrow. "Anything you want to know before we move on?" but Rhonda is mute. "How about you, Darla? Any questions?"

I press Rhonda's limp hand to my chest and squeeze hard. I'm cold to the bone, terrified to the core of my soul that the rat in her head, assuming there is one, will eat its way through her brain like it was cheese, leaving nothing behind 'cept bone and hair.

Any questions, he wants to know. Hell, I've got dozens. Will my legs support me when I stand? Is it possible to swallow all the tears behind my eyes without drowning? And if the rat is dangerous, does Rhonda have what it takes to fight it off? And what in God's name am I supposed to tell Pearl and Jessie and Elijah when I get home? And where in the hell is Momma?

"Any questions, Darla?" he asks again.

I lean across his desk and look him in the eye. "Yes, Dr. Manson, just one," I reply. "Have you ever shit in an outhouse?" and out of the blue, Rhonda says, "I want Frank."

While nurses tuck Rhonda in and draw blood, I wander through an orderly battlefield, traipse along interminable, odd-smelling hallways, climb deserted stairways, ride humming elevators, my fingers hitting one button after another as I search in vain for a friendly face. White uniforms, green scrubs, American Indians, East Indians, men with mops, others with stethoscopes, an oriental lady on crutches, a woman with no legs at all, steel carts, plastic meals, plastic cups, plastic bed-pans, soap holders, washbasins—and floating past, ghostlike figures toting fluid-filled jars. Ceilings too high for comfort, corridors too wide for conversation, wet floors, sick and dying people in steel beds under stiff sheets. In the waiting rooms, agitated adults wrestle with sick kids and argue with each other.

When I smile, they turn away—like they fear I'll ask a question they can't or mustn't answer, and when I find a place to sit, I am scru-tinized by countless eyes, analyzed and studied, from my wild mane right down to my sandals, until a diagnosis is made.

The hospital cafeteria is almost deserted and the two-dollar daily special, beans and corn bread, brings no comfort. I locate my compact and fix my lipstick—reluctantly examine my eyes, the well-defined creases. I'm at another curve in the road. I will never again be the same as I am now, never as pretty, breasts never as firm, muscles never as tight, skin never as smooth, because time is passing with the speed of light, and years are piling up behind me, nudging me toward an inevitable middle age.

My future skitters ahead, just out of reach. If I wait too long I'll never catch up. At age sixty-five, I could be childless, my fingers red and swollen, my eyes weak, bristles sprouting from my nose. I see myself hunched over an outdated sewing machine making prom dresses for the girls of Paradise High while listening to a long-dead opera singer whose name escapes me, whose voice fades into oblivion one faint, screwed-up note at a time . . . at a time . . . at a time.

If Spirit were here, I could lose myself in his arms for an hour or so, rejuvenate, jump the next hurdle with ease. I locate a phone and almost call him, but change my mind. Instead, I dial Billy Joe's Auto Repair. "Get started on Rhonda's truck, Billy Joe," I tell him. "She's gonna need it soon."

I phone Dr. Manson's office. The gold-trimmed receptionist recognizes my voice, says, "Hold just a minute, Darla, he'll be right with you," and when he answers, I say, "You're gonna be eating your words, Doc, 'cause Rhonda's not as sick as you think. Simple reason being, for the past ten years I've pumped her full of One-A-Day vitamins plus iron. Besides, she's too young to die, I'm in love, and I've got business in New York."

Back on Rhonda's floor, I detect the faint smell of urine and liquid soap. In a room across the hall, a candy striper introduces a sickly-looking little boy to a bear that talks and sings, whose eyes move back and forth in a grotesque manner. Everyone knows bears are sedate creatures with sewn-on grins and fixed glass eyes—friends who merely sit and listen.

Across from Rhonda, motionless and snoring, a much older woman is hooked up to a couple of IVs and other gadgets.

With the blinds half-closed, the walls, floor, and ceiling have taken on an algaelike hue. Even Rhonda, sitting on the bed clutching her knees with her back to me, her gown open, her spine a knotted rod, looks sur-real—a green ghost, slightly blurred and pallid, her skin's so thin I think I see her heart beating, the blood trickling in and out all too slowly.

"I've been thinking about the kids," she says, as if she has eyes in the back of her head, "how when I was pregnant with Pearl she moved around inside me like a butterfly stretching its wings. Jessie was differ-ent. He barely moved, just sat there, like he'd found a good book to read."

"I remember you saying that."

"I'm not fucking dying, Darla, y'hear?"

Disheveled, she peers over her shoulder, her wet eyes reflecting something so vague I can't put my finger on it.

"And you know what else, Darla?"

"What?"

"We don't have any snapshots. Not a goddamned one."

I climb on the bed with her and tie the gown, take her in my arms and feel how small and defenseless and shockingly cold she is. This is how it's always been, right from the beginning, 'cept when Elijah's with us, me and Rhonda fighting the odds, all alone in a cold hard box. Eyes closed, she turns and curls against me, as she has hundreds of times, like we're a statue—like Mary and Jesus in Michelangelo's *Pietà*.

"I mean it, Darla," she whispers, like her throat's dry. "I don't care what anyone says, I ain't dying."

I pray she doesn't feel my pulse throbbing—that she doesn't detect the doubt in my voice. "I know you're not. It'll snow in hell 'fore I allow it."

★   ★   ★

Hours later, Dr. Jeffers, an elderly surgeon in rumpled clothes, says, "I don't have the heart to tell her yet, but Rhonda's cancer is advanced."

The word strikes like a snake. The smell and taste of it shoves dreams of freedom aside. "She's had a rough life," I say, like that's got anything to do with it—yet I feel compelled to tell him she got short-changed from the start, that she's entitled to a hell of a lot more time on this earth, that these things are supposed to happen to other people, to people I don't know, that he must take heroic measures to save her, but I can only say, "She's had a rough life" again.

He nods as if he knows—as if I'd shown him pictures. "Life is brutal."

"Life is shit, Doctor. Death is brutal. She's only twenty-eight, for Christ's sake. She deserves a chance."

"New drugs are being tested as we speak, Darla. Direct infusion of cancer-shrinking chemicals looks promising. Scientists have used cold viruses to transmit cancer-fighting white cells, and one day we'll have a cure, but—"

"But?"

"I can't promise anything, but we'll try," he says.

Now I know what it was I saw in Rhonda's eyes an hour ago.

It was cancer, drawn on her face like a map of hell.

"Why her?" I ask. "Why her and not me?" but he can't answer that question either.

Outside, the deafening roar of heat and rush-hour traffic is almost welcome, euphoric. The sky is white and luminous, the sun acid on my face. Ugly buses and a million cars rush by in all directions. Exhaust fumes, a compound of tar and oil that coats my throat. Shimmering towers of glass and steel. The stink of asphalt and, simmering underneath it all, the wide-eyed, burning enthusiasm of men and women who are on the move, making plans, climbing up, and improving their lot. The red, white, and blue excitement of go-get-'em city folk.

And God help me, because I want to be just like them, I squint at the sun and join in, let the horde carry me and Miss Ladybug along, stop and start with everyone else, drum my fingers on the steering wheel, observe sloe-eyed beauties as they apply their makeup in pull-down mirrors, watch executives talk on their cellular phones and pull into car washes for a weekend wash and wax—pretend for a short period of time that I live much like they do, which is no easy task considering I'm headed back to the sticks in 102-degree heat in a beat-up, polka-dotted Super Beetle with no air conditioner, and my baby sister is fucking well dying.

I locate a phone booth outside a Git 'N' Go market. It is stifling inside. The floor is tacky with gum, littered with scrunched-up candy wrappers and cigarette butts. Graffiti everywhere. I call Elijah, tell him I'm on my way, that I'll talk to him and the kids about Rhonda when I get there. "It's bad news," I warn him, "but I won't tell Pearl and Jessie just how bad. Not yet, anyway."

I hear a noise—imagine Elijah choking back tears, afraid the kids will see him. "You know best, hon," he says with a sniffle, "and in case you're interested, your preacher friend just showed up. Wondered if I'd heard from you."

"Tell him you have."

"This is her now, Spirit," Elijah says with a trace of annoyance, then, "Now he wants to know if you've got time to talk to him, Darla. Do you?"

"Sure I do."

Panting sparrows hunt for crumbs under parked cars. Red dust and scraps of paper swirl through the parking lot. Lasers of sun bounce off windshields and blind me, burn my eyes. Sweat runs down my back. My breathing is ragged.

I see Spirit before he speaks, his eyes wrinkled at the corners, sleeves pushed up, sturdy arms, tan skin reflecting the light coming through Elijah's kitchen window. Smell him—faintly soapy, taste him—sweet, and feel those magical fingers. I'm spellbound, caught up in the sorcery of the Reverend Spirit E. Jackson, alive and madly in love while Rhonda rots away in a metal bed.

"What did you find out?" he asks.

"If I tried to tell you right now, I'd only—"

"I understand. See you later?"

"Yes, see you later." Standing in this airless cubicle, the traffic so loud I barely can hear, I long to reach out and grab him, lose myself in him, become someone else, have someone else's memories, live in another time, another place, and start anew—and not even know the meaning of guilt.

"I miss you, Darla," he says.

"I miss you, too. You okay?"

"I'm fine."

"You sound different."

"I am different," he says in a hushed voice. "A beautiful woman worked a miracle in my life, altered it forever."

"No, something else."

"You're something else."

"What's wrong? Tell me."

"I was fired today," he says. "Two Lamb of God deacons gently, but firmly, asked me to leave."

I know why without even asking, and I am numb with the realization that Spirit must be devastated. How could we have been so naive? What was I thinking?

"Needless to say," he goes on, "I'm no longer welcome at Trudy Spencer's—but that's no problem."

"Where will you stay?"

"I checked in at the Ponderosa Motel, room twenty-four."

My heart shudders, goes cold. "This isn't happening. It's not possible."

"What's not possible?"

"Everything.

"Everything?"

"But love does that."

"Does what?"

"Blinds you."

Somewhere between Oklahoma City and Paradise, I gas up and buy four large Milky Ways, Rhonda's favorite. Back on the highway, I consume one after another until they're all gone. Fifteen minutes later, I bring Miss Ladybug to a screeching halt on the shoulder of I–40 and throw up. Shuddering at the smell and taste of undigested chocolate and bile, I swear off Milky Ways forever.

Who Turned Up the Heat?

. . . .

Elijah doesn't wait for me to get inside. Smelling of hot grease and pepper gravy, he meets me in his front yard. The diagnosis dazes him. He totters slightly, even touches his forehead and strokes it, frowns—as if he knows exactly where Rhonda's rat had settled, that by touching the spot he can make it go away.

He rubs harder. "Why, God, why?"

"Don't ask Him why. Ask Him what the frigging message is."

He touches my arm, draws me back inside, to the kitchen. I collapse into a chair.

"We got some serious praying to do, hon," he says, "but you already know that."

"Where are the kids?"

"Front bedroom, watching TV. What about Rhonda's truck?"

"Billy Joe's working on it."

"How 'bout letting me pay?"

"Paid already. Stopped on the way here."

"Got Rhonda's rent caught up. Fact is, she's a month ahead right now."

"You shouldn't have."

"Not another word." He pulls a small Sunny Delight from the fridge and sets it in front of me.

"So how's things going with the preacher? He looked kinda down when he left here."

"The way I see it, Elijah, you enter a relationship same way you put dirty clothes in a washer. You expect all the whites to come out sparkling clean with nary a mark or stain on 'em—so nothing, absolutely nothing, prepares a person for what happens when one red sock meets up with a cup of Clorox bleach."

"Clorox bleach?"

"Trudy Spencer."

"Red sock?"

"Lamb of God."

"Problem?"

"The preacher and me—together, at my place."

"Lawd have mercy. He nevah said."

"They fired him."

"Lawdy, Lawdy, give us strength."

My stomach heaves and pitches as I try my damnedest to figure out what I should say and how I'm supposed to say it when the kids walk in. Poor little things. They're so worried they're pale. Their little hands are clasped tight, their lips are pulled tight and thin, and they're looking at me as if I'm a stranger—someone they're scared of.

"Y'momma's ailing," I say, "but she's got some wonderful doctors, and they'll get her well."

"I don't believe you," Jessie says, a raspy catch in his throat. "I wanna go home."

I see my reflection in his pupils, the tangle of hair, the somber expression, and I know I've gotta appear strong and safe and in charge for these kids. "It's true, Jessie, and she wants you and Pearl to stay with me until she gets well. That way, I can take care of you. You know, make sure you eat right and stuff, okay?"

"They can stay here with me and Sophie, Darla," Elijah says, looking hopeful. "I got plenty o' room."

"You've got enough to worry about."

"Y'granny ain't no trouble."

"Pearl and Jessie are my responsibility, Elijah. We'll have a great time, won't we kids?" No response. "By the way, where is Granny?"

"Taking a nap," Elijah says. He pads around the supper table, spoons leftover mashed potatoes and oven-baked chicken into his treasured Tupperware, pours gravy into a jar. "Kept her busy today, didn't we kids? Went and checked on the creek—sure is low—and collected some stones. Even talked her into leaving them durned frogs at the house."

"Soon as we have a good rain," Granny yells from the back bedroom, "I'm taking 'em back for a swim, y'hear?"

"Hear ya, Sophie," Elijah yells back. "Thought you was sleeping. Anyways, Darla, we all had us a fine ol' time till the heat forced us home."

"None of our things are at your place, Aunt Darla," Pearl whines as she twists and turns on the balls of her feet, "and seeing as I'm thirteen years old and school's out, I don't see why I can't take care of Jessie at home till Momma gets back."

"You're crazy if you think I'd let you stay there alone. Y'momma would worry herself silly."

"So don't tell her."

"That wouldn't be honest."

"But I could have the place all clean and tidy before she got back. You know, wash windows, vacuum, mop floors—that sorta stuff." She hugs me, squeezes me, gazes into my eyes. "Please, please, pretty please. I can do it."

I squeeze back. "I know you can, honest I do, but that's not what y'momma wants. Soon as we know she's being discharged, we'll clean house together," and out of the blue I realize something that almost chokes me. Should Rhonda pass on, Jessie and Pearl will be my responsibility, my kids, and the idea terrifies me—freezes me to the chair. Why, on that long drive back to Paradise, facing that endless stretch of concrete, love grass, and scrub oaks, didn't it occur to me? I was preoccupied with pain and decay, that's why. Couldn't stop wondering what kind of miracles doctors pull out of their bags when folks start thrashing about in agony.

"Things'll work out, Darla," Elijah says like he's reading my mind. "May not happen the way you want, but it will be the way God planned, y'hear?" which leaves me wondering why His plans so often include pain and suffering. Seems to me He could have left such things out of life's equation with no detectable effect on the balance of nature—along with tornadoes, hurricanes, earthquakes, roaches, and wrinkles.

"I know what, Aunt Darla," Jessie pipes up. "Why don't you stay at the trailer with us?"

"I can't, sweetheart," I tell him. "Everything I work with is at my apartment. Sewing machine, cutting table, material—everything."

Frustrated, he shoves his hands deep into his pockets and sighs. "Oh yeah, I forgot."

"Trust me on this, okay? We'll use Elijah's truck to pick up your mattresses and your clothes. It'll be fun. Sorta like camping out in the wilderness. We'll fix popcorn and hamburgers and—"

"What exactly's wrong with Mommy anyway?" Jessie asks as Pearl, her expression one of indifference, leaves my arms to help Elijah. She stacks dirty dishes and returns unused cutlery to the drawer—looking for all the world like she's got every piece of necessary information.

I move from the table, put distance between me and the kids, plant myself closer to the living room in case they catch wind of it—not the lies, but the stink of fear. It's weighing me down like a wet coat.

"We'll have you evaluated and your treatment mapped out in five to seven days," Dr. Jeffers told Rhonda as we left. "Then we'll transfer you to a facility in your area. Might even discharge you home with outpatient care."

Jessie, staring directly up at me with eyes pale as opals, almost brings me to tears.

"If she's ill like you say, Darling Darla, you gotta know where the sickness is. What part of her body it's in, I mean."

"It's in her head, a little lump," I say, believing this will satisfy his curiosity, but he continues to stare, as if he's calculating the risk of going one step further—as if I'm glass in winter, frosted over with rime, that waiting on the other side of this chasm is a reward for his patience. I'm about to disappoint him. I'm guessing I'll disappoint him many times in the months to come. He's too little for the truth.

"In her head?" Jessie says. "You mean like that sinus infection she had?"

"Kind of."

"Whereabouts in her head? How big is it?"

"You don't have to know every little detail, Jess," Pearl says. "It's probably one of them nothing lumps—the kind that pop up overnight like a toadstool and vanish come morning. Right, Aunt Darla?"

I clear my throat, swallow the bitter taste on my tongue, and concentrate on my casual reply. "Right, a nothing lump," and I wonder what Rhonda is doing right now. Is she still curled up under the sheets, sobbing, refusing to be consoled? Or is she asleep? I pray to God she's asleep. I pray she's asleep every time time I think of her, 'cause if she's not, you can bet she's dwelling on that rat behind her eyeball, a cancer so goddamned powerful no one knows how to destroy it, which totally amazes me. "They can put men on the moon," I say without thinking, "send entire crews of astronauts into space for weeks at a time, yet they don't know how to—"

"'Nuff said, Darla," Elijah interrupts. "How 'bout a bite of supper 'fore we put it away?"

I tell him no, that I'd like to borrow his truck and pick up some things from the trailer.

"No problem. Can I help?"

I shake my head.

Jessie tugs on my blouse. "Whereabouts in her head?" he asks again.

"Would you like me to draw a picture?"

Pearl rattles cutlery and swings around. "You don't need no picture, Jess," she says, her eyes flashing. "Momma's got a lump in her head, the doctor will fix it, and she'll be home 'fore we know it, okay?"

Jessie purses his lips and wipes his nose on his sleeve.

"Okay," he says. "Just so's we don't have to stay with Frank."

"He's in jail, Jess," says Pearl. "Remember?"

Elijah clears his throat. "You kids go back and watch TV awhile while me and Darla talk, okay?"

When they're out of hearing range, Elijah says, "Spirit said call him if you need anything."

"I'd rather he wasn't involved."

"Looks to me like he's more involved than I care to know. Hope you know what you're doing."

I take his face in my hands and kiss him. "All I know at this point is, I don't want to burden Spirit with *my* problems. I'm strong. I'll manage. Always have, right? What about you? Will you be okay?"

"I can handle it," he replies, but I spy a tear in his eye, and he's chewing his lip, which tells me he's biding his time, waiting for us to leave so he can mourn in private.

A hot devil wind blasts across the prairie, grabs the windows and makes them rattle. It's miserable outside. It's close to ten at night, still 93 degrees, and every clematis, marigold, crepe myrtle, and honeysuckle bush in Paradise has shriveled to nothing. The only folks who can water their yards when the fancy takes them are those with a well. If you're hooked up to the city, you're limited to odd or even days, depending on the first number of your mailing address.

Grasshoppers the size of greyhounds are everywhere. Weeds choke out flower beds and cover fences. Tough woody vines have twisted themselves around telephone poles, inched up trees, stretched across railway lines, and climbed over crumbling walls with alarming speed, fastened themselves to whatever's available—the tires of a car not driven for weeks, abandoned tricycles, and rotting sheds. A particularly strange plant, covered with ugly purple flowers and long thorns, wormed its way into the Dead Bolt Cafe's air conditioner and blew the motor—prompting customers, including Pearl, Jessie, and me, to leave the evening special, hamburger patty with fried okra and butter beans, cooling on the tables so we could run home and cool off.

Troubled by the incessant heat, how the blast furnace makes their hearts race and their legs tremble, most folk don't step outside after ten o'clock in the morning, not even to answer the doorbell, check their mailbox, or look for their kids—and when they resurface after supper, listless expressions on their faces, their eyes blinking, they sit on shaded porches fanning themselves, guzzling tall glasses of iced tea and lemonade. Some women, I'm told, have taken to cooling themselves off in tubs of cool water brimming with ice cubes. Men wrap frozen towels around their necks and gorge on the latest fad—white grapes and whole peeled bananas dipped in chocolate syrup, then frozen solid in the freezer.

With Paradise deep in drought, stores stay empty, parking spaces go unused, and hundreds of trees, bradford pear, redbud, maple, and oak, including Momma's goldenrain tree, are bare, having dropped their leaves, which then scattered in all directions depending on the strength and inclination of the wind. Peaches are rotting on the ground 'longside tomatoes. Entire strawberry patches have vanished, leaving behind sun-baked strips of clay that cats and dogs refuse to walk on.

Chickens stopped laying and fled with the turkeys. Cows are running loose and pigs are suffering. Intent on finding a decent mud hole to wallow in, three of Mr. Harper's prize-winning porkers broke out of their pen, burst through his back door, charged into the bathroom, and piled in the tub with his wife. Mrs. Harper promptly had a stroke and was hospitalized. Red dust stings your eyes and piles up in gutters. Ponds are dry. Every bird, 'cept a sparrow or two, has fled north in search of water. And at day's end, when the smell of hot tar is at its worst, religious folk gather in churches 'longside the sinners, and pray for a downpour.

Grim-faced, Gary England opens the late-night news. "I'm mighty sorry, folks," Jessie's favorite weatherman says, like it's all his fault, "but there's no relief in sight, no sign of precipitation in the state. All I can promise is three-digit temperatures, high dusty winds, and an increased danger of grass fires."

"There was a time," I say to Spirit, "back when me and Rhonda were just tykes, when I believed God was the only answer, that my ticket into those pearly gates was saying my prayers, doing good deeds, and living a clean life. I also believed that if I steeled myself against reality His hand would seek me out, raise me to a higher plane away from all the dirt and misery, that He'd save me, save us—me and Rhonda."

"And now?"

I glance over at Pearl and Jessie. Sound asleep on their mattresses, ignorant of what lies ahead, they resemble life-size dolls—their cotton-filled arms and legs flung out, their tummies bulging with chocolate milk and Oreo cookies.

"I'm not sure what I believe anymore, and I won't debate the subject with a preacher, but I can't help but ask why this happened to Rhonda of all people—to those two little monkeys. I mean, look at those precious kids. They deserve better."

Leaning forward, he sweeps the hair from my face, touches my cheek, and says, "Next to their mother, they have the best."

I have not a doubt in my mind that Spirit's the finest man I've ever known. This man prompts dreams. This man sits in my head and creates dreams. But he arrived at the wrong time.

With all that's going on, I don't know how I'll keep this relationship going. A chill slides across the back of my legs and shoulders—and though I'm tempted to say "Someone just walked over my grave," I doubt I'll ever say those words again.

"Where's the justice, where's the mercy, that's what I want to know," I say, struggling to keep my voice low. "I mean, look at you. You dedicate your life to God, of your own free will you come to this miserable town to preach the word, and how are you repaid? A bunch of cold-hearted, pious hypocrites give you your walking papers, force you to spend a fortune on long-distance calls to salvage your professional neck. Why? That's what I'd like to know."

He sits back in his chair and for a second it's as if he's extracted himself, as if we have nothing to share but a deep rift of caution. "Impropriety," he says.

"Meaning?"

In the quiet that follows, I hear only the wind, the blunted hum of the old air conditioner, Pearl and Jessie's steady breathing—our breathing.

"Meaning my behavior *appeared* unbecoming a man of God."

"*Appeared?* Some mean-spirited Lamb of God sister, name of Trudy Spencer, saw your Cadillac parked behind the bakery at odd hours, saw it next to Miss Ladybug over at Elijah's, or over at Muff and Freda's, and it *appeared* like you were screwing around? Excuse my language. Is that what you mean?"

"That's exactly what I mean."

"But no one knows for sure."

"Three of us know for sure, Darla. Me, you, and our maker."

"But—"

"Whoever reported it had every right to be suspicious, and the church had every right to remove me from my post. I take full responsibility. Better still, I should have listened to you. 'We're oil and water,' you said. 'Let's leave things as they are before the new-car smell wears off,' you said, but did I listen? No, I came looking for you."

His words are as vague as "approximately six yards of fabric," or "five acres, more or less." They leave a body wondering what he really means—and I daren't ask.

I rub my eyes, stretch out my legs, and rotate my head in a feeble effort to work the day's stress out of my aching body. I don't want to talk about Spirit's job, or how I figure into its demise, or what headquarters in New Mexico said. Too painful. Don't want to contemplate that when we make love we're committing a sin. Don't want to discuss what he'll do now, how long he'll stay in the motel or in Paradise, or how many more phone calls he plans to make—or where our relationship is headed. Oh, no. Too painful.

I want to talk about Rhonda. I want to tell him how helpless and angry I felt when I caught her with Uncle Dave. Want to show him the scars Uncle Phil made on our backs with his belt buckle when we caught that old couch on fire. Want to tell him about the time me and Rhonda poured an entire bottle of corn syrup into the mayor's shiny new boots while he romped in bed with Momma, how when Muff and Freda showed up unexpected, he told them he'd just stopped to use the bathroom, and marched to his truck, his feet squishing and squashing around in all that goo. Me and Rhonda stood on the porch laughing so hard we made our sides ache.

Jessie groans, flings out an arm. Pearl stirs and says, "Don't go, Momma. Don't go," and I wonder how often they dream of Rhonda.

Spirit pulls me onto his lap, and for one dizzy instant I am lost in the open neck of his shirt, in the aroma of warm flesh and soap rising from that dark place.

"You're all tuckered out, luv," he says, "and I'm not helping matters."

No ice in this man's eyes. Nothing up his sleeve but an arm. "You're helping more than you know."

"Don't say anything, just listen, okay?"

"Okay."

"I love you, Darla Moon. Love you so much that seeing you hurt like this breaks my heart, so please, don't worry about me and the church. I'm deeply, deeply sorry it happened, that I wasn't strong enough to resist, but I will not, cannot deny I love you with all my heart. God knows our deepest thoughts. God knows we're imperfect. And He alone will judge, okay? Understood?"

"Understood."

"From now on, I'll drive you to the city in my car. Yours could have a stroke traveling all that way in this heat. I want to help you and Rhonda."

"We have no photos," I hear myself say.

"Of who?"

"Of relatives, of our childhood, of us growing up. Elijah has a couple that were taken at school, but that's all. It's as if me and Rhonda never existed 'cept in each other's eyes—like puffs of smoke moving from one address to another—no shape, no rhythm, no beat, just a long disjointed song looking for a mouth to sing it."

The phone rings. I grab it before it has a chance to ring again.

"Darla? Billy Joe Comfort. You alone?"

"No, I'm not."

"Well, I was working late and—can I come over?"

"This isn't a good time, Billy Joe. Is something wrong?"

"You've got a problem, that's for damned sure."

"What else is new?"

"Frank Slater's loose."

"Loose?"

"Ten minutes ago, I'm here at the garage working late, and the bastard shows up, says something about the girl dropping charges, then peels outa here like his ass is on fire. What could I do, Darla? It's his truck. He's got keys."

"Say where he's headed?"

"The city, to see Rhonda. Say, Darla, I know this isn't a good time, what with y'sister bad off and all, but is there any chance you'd go out for dinner with me some evening?"

"Can't even think about that right now, Billy Joe, but thanks for calling."

The atmosphere turns bacterial, thriving, it seems, on what has taken root in my apartment—a clot of subdued fear and pandemonium.

A Touch of Magic

. . . .

The sky is harder than a corpse's tit this morning and just as empty. If there is a bird in it, a cloud or a rainbow in it, let others look. I don't care. The air is too thin, the sun is too hot, every breath an effort, and this gray, gut-sucking misery I've felt for weeks and weeks won't let go. But, thank God, in spite of all the hospital visits, I've managed to avoid the one virus I despise the most. Frank Slater.

And thank God for Spirit. Between arduous, almost daily telephone conversations to and from New Mexico, not to mention all the letters he's written, he has supported me, shopped for me, and been at my side—driven me wherever I've had to go—phoned me from the motel when he gets up, and before he goes to bed each night. I couldn't ask for more—yet I'm too exhausted, too worried, too mentally weary to give much in return. Nerves shot, too. A highway I once found exciting, the one between Palm Grove and Oklahoma City, has turned dangerous, and every driver a threat—a horn-blowing road hog who wants to cut us off, spit rocks at the windshield, and reach his destination before we reach ours.

Early morning, the sound of nesting robins outside my window makes my head throb. At night, the moon blinds me. Even with my eyes closed, with Pearl and Jessie asleep just steps away, I feel ice in my veins. Under my bed, a great slab of it shifts with the tide. I once felt safe here in my apartment. No more. If I don't hang onto something, the quilt, the pillow, Spirit, my own knees, I fear some awful thing will sweep me away.

The apartment is too quiet. I hear air currents move through the room, around and under the curtains, across bolts of fabric, over the sleeping children, into their mouths, and down their throats where the sharpness of it makes them cough and sniff. The brightest fabrics have turned coarse and dull under my fingers, and I'm often attacked by a weakness so severe I wonder if my legs will ever feel the same again. Only by saying "Jessie and Pearl, Jessie and Pearl," over and over again, does the feeling pass. Stars hide when I look at them. When, after hours of tossing and turning and thrashing about, I fall asleep, I tumble into a bleak predatory place inhabited by bats and cockroaches, a place where nightmares live, where Pearl and Jessie are locked in a trailer with a madman, and Rhonda, her hospital gown bloodstained, forever boards a train without so much as a hug or a kiss goodbye.

Determined to shift the gloom, I made school clothes for the kids: shirts and pants for Jessie, short tunics for Pearl, using patterns and fabrics she picked out. I've eaten cartons of ice cream and not tasted a bite. I pricked my finger with a needle, jabbed my hand with the point of the scissors, showered in steaming hot water, raked huge tangles out of my hair with a fine-toothed comb, but the feeling won't budge—and in a dark undusted corner of my mind, unspeakable thoughts keep stirring.

Elijah, me, the kids, and Granny, along with her new "recruit," attached to a leash, have attended Fountain Baptist Church four times. Four times, amid tumultuous amens and hallelujahs, my heart broke anew as a young black girl in a long white dress sang manna down from heaven. And four times or more, Preacher Lazarus Brown and the entire congregation *claimed* Sister Rhonda's healing, convinced that when we all joined hands, the "devil cells" in Rhonda's head stopped multiplying—that the blood in her veins immediately ran pure and clean.

But the rat keeps growing, faster than the doctors imagined, and everywhere I look, everything I hear, smell, taste, and touch reminds me of death. A robin's egg smashed on the sidewalk. A hawk moth, its life dust flying in all directions, beating itself into oblivion against my lighted window. The cry of a mourning dove. Rhonda's cold, waxlike hands clutching Pearl and Jessie's—their eyelashes roped with tears, their small chins quivering.

My obsession with mortality even prompted me to ask poor Granny if she feared dying.

She batted her eyes, as if her answer required a great deal of thought, and said, "Imagine it scairt me when I was young, knowing it could end all the fun I prob'ly was havin', but now? Well, the Headbreakers wiped out any notions I had of fun and got me mostly familiar with confusion and mizry. Dyin' can't be no worse'n that, can it?" Then she added, "The trick is t'keep moving. Sit still too long and with a snap of his fingers the old man'll take you out."

"The old man?"

"Old man Death," she explained.

The next morning, after sleeping so hard I woke believing I was naked, dead, and buried in a cave, I phoned Elijah and asked him the same question. "No, baby," he replied. "I ain't afraid o' dyin'. What I fear most is bein' lonely."

I hung up the phone feeling more depressed than ever and so cold, I broke out in goose bumps. My bones ached, my teeth chattered and my nose ran, so I switched off the air conditioner, hustled Pearl and Jessie off to the Dead Bolt Cafe with enough money to buy breakfast, wrapped myself up in an old comforter, and sat on the bed drinking hot chocolate from my favorite Big Bird mug. Who will comfort me when I turned seventy years old, assuming I live that long, I wondered.

Spirit, I reasoned, who's more than ten years older than I am, might be dead, as would everyone else I know—'cept, hopefully, Pearl and Jessie, but who wants to burden loved ones when you're bloated with gas and your bones snap like chalk?

I felt so bad that day, I lied to Spirit. I told him I had errands to run then drove to Muff and Freda's for a tarot card reading. Halfway there, I prayed they'd tell me what I most wanted to hear, that Rhonda would recover, that Momma would never be heard from again, that success waited for me in New York and Spirit and I would, somehow, live happily ever after.

When I told Muff and Freda why I'd come, they shook their heads and insisted the planets were in the wrong orbit, that it wasn't a good time for looking into the future, but would I join them for tea and scones? The sight of those anemic, current-studded cakes turned my stomach, and the smell of sugary hot tea rendered me weak and clammy, so I rushed home to the welcome aroma of black-eyed peas simmering on the stove—to jalapeño corn bread wrapped in a towel, still warm from the oven.

Then, fearing the worst, that Muff and Freda knew something they were too scared to reveal, I grabbed a warm dressing gown, pocketed a large bottle of generic One-A-Day vitamins, drove Miss Ladybug to Oklahoma City as fast as she'd go, ran up three flights of hospital stairs because the elevators were slow, and was grateful beyond belief to find Rhonda alive.

"Frank's still so mad at you," she said, as I wrapped her up in my robe. "He can't think of nothin' else. That stint in jail has made him mean as a snake."

"What caused it before they locked him up?" I asked, which I shouldn't have, 'cause she started bawling.

When I told her I was sorry, she calmed down. "He wants the kids home with him," she said, which made me want to bend nails with my teeth. "Well, he's not having 'em," I told her. "If he comes within hollerin' distance, I'll get a restraining order. He has no legal right, and no judge in the world'll let Pearl and Jessie stay with him if I tell everything I know."

She cried again, claiming the hospital tests made her worse, that the medicines she took four times a day made her vomit, that nurses kept punching her full of holes, and a headache wouldn't let her sleep. Then she told me she was getting palliative treatment, whatever that is, which made me happy. Maybe, I thought, just maybe, they'd discovered something that would fix her—but outside in the corridor, where Rhonda couldn't hear, Dr. Jeffers said she'd had another seizure, the vision in her left eye was failing fast, and surgery was out of the question.

A week has passed since then, and I'm thinking more and more of Mandy, how Doc Hartley scraped her from my womb with such speed and accuracy, her death surely was instantaneous—which makes me wonder why, after all these years, awake or asleep, moving or still, windows open or closed, out on the street or under the covers with a finger stuffed into each ear, I hear her—laughing, walking, running, as if she's old enough to play hide-and-seek.

She remains hidden, yet I feel her everywhere. One evening, at sunset, I ventured down to the Rattler to check the water level, and I swear she sat on the bank beside me, hardly moving, barely breathing, as fireflies danced around us and an owl hooted up in a tree. But when a moon that, night after night, had leapfrogged over empty clouds failed to appear, when fireflies fled and light was drowned by shadows, she darted away, leaving only the shape of her small head in her momma's lap.

I've noticed other odd things. My skin is dry, my eyes feel gritty, whole milk tastes sour, and I have lost my desire for sex and calories. I smell Momma's cheap perfume in the shower, in drawers and closets, in a half-empty can of Folger's coffee—and when I walk across Main Street, that same smell rises like steam from the asphalt. Something else, too. I have yet to come face-to-face with Frank since he got out of jail, but his smell, a combination of soured laundry and beer, lingers in Rhonda's hospital room, in the neck of her shapeless gown, on her skin, in lifeless strands of pale red hair above her ears. I see his shadow at every turn, hear his footsteps fade, and after I've kissed and hugged Rhonda goodbye, I catch his stink in the elevator, and must lean against the wall to steady myself.

Stranger still are the dragonflies: brilliant blue ones and green ones with transparent wings that, no matter where I've been—the Dead Bolt Cafe, Elijah's, visiting Brandy at the beauty shop—follow me home, dipping and diving, to rest on the window ledges, in the shade.

Even stranger are the animals on Main Street. They arrived a week ago, close to three in the morning, when the only other sounds to be heard were chirping crickets, tree frogs, and the incessant click, click, click of the traffic light. Bathed in moonlight, they ambled single file down the middle of the road—the deer first, then the fawn, followed by two cottontail rabbits, a skunk with three legs, a small possum, and a large armadillo. They came with a breeze that scattered leaves from one end of Main Street to the other, and when I opened the window to get a better look, I smelled wild mint and rosemary. The critters stopped a moment or two outside the bakery, and while I rubbed my eyes in disbelief, they trotted right back in the direction they'd come from.

When they returned a second, third, and fourth night, when I knew I'd witnessed something rare, I woke Pearl and Jessie so they could watch the miracle with me. They weren't the least bit surprised. Didn't even get out of bed.

Jessie yawned. "Don't worry, Aunt Darla," he said. "They're Pearl's friends."

I knelt between them on the floor, my eyes piercing the darkness to study hers. "You know them, hon?"

Pearl buried her head in the pillow and mumbled, "Uh-huh. They live in the woods along the railway track."

"So why are they parading through town in the middle of the night?"

"Because they miss me," she replied, as if that explained everything, and went right back to sleep.

That's when Jessie hugged my neck and whispered, "You can sleep with me if you're scared, Darling Darla, okay?" and I did.

I found myself in Lourdes, France, pushing Rhonda down a narrow pathway in a dilapidated wheelchair. As we neared the holy grotto, I expected a miracle to occur, that Rhonda would be cured. Suddenly, the sky turned purple and huge black birds dive-bombed our heads, and when I raised my arms to wave them off, the wheelchair slipped from my grasp. Rhonda screamed and screamed, but I was helpless to stop her from falling down an embankment and off a high cliff into the ocean. The wheelchair, Rhonda strapped in it, disappeared beneath the waves.

I woke in a panic, the dream fresh in my mind, and immediately telephoned Rhonda.

"I'm bone tired," she said, "and last night I dreamed I was lost, that I was suffocating. I heard you calling my name, but I couldn't see you. It was too dark."

Decisions, Decisions

· ·

As I sit drinking coffee with Brandy inside the Dead Bolt Cafe, I can't help but wish Spirit and I were off spending the day together, alone—that we were back at Marshall's Steak House with its white napkins and skinny-necked waiter, eating off the same sweet sliver of cheesecake, and looking forward to a movie. But Frank's on the move, so I'm here with a crazy plan in my head, while Spirit makes more phone calls from the Ponderosa Motel.

"Ain't never seen you like this, Darla," Brandy says. "It's not a pretty sight."

I squint at the menu scrawled on the chalkboard. "I know, but I'm trying."

"Melba's field peas and ham will put a smile on y'face, and she just took a coconut meringue pie out the oven."

I tell her I'm not hungry, but it's more than that. Out front sits a perfect target for one of Leroy Poteet's high-priced parking tickets, a fancy, thirty-foot Starlight motor home with Michigan license plates. The owners, a well-dressed, middle-aged couple in the front booth, are whispering and snickering among themselves. Don't have to be a genius to figure out what's so funny. The rustic charm of Paradise's lone cafe amuses them—particularly the old plank floor and Melba's hair—two long brown braids wrapped around her head like a waffle cone.

When they first came in and the man saw me, his eyes narrowed with sudden interest—a look I've seen before. So had his wife, apparently. She tapped his hand with the menu and glared at me, believing, I'm sure, that I'd encouraged him.

But it's not only them. I realized this morning just how much the added responsibility of Pearl and Jessie will dwindle my savings—how, during the next few weeks and beyond, folders, three-ring binders, loose-leaf paper, lunches, pens, pencils, shoes, and clothes will deplete those savings further—push New York off the map.

The bright, saffron-tinted light pouring through the window, the ceiling fans rocking on their long poles, and the racket behind the counter as Melba sorts through plates and silverware, makes my head pound.

I put my sunglasses back on. "Who'd have guessed something gray and evil was growing behind Rhonda's forehead?"

"Not me, that's for sure," says Brandy. "Her being so thin and nervous made me think of thyroid trouble."

"I'm convinced they'll find a cure for it before long. Out of the blue, a doctor will say, 'Why didn't we think of this before? It always works.'"

"You reckon?"

"They've got to. I've got no photos."

"Huh?"

"I've got no photos of me and Rhonda. Not a goddamned one 'cept a couple of group shots from school that Elijah paid for."

"It's not too late."

"It will be if all I'm left with is heartache and a headstone. If Momma was here, I'd wring her goddamn neck."

"Where's the kids?"

"My place, watching a video. Me and Jessie's gotten real close these past few weeks—but Pearl? I just don't know about her. She seems preoccupied—quiet—pulled back, y'know?"

"Worried about her momma, don't y'reckon?"

"Yeah, I know that's what it is, and I've encouraged her to talk about it, but—"

"She'll come around."

"I'm gonna go see Frank, Brandy."

"What the hell for?"

"To straighten things out. He keeps bugging Rhonda about Pearl and Jessie moving back in with him. I think he's doing it just to be a horse's butt—to get back at me."

"After that business with Mardel, you don't want him around the kids unless Rhonda's there."

"Fact is, he came by my place the other night."

"Oh my, you never said."

"Haven't told anyone till now. He stood out on the steps cussing and yelling like a crazy person. I turned all the lights off and pretended I wasn't home. Hated the kids seeing me like that."

"Like what?"

"Pressed against the door, still as a mouse, concentrating so hard on being quiet I almost passed out. He was so close, Brandy, I swear I heard his heart beating through the door. Scared Pearl and Jessie half to death."

"You were trying to protect 'em, Darla. They know that."

"Doesn't make it right."

"And this preacher guy, this Spirit what's-his-name," says Brandy, staring into her cup, "you never told me about him, either."

"So who told you?"

"Trudy Spencer was blabbing about you and him in the beauty shop, but I smiled real nice and said, 'Let he who is without sin cast the first stone,' et cetera, et cetera."

"You can't beat a basic Sunday school education when you're dealing with a hypocrite."

"He sure is good looking. Saw him in the drugstore, and I don't mind telling you, he's a handsome devil."

"He's a *good* man, and I gave up looking for one of them years ago."

"You and me both."

"Oh, I cut up with all of 'em at the Dance Barn and I've slept with some, but I sure am tired of those 'add two eggs and one stick of margarine' relationships."

"Truer words never spoken."

"And I thought the slow-cooked, homemade variety was a thing of the past, till Spirit came along."

"So the famine's over?"

"Lamb of God fired him, Trudy Spencer evicted him, now he's at the Ponderosa Motel."

"Are you kidding me?"

"Wish I was. Room twenty-four, can you believe it? Just thinking about him and me in the same bed that me and that highway patrolman shared gives me heartburn."

"Your pot *is* full."

"Confused, too. I'm still hell-bent on going to New York, but I'm crazy about Spirit, and I can't bear the thought of leaving Elijah—and Rhonda's *really* sick."

"Take it one day at a time, that's what you always tell me. You're strong, Darla, nothing'll change that, right?"

"Don't bet on it. They're getting Rhonda ready to come home, putting a shunt in her neck, whatever that is, arranging for nurses, changing all her medicines around. So, if I'm to get a foot in her front door, I'd best be on speaking terms with Frank. I've gotta go talk to him—no choice."

"I'll go with you."

"Can't ask you to do that."

"You can't go alone."

"Spirit's got enough to worry about. Don't want him involved."

"Well then, I'm all you've got."

Friends and Loved Ones

. . . .

The trailer looks deserted. The curtains are drawn, weeds have sprouted from every crevice, tinder-brown grass a foot tall, and Rhonda's lawn mower is under the steps, in pieces. And there, parked next to Frank's truck, sits Momma's old Pontiac. "What the heck is that doing here?"

Brandy stops smacking her gum and says, "This is a bad idea, 'specially if your momma's inside."

"She can't be, she's with old Dusty Duke." The instant I step out of Miss Ladybug, I catch a whiff of Frank. "If he lets me in and I'm not back out in five minutes, go phone the marshal. Don't tell him it's me in trouble, though, 'cause he might not come."

Bowzer appears, waits for the obligatory head scratch, drinks from a large basin, and retreats beneath the trailer. The door opens, and out steps Momma, barefoot, wearing one of her long red, yellow, and turquoise Mexican dresses. She's got a three or four day old black eye and a swollen bottom lip.

"You looking for me," she says, one hand on her hip, "or trouble?"

"Find one and you've found the other," I reply, "and aren't you the picture of health? What you doing here? Did ol' Dusty Duke give you amnesia and you forgot where you live?"

Frank, hair disheveled, peers over Momma's shoulder, an open beer can in his hand. "He dumped your poor momma in Colorado. Be thankful she made it back safe."

"Yeah, right, Frank. This sudden sympathy for your mother-in-law's got nothin' to do with what you're drinking, does it?"

"Mind your fucking business, Darla," he growls, "and get off my property."

"Don't be ignorant, Frank. We're in a trailer park, for Christ's sake. I came over to see if I can help you get the place ready for when Rhonda comes home. Frank did tell you Rhonda's bad off, didn't he, Momma—or have you two been discussing more important stuff, like desirable vacation spots on the West Coast?"

"Frank told me," she says. Her speech is slurred. "I'm real sorry to hear it."

They've been boozing it up in that trailer—and God knows what else. "Real sorry? You should be frigging well devastated. Is *real sorry* the best you can do, for Christ's sake?"

She shifts her weight, runs her fingers through her untidy hair, brushes it back from her forehead. "What d'ya want me to say?"

"Hell, I don't know. You dump Granny on Elijah's doorstep like a sack o' laundry, you take off with a bald-headed trucker like you don't have a care in the world, no forwarding address, no phone numbers, not a word about where you're going or for how long, and why that surprised me, I don't know, 'cause you've done it so many times before I should be used to it, right?"

Momma laughs nervously. "Listen to Miss High and Mighty here, and her messing around with a preacher. Like mother like daughter, eh?"

"I'm nothing like you."

"Thank God he ain't Jewish," she retorts, grinning at Frank.

"Meaning?"

"Well, Jews have such a poor sense of direction, don't they? Wandered about that desert for forty years without a clue, and you're as bad. Can't never make up your mind what part of the country you want to be in, so you and a Jew together—"

"You're sick, y'know that? You two make a fine pair."

Bleary-eyed, Frank waves the beer can at me. "Get off my property 'fore I throw you off."

I hear Miss Ladybug's door open, Brandy's footsteps on the gravel behind me, feel her hand on my shoulder.

"Let's go, Darla," she says. "How's about a ride home, Mrs. Moon?"

Momma fires up her Elvis lighter and lights a Camel. "I'll drive m'self when I'm damn good and ready," she says.

Frank shoves Momma aside and leans on the railing. He's wearing a Coors Beer T-shirt, grimy boxer shorts, and black socks. Lord only knows what Rhonda sees in him.

"Don't need your goddamned help cleaning this place up, either," he says, waving his beer in my direction. "I'll hire someone. I got money."

"Then Momma gave it to you—or you stole it."

"None of your business. Besides, Rhonda won't be coming back here. She's going straight to the nursing home—right here in town."

I feel the color drain from my face. "Paradise Acres? The doctor told me she could be nursed at home."

Frank shoves Momma aside and starts down the steps. "I can't watch her and work too."

"Excuse me?"

"I said I can't watch her and work too."

"You haven't worked in six fucking months, you miserable bastard, and you owe me two hundred dollars for repairs on your truck. I'll take you to small claims court if I have to."

"Let's go," Brandy says, but I'm not through with him.

"You're dumb as a hammer, Frank Slater. If breathing wasn't involuntary you'd have suffocated years ago."

"Darla, get your ass outa here," Momma says, "'fore things turn nasty."

"If you're too damn lazy to take care of Rhonda, Frank, you can be sure I will."

"Like hell you will."

I stand my ground. "If a snake could talk it'd sound just like you."

Brandy pulls my arm. "C'mon, Darla," she says, but I'll not move till I'm ready. Out of the corner of my eye I spy Mardel, standing at the door of her trailer with an older woman. Her mother, I imagine. They look just alike.

"You two nosy bitches get back inside where you belong," Frank yells at them, lumbering down the steps. They vanish so fast it's hard to believe they were ever there.

"That girl's sixteen," I tell Momma as she trails behind Frank, the cigarette in her mouth. "If her and her mother weren't so scared o' this bag o' shit, if they hadn't dropped charges, he'd still be in jail on rape charges. Bet he didn't tell you that, did he?"

"I made a fucking mistake, is all," Frank hisses into my face.

"A mistake? A mistake is wearing white after Labor Day, Frank. Raping a sixteen-year-old is a filthy, despicable crime."

"Stay outa my life and bring them two miserable kids back here where they belong, you understand?"

"Won't never happen, Frank. The stuff I got on you would fill a thirty-pound turkey."

"Bring 'em back."

"Hear that, Momma? The rapist wants your grandchildren back under his roof. Hell, I'd slit m'own throat first."

Frank's eyes are tiny, glinting holes. "Given the opportunity, I'd slit it for you."

I suppress a shiver. That's when I hear the train, feel the first tremors under my feet, hear the warning horn. "Do everyone a favor, Frank, go lay on those tracks out yonder."

He grabs me by the throat, squeezes hard, and throws me to the ground. I'm dazed and coughing, and my ears ring as the train roars through the crossing. Frank glares down at me, a clone of all Momma's boyfriends, 'cept there's no way in hell I'm gonna let him get away with this.

I jump to my feet, grab a board, draw back, and with both hands, I summon every ounce of strength I can muster and whop him up the side of the head. Frank reels backward and bounces off the trailer. Momma and Brandy scream in unison as he rolls over, scrambles to his feet, and recovers. He starts toward me again, blood trickling down his face, but Momma grabs him round the middle and pulls him toward the trailer. Brandy shoves me toward the car.

"Get outa here before you kill each other," Momma screams. "Go on, get the hell outa here."

I clamber in and start the ignition. "And you get your no-account ass home where it belongs."

"How's about Big Bucks Bingo tonight?" she yells, like we just exchanged pecan pie recipes.

I peel out, sending plumes of sand and gravel flying in the air, while Mardel, pasty and tired looking, watches us through a gap in the lace curtains.

"Bingo. That's all that woman thinks about." I pull onto the narrow dirt road with Frank's drunken arrogance stuck in my throat like a fish bone. "Useless, no-good slimeball. Won't even care for a sick wife. I gotta talk to them, that's the only thing I can do."

"Talk to who?"

"Mardel and her mother. Maybe we can get those rape charges reinstated."

"I doubt it."

"They've got a phone. I'll give Mardel's mom a call and—"

"Won't do no good."

The line of Brandy's jaw and the way she's blinking her eyes tells me she knows something I don't. "Okay, out with it."

"You won't like it."

"Don't like Ex-Lax either, but it has its uses."

"Pearl didn't want you to worry."

I pull off the road and let Miss Ladybug idle. "What's Pearl got to do with it?"

"I'm not s'posed to say."

"What's Pearl got to do with it, Brandy?"

"Okay, okay. She let it slip that Mardel phoned her last week."

"And?"

"The only reason her momma dropped the rape charges is—"

"What?"

"Mardel's three months pregnant. It's Frank's."

My head explodes. If the world would just stop spinning for a minute, I'd fling myself off.

"It'll be over 'fore anyone knows about it, Darla. Her momma's about convinced her to go to old Doc Hartley out on the highway. Frank told 'em he'd pay to get it done."

Other than Rhonda's sickness, nothing, absolutely nothing, could be worse than this. The idea of that young girl strapped to the table in that shabby room of horrors, reliving my nightmare, tears at my heart.

Neither of us says another word until, halfway between the trailer and her one-bed duplex, Brandy says, "You shouldn't have made me tell you."

The heat rolls over us like lava. Paradise smells like hell in August—dusty and dry, a bed of glowing coals. I try my damnedest to imagine ice cubes, a mountain stream, cold showers, and cool white linen. Instead, I envision giant African crocodiles defending a swampy hole, prehistoric lovers 'neath a giant acacia tree, knifing each other for the last sip of water.

If I didn't believe that beyond the plains, north of Tonkowa and the Arkansas River, west of the great Black Mesa, weather had already been made, that rain will, eventually, fall, that Frank Slater will die one day, before I do—I'd question the point of living.

I can breathe again inside Brandy's air-conditioned duplex. Stripped to our undies, we fall into battered easy chairs, our arms and legs sprawled. Panting and drenched with sweat, we sip on a beer. Brandy holds up her latest triumph. A baby's jacket, knitted in pale lemon wool.

"Cute," I say. "Who's it for?"

"My little kiddo—if I ever have one." She spits out her gum, rips open a large bag of Fritos. "God, I envy you."

"Yeah, right. You and Ivana Trump."

"I'm serious."

"What the hell do you envy me for?"

"For leaving this burned-out, dried-up excuse of a town."

"I haven't left yet—and I'm beginning to wonder if I ever will. Even worse, I haven't seen Spirit in a couple of days. Too busy catching up on my work."

"Call him," she mumbles through a mouthful of chips.

"And tell him what? That Momma's drunk over at Rhonda's? That I clobbered Frank? That he got a sixteen-year-old pregnant and young Pearl knows?"

Brandy shrugs and kicks her loafers across the room. "If that's a multiple-choice question, I'd say none of the above."

"My gut instinct says all the above."

"Why don't you two go somewhere and do something while I watch the kids here?" She throws me the Frito bag.

"I'll think about it." I nibble a Frito, but I'm not hungry. "We're s'posed to visit Rhonda this evening, but I'll phone her—tell her it'll be tomorrow."

"How come?"

I fold down the top of the bag and toss it back. "I've gotta think. Hearing about this baby has thrown me. I can't imagine what's going on in Pearl's little head. And if she tells Rhonda—"

"What'll you do when you leave here?"

"Feed the kids, take 'em to Elijah's, see how Granny's doing—if Momma made it home."

She struggles out of her chair. "I need another beer. And what if y'momma isn't? Home, I mean."

"I'll find me another gun and shoot her ass off."

"Old Leroy Poteet still got that one you bought in the city?"

I pick up the phone and dial Elijah's number. "Yep, and that bothers me. If I go buy another one legal, is someone gonna ask me what happened to the first one? And if they do, do I tell 'em?"

Elijah says, "Guess what? Pearl and Jessie's here."

"How come? I left 'em home."

"Spirit brought 'em. He went by your place and those little devils wormed a ride. They left a note so you wouldn't worry."

"What if I'd phoned? I'd have had a stroke if they hadn't answered."

"Nevuh thought o' that."

"Seems no else did either. Anyway, guess who's back."

"Y'momma?"

"Give that man the door prize. She's at Frank's—boozing."

"Have mercy. What made you go over there?"

"Being friendly, so's I can visit Rhonda when she comes home."

"And?"

"Me and him tangled."

"And?"

"He bled some."

"Oh, my. Don't tell me why or how, just tell me how you think you gonna get in his door now?"

"Won't have to. He's putting Rhonda in the nursing home."

The silence is more than I can bear. "Elijah. You okay?"

He sniffles a bit, and says, "Nevuh mind about me. Listen, Darla, Pearl took me aside a while ago and said she knew an awful secret. Wondered if she should tell you. I got her to confide in me, and you'll nevuh guess—"

"Yes I would. Heard about the baby myself a short time ago. See you soon, all right?"

"What'll you do tonight?" I ask Brandy after I hang up. "Got a date?"

"Hell no," she says, lighting a Salem. "I've started taking better care of m'self. I'd join a nunnery if they'd let me smoke."

I take my last swig of the beer. "You're Baptist, for mercy's sake. Nuns are Catholic."

"So I'll switch."

"Gotta be a virgin too."

Brandy's eyes widen with surprise. "Who checks that out?"

"The head nun."

"The *head nun*?"

"The boss of all the other nuns."

"Oh—when you said *head* nun, I thought you meant the one in charge of the bathroom."

We snicker like idiots.

Brandy extinguishes her cigarette into a Miracle Whip lid. "Think I'll give up smokes *and* sex."

"They've got a patch for that, too?"

She chuckles. "Don't I wish."

"Yeah, cost a bomb, wouldn't it? You'd have to slap one on y'head, heart, and crotch."

Brandy laughs so hard her breasts jiggle. "I met this weirdo at the Dance Barn the other night," she finally says. "Tattoos everywhere, so much hair on its head and face I couldn't tell if it was coming or going. Reminded me of the scientist who crossed a parrot with a lion. Didn't know what it was, but when it talked, I sure as hell listened."

I spit and spew beer all over myself.

"I honestly believe," Brandy says, toying with another Salem, "that men have got just one damned thing on their minds."

"Yeah, but for some crazy reason women think they can tame that

Tasmanian devil 'tween their legs—make it sit up and beg like a French poodle."

Brandy chokes on her beer. "And they're such phonies."

"Yeah, like the golden arches."

"Huh?"

"When me and Rhonda were little tykes, Elijah took us to the new McDonald's in Layton. We'd never seen one 'cept on TV, and up close, those golden arches looked enormous. Me and Rhonda were crazy with excitement, but when we got inside and started eating them scrawny burgers and fries, I decided they were frauds, that the TV ads and the golden arches hadn't delivered what they promised—that McDonald's was no different than all the other hamburger joints."

"So?"

"Well, that's how it is with men. Golden arches on the outside, same old mystery meat inside the bun."

Tipsy from heat and beer, we compare penises to fruits and vegetables, and laugh so hard we wet our pants.

Lying Comes Easy

Rhonda says she'd rather me and Spirit didn't come visit her tonight anyway. Says she's been nauseated, that she looks bad. Says she'd rather sleep than stare across the bed at folks whose eyes pity her—'specially if it's a preacher she hardly knows. I don't mention Momma. Rhonda might expect her to show up.

I strip down, pile my hair on top of my head, and climb into luke-warm water. No bubble bath, no bath salts, just me, an old claw-footed bathtub, a bar of unscented soap, and Pavarotti singing Verdi's "Di Quella Pira."

The aroma of yeast and hot bread rises like steam from the bakery, and all is quiet—'cept for the fluorescent light over the cutting table, buzzing like a swarm of angry hornets, and blue jays squawking in the elms. Frank is stuck in my head. Smelly, unkempt, he's on his porch with Momma, who's pounds heavier than when I last saw her. They stand side by side like two dirty jokes. Behind them, the trailer's dark mouth bulges with nasty questions.

Momma's reaction to Rhonda's problem angers me more than anything else, but indifference is her middle name. I recall a bitterly cold afternoon when I was about seven—how me and Rhonda stood shivering on the front steps of a run-down farmhouse while Momma talked to a beefy, red-faced man with dirt under his fingernails. She told us to wait for her in the car while she went inside to *take care of business,* and we almost froze to death before she came back out smelling of sweat and bay rum, toting two dozen eggs and a slab of bacon. But her and Frank Slater? I still find that hard to believe.

I brush my teeth and tongue with toothpaste and Listerine. God forbid Spirit should smell beer on my breath. In preparation for another hot drive, I slip into leather sandals and a cool lime-green sundress, and walk through a cloud of White Shoulders. Then something, I don't know what, prompts me to unlock the closet door and switch on the light. The Lincoln Center Gown is stunning, so outrageous and elegant, I'd like to fix my hair in an elegant topknot, step inside the luxurious folds, and pretend I'm in New York, on my way to a Pavarotti concert.

I pull into Elijah's driveway and park behind Spirit's Cadillac. Momma's back home. I can see her car from here. Bet she's holed up with a six-pack, her Camels, and a box of Moon Pies.

The kids are outside. Pearl, wearing a white top and the teal-blue scooter skirt I made her last spring, sits under Elijah's mulberry tree, watching Jessie twirl on the tire swing.

Jessie comes running. "Guess what?" he screams. "Gary England said it's raining in the panhandle. Says it'll rain here, too. Thunder and lightning, maybe. See the clouds?"

I look where he's pointing and sure enough, the northwest sky is black and roiling—clouds stacked ten miles high, one on top of the other like dollops of Cool Whip. I grab Jessie under the arms and swing him around. He smells of grass and Elijah's strawberry jam.

"Well, who can argue with Gary England? He's an expert, isn't he? If he tells you something, you know it'll happen—right, Pearl?"

She merely shrugs. "A little rain's nothing to get excited about."

"Is too," says Jessie. "I'll have puddles to jump in—and that's not the onliest thing. There'll be frogs in the creek."

I hug him. "The only thing, Jessie."

"Huh?"

"Onliest isn't a real word," I whisper.

"Everyone I know says onliest."

"Maybe so, but it's not a real word. When you go out into the big wide world, you don't want folks laughing at how you talk, do you?"

"I ain't going out into no big wide world," he says, charging toward the house. "I'm staying in Paradise with my momma forever."

Hearing him say that puts a big old dent in my heart. I sit beside Pearl, arm around her shoulder, and kiss her cheek, smell her skin—a hint of Johnson's baby powder and shampoo—her fingers and toes painted with a coat or two of my hot-pink nail polish. "Have I told you lately that I love you, Pearl?"

"Every night and morning," she says, but there's no fire in her eyes. I see worry instead, and a girl her age shouldn't have so many things to fret about.

I pull her close. "How about us going to a nice restaurant in Palm Grove tonight? You and Jessie can order anything you want."

"No thanks. I'm not hungry."

"Did you eat the sandwiches I left you?"

"No. Jessie ate mine and his."

"A good wind'll blow you over. Wanna tell me what's bothering you?"

"Maybe."

"Whatever it is, I'm a big girl, Pearl. I can handle it."

"It's about Mardel," she begins tentatively. "Something scary happened to her."

"I know, I heard—about the baby, I mean. And you're right. She must be awful scared, bless her heart."

Pearl shudders. "Do you know who the baby's daddy is?"

"Yes, I do."

She wipes at the tears in her eyes. "If Momma finds out, it'll make her sicker, I just know it will."

"Well, we won't tell her, will we?"

"If I hadn't felt so sorry for Mardel and invited her over, maybe it wouldn't have happened."

"Honey, it's not your fault. Frank's to blame. What he did was wicked and inexcusable—and against the law."

She's quiet for a moment too, then says, "Are you and Spirit going to see Momma tonight?"

"No, baby, I called her. She's awful tired, and said she'd rather we waited till tomorrow. You and Jessie can go with us—unless you've got something else planned."

"I got invited to a slumber party, but I'm not going. Be different if Momma was home and she felt good."

"I think she'll feel better when she leaves that hospital."

Pearl's face lights up. "She's coming home?"

I juggle words, try to get them right before I say them. "They'll discharge her soon, I think. I'm just not sure if she'll come straight home."

"Where else would she go?"

"To a convalescent home till she gets her strength back—a nice place. Maybe Paradise Acres."

"That's an old people's home. Nobody gets out of there alive."

"I know lots of folks who've stayed a while and gone home later."

"How many?"

Lying comes easy. "Dozens, at least."

"Aunt Darla, if I ask you a question, will you tell me the cross-your-heart-and-hope-to-die truth?"

"Sure I will," the liar says.

She closes her eyes and stiffens under my arm.

"Is my momma gonna die?"

Searching for an answer, I gaze toward Momma's place. My heart screeches to a halt. Under the goldenrain tree, looking this way, a small, curly-haired child in a pink dress stands hand-in-hand with a tall, transparent apparition. It's Mandy and Shamir. I try like the devil not to blink, and for the longest time I don't—but the instant I do, they vanish.

"Is she, Aunt Darla?" I hear Pearl say. "Is my momma gonna die?"

I shift my gaze to Lamb of God Church, to Momma's house, down the road, beyond the haze shimmering on the crest of the black-top. Not a soul in sight—living or dead.

"Yes, Pearl, she is gonna die, but there's no one on earth who knows when—no more than anyone knows when you or me's gonna die."

"But seeing as she's real sick and we're not," she says, wiping away a tear, "she's more likely to die 'fore us, right?"

I give her a big squeeze. "It's possible, baby, yes."

"You know what I worry about most, Aunt Darla?"

"What, baby?"

"Well, two things really. One is, I'm scared me and Jessie will have to move back with Frank."

"Won't happen. You have my word on that."

"And the second thing is, I'm scared Momma's gonna be the first one in our family to die. I don't want her waking up in a strange place not knowing anyone."

I'm so moved I can barely speak. "Heaven's not a strange place," I whisper. "When we get there it's like going home—like waking up from a bad dream and finding you're in your own bed. Besides, if y'momma gets there 'fore me or you she'll know scads of folks from right here in Paradise—all those people from Elijah's church who passed on, not to mention those folks who used to work in the stores downtown—and Billy Joe, the mechanic—and his mom and dad. Lots of people."

"What about your daddy, Aunt Darla? You reckon he's there?"

I scan the area again. No sign of them. "God only knows. I've no clue where he is."

As I near the front door, a flock of sparrows flies into a thicket of thriving honeysuckle growing against the house. Overhead, soaring like a kite, a red-tailed hawk searches in vain for his dinner. God's creatures amaze me. They're so alert, so vigilant. Us humans, on the other hand, can shake hands with the Devil himself and be blind to the color of his eyes.

Seeing Spirit affects me like the Lincoln Center Gown. Every time I slap eyes on him it's like the first time. The easy smile, the eager swagger as he approaches me, arms wide open, the way he draws me in and wraps me up, the way he sighs—like I'm all that he needs in this crazy world. Everything he does, everything he is, the way he makes me feel, renders me weak and breathless and trembly at the knees.

"You look great," he whispers, unaware that in the kitchen, Elijah watches us. "I've tried to reach you all day."

"Did Elijah tell you Momma's back?"

"He mentioned it. Where have you been? Feels like I haven't seen you in weeks."

"If you weren't here now I may not have seen you today, either."

He draws back, a look of concern and surprise on his face. "We're not going to see Rhonda?"

"She's not up to it, and neither am I."

"Something wrong?"

"Things on my mind, that's all."

"Me too," he says, suddenly buoyant. "Look, I don't know how to tell you this, Darla, but I got a call from New Mexico. Headquarters wants me back now—if not sooner—to discuss what's happened."

"What's happened?"

He turns around, checks on Elijah's whereabouts, and says in a muffled voice, "This business with Lamb of God."

"And me?"

"And you. Told them the truth straight up, right from the beginning, and the good news is, the board wants to discuss my next assignment."

"Thank heaven."

"I'll come back here before I go anywhere else. At the most, I'll be gone eight to ten days."

I miss him already—start counting his eyelashes. My body aches for him, for the way he feels when he's inside me—but I have two kids to think about, and the time for lovemaking has run out.

"I know I shouldn't leave you like this—what with Rhonda so sick."

"I've got Elijah, I'll be fine."

"Wish you could go with me."

"Me too." I raise my lips for a brief kiss and wriggle free.

In the kitchen, I glance back. He looks comfortable, almost fatherly, sitting on the couch between Pearl and Jessie. He listens intently as Jessie rattles on about the weather—but for all I know, he may have a slew of kids in every rinky-dink town between here and New Mexico. Sadness moves in—as if I'm alone in the world and God is shrugging his shoulders.

I kiss Elijah's cheek and sip the iced tea he puts in my hand. "Mmmmm. This beats Miss Cissy's. Perfect, in fact."

He beams, tussles my hair with one large hand, and says, "You're perfect. Like a slice o' key lime pie in that dress."

I snap the suspenders on his denim overalls. "Pretty cute y'self, big boy. Where's Granny?"

His eyes turn flinty. "Y'momma came and got her right 'fore Spirit showed up."

"And?"

He grabs a tea towel, angrily wipes out a Teflon saucepan, and slams it on a hook. "I tried to talk her out of it," he whispers, "but she got loud and antsy, insisted she was sober as a nun, which she wasn't, so against my better judgment I let Sophie go."

"Not a word to Spirit," I whisper back, "about Momma's drinking or this Mardel business, hear?"

"Whatever you say, but I don't trust Roxie when she's on the bottle."

"And I do?"

He grabs a cast-iron skillet from the stove. Dries it. Hangs it up, rattles a few pots and pans like he's nervous. "Nevuh know what trouble she's gonna get into, her smoking and all. I worry about fire, y'see."

"Tell me about it."

"I keep telling m'self it don't do no good to stew over sump'n you got no control over, so I peek out the window now and then, drop by a coupla times a day, and give the rest t'Jesus, along with this unborn baby I jest learned about." He stops a moment to shake his head, then adds, "You know, as much trouble as I've laid at His feet over the years, it's a wonder He ain't had His number changed."

I gaze across the field to Momma's place, at the goldenrain tree. "Long time since I asked Him for anything."

"Is that 'cause you've got everything, Darla Moon?" he asks, heading for his bedroom. "Or 'cause you're too proud?"

I leave by the back door, and seein' as I don't want to walk that scorched stretch of sunbaked blacktop, I traipse through knee-high weeds and meager shade to knock on Momma's front door. The cooler's running, and Granny, coat-hanger crown on head, finally peers through the blinds. I coax her to let me in.

"You okay?" I ask, but she doesn't answer. Her eyes, dark reflections of an even darker pond, stare hard and serious at the palm of her right hand, like it's a map of the world and she's figuring a shortcut to China.

"What're you doing, hon?"

"Just checking," she says, shuffling off to her room. Ball of twine in hand, she's half watching the static on channel 3 as she sorts through her newspapers, preparing for her leg-wrapping ritual. She stares at the ceiling, smiles, and I can only imagine what she sees. Her own guardian angel, for all I know.

The house smells stale. In the fridge, I find a couple of beers, two Moon Pies, and sliced cheese. Momma is sprawled on her bed, fully clothed and snoring, as though she staggered in and stayed where she fell. Suzy Boggus is singing "No Way Out" on the clock-radio, but that's a bucket of shit if ever I heard one. Time and cross-country roads provide all the way outs any man or woman might need. I rinse my hands in the bathroom sink. The overhead light reflects in the water as it drains away, and creates a striped illusion. Granny's right. There are zebras in the sink. I phone Elijah.

"Momma's out for the count. I'm bringing Granny back."

"I'll pick you up."

"Thanks."

"What'll I tell Spirit?"

"Not a damn thing."

And the Rains Came

· ·

Since Spirit left, more than a week ago, we've been bombarded by thunderstorms. TV reception is poor, and the air is wet and full of whispers—so thick and heavy it plugs the ears and clings to the back of the throat. The whispers, some say, are the result of inflamed eardrums, while others claim the dead are uttering up evil curses from various and soggy cemeteries around town. Muff and Freda insist they have a cure. A twenty-dollar tarot-card reading, plus ten dollars worth of mixed-herb tea, will, they say, guarantee a flu-free winter and silence the voices—an offer many desperate souls can't refuse.

Headaches run rampant—not the knotty type behind an eye or above an ear, but the screaming, agonizing, viselike variety that renders the body useless. Their source has been hotly debated. One rumor has the bakery falling on hard times, so Mr. Coombs must use a cheap yeast and inferior flour. Ghostly apparitions seen on television screens late at night have also been blamed, while others point their fingers at high-voltage power lines. Random electricity, they claim, triggers brain tumors, makes hair and teeth fall out, and causes wombs to drop. The headaches, men say, render their wives lazy. They say they come home after a hard day's work and find them exactly where they left them that morning, in bed, their hair still in rollers, surrounded by candy wrappers and *True Love Story* magazines, not to mention the occasional empty bottle of wine. The women blame the headaches on their husbands—saying they don't put out the garbage and won't watch the kids, that entire paychecks vanish between work and home, that strange females call their men at home and hang up without identifying themselves.

Kids are rebellious. Some girls have dyed their hair carroty red, some brilliant green, lathered it so heavy with gel it sticks straight up, in spikes. And when they parade down Main Street in short shorts with their midriffs showing, boys trip over their own feet and howl like wolves.

The heat, the drizzle, and the waterlogged streets are, according to some, also responsible for a sickness that turns flesh so hot it glows. A powerful sense of desperation seems to hang in the air. Folks are questioning their religion, their children's loyalty, and their purpose in life. They're moving to Tulsa, to Little Rock, Arkansas, and beyond. And who can blame them? In a big city, surrounded by food at Hometown Buffet, or dipping into a sundae inside Braum's Ice Cream Store, or in a mall while you try on red spike-heeled shoes that cost a week's wages, or in a fancy brown paper bag, its bottom thick with expensive cookie crumbs and loose sugar, a woman can forget her troubles. In Paradise, reality stares back at her from every dirty flat surface like a bad dream.

For the most part, Momma has avoided me since we met at Frank's. In spite of the constant drizzle, or because of it, no one knows which, she walked across the street to Lamb of God last Sunday night and got herself saved.

She told Elijah, "I'd have done it that morning if I hadn't got up with a hangover," and Elijah is furious.

"Me and Sophie was watching Billy Graham on channel fourteen," he says, "but I know exactly when the *insult* to God's face occurred, 'cause we could hear the congregation whooping and hollerin' all the way down here."

"Well, well, well," I say. "Sure is hard to believe."

"Nothin'll come of it," he predicts. "Might as well put a hundred-dollar hat on a ten-cent head."

Yesterday evening, right after I dropped in on Momma and found her cleaning house, a miracle in itself, women showed up looking like vampires. Dressed in black, their skin powder-white, their hair stiff with spray, their eyes hollow and expectant, Mrs. Salmon and Mrs. Curtis arrived first.

Deacons' wives and a sprinkling of dewy-eyed converts in flowery go-to-meeting dresses followed. They descended on Momma's living room like a flock of starlings and packed themselves into every chair and corner, for a prayer meeting, no less. Curious, I retreated to the kitchen and watched.

Above the Bibles, the bookmarks, and the hairdos of steel hung the thicker-than-sludge smell of Lysol, Old English furniture polish, and sweaty underarms. Cheeks red with passion, hands raised and flutter-ing, eyes glittering with some only-to-be-imagined madness, they rat-tled off prayers and Bible verses like mantras.

"My sweet Lord . . . ," "Dear Jesus . . . ," "Beloved Saviour . . . ," "He promised . . . ," "He gave me . . . ," "He blessed me with . . . ," they cried, as if Jesus Christ himself, bearing gifts, made regular visits to their breakfast tables, as if He marched in and out of their front doors with impunity. When at last they were quiet, when someone voiced concern for a missionary couple in the rain forests of South America, Momma raised her voice and said, "Well, I don't care what the preacher says about pollutin' the jungle, if it's the last thing I do on this earth, I'm gonna mail them precious folk a dozen cans of Raid insect spray for Christmas." I rushed outside, sick to my stomach.

Poor Rhonda. She seizes at least once a day, then flounders around her empty world like a nightmare—knowing us one minute, and claim-ing she's never laid eyes on us the next—and me never knowing which of the two I prefer. But they've started her on two experimental drugs and, we're told, drastic improvement is possible. Improvement? What the hell's improvement?

Pearl and Jessie, brave beyond their years, seem oblivious to the change in their momma's appearance, to the tangle of tubes and catheters under the covers and at the side of the bed. They spend visiting hours fixing her hair, kissing her cheeks, and telling her stories. As for me, I wish I could have the nervous breakdown I so richly deserve.

School Days

· ·

August is winding down, yet the soil is soaked, roses and wild flowers have rebloomed in every yard, and Spirit is exiled in Elba—banished by headquarters to Roswell, New Mexico.

"Not banished," he said, a tad reproachful. "I'm conducting a revival, and it's only for a couple of weeks, right?"

I imagined for a couple of seconds I was his wife—saw myself teaching Sunday school—wondered if, while reading this verse or another, I'd still crave a beer. "Right," I replied. "What's a couple of weeks? I've had headaches longer than that," and we laughed, but I hurt like hell inside.

And last week, as me and Pearl stood outside staring at a thumbnail of a moon, a trickle of bright red blood turned her into a woman. After she showered, we left Jessie at the kitchen table drawing pictures of storms and lightning and aliens while we sat on my fluffy blue bathmat to discuss life, love, and babies—all the things Rhonda planned on telling her.

"Babies are precious," I told her. "They are the most perfect, sweet-smelling creatures on earth. They are to be cherished, fed, and powdered, and the only time a woman should consider conceiving one is when she's mature enough to love and raise it." Then the hypocrite said, "Hurting or destroying such a gift is unthinkable, a sin."

★   ★   ★

Today, the first day of school, Pearl comes home early.

"You have an appointment with a school counselor tomorrow," she says, and hands me a crisp slip of paper. "But it's not 'cause of anything *I've* done, honest."

"So why—?"

"Haven't a clue."

"And how come you're home this time of day?"

She heads for my bed, pulls the patchwork quilt across her legs, and curls up. "Stomachache."

I sit beside her and peer into her eyes. "You sure that's all it is, a stomachache?"

Taking my face in her hands, she kisses the tip of my nose.

"Positive," she replies. "Don't worry, okay?"

Within minutes, she's asleep, and I'm left staring at Spirit's first gift to me, a burgundy leather Bible with gold letters on the front. It sits on the table alongside his second gift, an African violet. The leaves have curled and turned brown. It clearly needs water, food, light or shadow—I'm not sure which.

The smell of chalk, burgers, and sweaty gym shoes revives no fond memories for this old student. Fact is, as I stride past a wall of gray metal lockers toward the counselor's office, I recall being manhandled after school in the mail room at the end of the hall by my English teacher. I was Pearl's age and well developed, and Mr. Pratt, a short man with blond hair, lured me in with the promise of free movie tickets if I would help him unpack books intended for the library. Once he had me inside, he threw me to the floor and straddled me. The wide crack of light under the door was enough for me to see Mr. Pratt's figure, his unzipped pants, his erect penis. With one hand clamped over my mouth, he used the other to pry my legs apart, but he'd overlooked one important thing—the giant-sized chip on my shoulder.

I bucked and kicked till he wore himself out, till his manhood resembled a cocktail sausage. "Don't come near me again," I said, rushing into the hall. "And if I hear you've done it to anyone else, I'll rip off y'balls and tell y'wife." He resigned a week later.

I find Cindy Harker in the counselor's office. She's wearing a Darling Darla Creation—navy blue shantung, sleeveless. Her blond hair is immaculately set, her ankles perfectly crossed, her gray eyes unflinching.

"Take a seat," she says. "Get comfy."

I sit, but I'm not comfortable. "What are you doing here?"

She smiles. "Meeting with you."

"You're the school counselor?"

"School District Twelve psychologist."

"How'd that happen?"

"Got myself a college education. Got my degree two years ago. It was in the paper."

"Don't read the paper much."

"Well, you're a busy woman."

The woman looks just like her miserable daddy around the nose and eyes. "That dress o' yours, Cindy."

"Excuse me?"

"I made it."

"I know. It's one of my favorites."

"Well, it's not right."

"For what?"

"For this job. It's stylish, but to my way of thinking it'll distract kids. Draws attention to your underarms and your collarbones. Sleeves and a collar would be more professional. And those sandals are wrong. You need pumps—plain navy pumps. So why am I here, Cindy?"

She clears her throat. "Well, it's regarding a high school student, a young lady by the name of Mardel Rogers—and the man who got her pregnant."

I feel queasy, light-headed. "I'm his sister-in-law, not his keeper."

"I understand, but there's something you ought to know. Mardel's mother wants to withdraw her from school and send her to Texas to live with an aunt—till the baby's born and adopted."

"Adopted?"

"Mardel, however, says she's not going anywhere. She plans to stay in school, work part-time, and raise her child with the father's help."

"With the father's help?" My mind races. "And I'm here because—?"

"I know your sister's ill and—"

"She's done better since they moved her to the nursing home—and she must never know about this."

"At first, I was concerned that Mardel's presence in school might have a serious effect on Pearl and her brother."

"Any suggestions?"

She leans forward, props her chin on her hands. "At this point, with your permission, I'd like to say a few things."

"Now what?"

"I admire you tremendously," she says out of the blue. "If it hadn't been for you, I wouldn't be sitting here."

"Excuse me?"

"I've always envied you, 'specially when we were kids."

"For what?"

"You were independent."

"I ran wild."

"Your mother was pretty."

"She was a whore."

"You ate candy bars for lunch."

"No money for the cafeteria."

"You weren't shy around boys."

"Didn't trust a one of 'em."

"You wore crazy outfits. Crazy colors."

"Goodwill's best."

"And no one pushed you around, not even teachers."

"Act submissive, they take advantage."

"Like Mr. Pratt?"

"What about him?"

"He victimized a lot of girls, but we were too scared to say anything. You weren't."

While I'm figuring that one out, she says, "Don't ask me how I know, I just do—and then I learned about my father and your mother. My mother told me. Things never were the same between us after that."

"I wondered if you knew."

"But you made your own success, and you seemed happy, so I thought, hell, if Darla Moon can do it, so can I, and I spent every penny of my dead daddy's money proving it. Which brings me to Pearl and Jessie. I'm not the least bit worried how they'll handle the situation. With you on their side, they'll do fine. Thought you should know what's going on, though, just in case."

It's as if someone has unplugged a hole in my chest. All the resentment I've ever felt for this woman seeps from the wound like vinegar. To my surprise, Cindy comes round the desk and hugs me, gives me a business card.

"Give this man a call. Gerald D'Angelo is a college friend. He started his own business in New York a year ago, and he's hunting a designer—someone with *zip* and *fizz* is how he put it, so I told him about you."

I don't know what to say.

"One other thing, Darla," she says, smiling. "More than anything, I envied your beautiful black hair."

I smile back. "And I'd have killed for your black patent leather shoes."

The Rattler's Revenge

· ·

The phone rings at three in the morning and fear runs through me like a hot knife. Rain, gallons of it, pours down—tumbles from the gutters like Niagara Falls. The sky grunts and groans, heavy and labored. Lightning flashes. One glorious, cracking strike after the other.

"Your momma says Sophie's not in her bed," Elijah hollers in my ear. "Don't have no idea where she is or how long she's been gone. Gotta go look for her, y'hear?"

"Where? Where?" I scream. "Where'll you be?"

"Y'momma's gonna drive up and down the road and I'll search along—"

"Oh God, Elijah. The Rattler."

"That's where I'm going."

"I'm coming," I yell, but he's gone.

I find my flashlight, wake the kids, throw on clothes, and slip into tennies. Minutes later, we're out the door and moving west through sheets of rain, the sky a black, yawning mouth over our heads.

Jaws so tense my teeth ache. Hands clenched so tight around the steering wheel they tingle, and we're all sobbing. I turn the windshield wipers as high as they'll go, but the road is barely visible. Every lightning flash, every roll of thunder summons an image of Granny, cold and drenched to the bone, out in the dark, terrified, not knowing where she is or how she got there.

We find Elijah's front door wide open and him gone. "Stay inside and lock the doors," I tell the kids, "and don't open them to anyone 'cept family."

Which way to go? Seth Dalton's old spread or the Rattler? I opt for the creek. Battered by wind and rain, I tear across the road, race down the incline, and start yelling for Granny. She's more familiar with the area behind Lamb of God, so I head in that direction.

"If there ever was a time to show yourself and surprise me, Shamir," I plead under my breath, "for God's sake, for Jesus Christ's sake, let it be now and lead me to Granny," but as my lamp pokes holes in the darkness, as I scramble through scrub and brush, time unreels in slow motion and shoves me toward the unknown.

Never known it to rain this heavy, and the wind must be blowing at forty miles an hour. I hear the Rattler before I see it. It has flooded its banks. Roaring like a jet engine, it thunders unchecked through the narrow waterway. I step ankle-deep in water and jump back, direct the lantern at the creek. It's roiling, exploding with tree limbs. Careful to stay above the waterline, I head in Lamb of God's direction, screaming Granny's name—but she will never hear me. I can't even hear myself.

Each lighting flash illuminates the sky and transforms the woods into an electrified white-and-blue landscape. The ground trembles beneath my feet. Twigs and flying debris sting my face. Suddenly, I see Elijah. He's bent over, flashlight in hand, looking at something. He picks it up and examines it. Sodden to the skin, arms limp at his side, he just stands there, staring back at me. I wade through muck and mire until I reach him.

"She's gone," he cries, shoving Granny's frog leash into my hand. "She's gone."

We're in the morgue at eight in the morning, shivering and unprepared. Deep gashes crisscross Granny's face and neck. I ask the attendant if I can see her legs. He pulls back the sheet. Her legs are scratched and gouged—she's barefoot.

"Newspaper and string still attached," I hear myself say. "Some, anyway."

Elijah reaches out to stroke her cheek, and with tears running down his face, says, "Without it she might have had a chance. The deputy who found her said the string got hung on a submerged log and held her fast."

Her hand is frigid. Same as the rest of her, I reckon. But she looks peaceful, despite the struggle she must have put up. "Why would you let Granny drown?" I ask God. "More than anyone she deserved to die in a warm bed, surrounded by people who love her. You shouldn't have snatched her up when she was alone."

Head down, shoulders slumped, grievously wounded, Elijah turns away and shuffles toward the swinging doors. "Her eternity dress is in m'closet, along with her slip and shoes," he says, his voice breaking, "and her restin' place is over at Fountain Baptist, next to mine."

Power in the Blood

. . . .

Sister Lottie Jordan, a blue-black woman of great size and substance, her stockings neatly rolled above her ample calves, starts playing "Rock of Ages" on the piano. At the heart of each note, throughout the hymn, lies a string of memories going back nigh on thirty years.

Eyes closed, hands clasped at their waists, the purple-robed twelve-woman choir sways and hums in unison—but the moment is fractured by someone a row or so behind us.

"She was an odd little thing," the woman says, and I immediately recognize Mrs. Salmon's voice, a Lamb of God sister.

Elijah's right hand grips my left one, Pearl and Jessie fix their eyes on the casket, and Momma—well, I don't give a damn one way or the other what she's doing.

"Way back," Mrs. Salmon continues, "I found her up a tree right off Main Street. Claimed she was picking oranges—and her in a pine tree with six inches of snow on the ground."

I recall the incident. I coaxed Granny down from that tree with a Hershey bar and a sack of invisible frogs. A week later, she got double pneumonia and almost died.

"And why on earth would they bury her at a colored church?"

Damn them. Damn the ones who laughed at her, who turned their hoses on her when she wandered into their yard, who called her a no-account, drunken squaw. Damn the ones who damaged her brain and stole her memory. Damn all of them for their imperfect eyesight.

I leave the pew and head for the heathens on the aisle, their faces stark white sails against a black sea. I smile, crook my finger at Mrs. Salmon, and whisper, "Would you follow me, please?" and to the sound of "Just a Closer Walk with Thee," Mrs. Salmon, and her female companion, oblige—follow me outside.

"If you come back in, Mrs. Salmon," I tell her, "I'll stuff that wicked tongue of yours down y'throat."

Pale and stunned, they freeze like pillars of salt.

Amid the smell of perfume, hair pomade, and fresh carnations, the congregation stands on its feet, waving and clapping in perfect time, as Sister Jordan starts playing "There Is Power, Power, Power in the Blood," and I stride down the aisle, singing louder than anyone. With the service over, everyone, about fifty of us, mostly black folk, file past Granny to pay their respects—and do they get a surprise.

Granny's humped back prevented her from sleeping on her back, so Mr. Bolton put her on her side. She's wearing a long-sleeved, baby-blue chiffon gown that covers her feet, and on her head sits the hat Elijah bought her years ago on a trip to Palm Grove—a white satin pill-box complete with spotted net veil. At first glance, one would think she was taking a nap, the way a child might—her favorite candy, a Tootsie Roll Pop, clasped in one hand, her frog leash in the other.

With the coffin closed, the pallbearers carry Granny to what Preacher Thompson claims is Fountain Baptist Cemetery's finest double plot. Purchased by Elijah some fifteen years ago, it sits atop a rise 'neath one of the few scarlet oaks to survive the drought. Chickadees chatter up in the branches, and Granny will face east, away from Paradise—a perfect site to spend eternity.

Elijah looks remarkably handsome in a double-breasted black suit and shiny leather shoes—but he moves with effort, his face a mask.

Pearl, pure perfection in the ankle-length dress I made for her last Easter, her long hair pinned back with red, heart-shaped clips, carries Granny's old white Bible—the one she brought from Arkansas. Granny lost the ability to read under the knife, but she enjoyed the colored pictures as Elijah read to her.

At first, Jessie didn't want to go to the funeral, and no one pressed him to do otherwise, but at the last minute he chose a white, short-sleeved shirt and freshly pressed denims. He now stands at my side, the perfect little gentleman.

Momma, her dull red hair in a crude French twist, her makeup smeared from crying, has squeezed herself into a long-discarded black skirt and blouse that smell faintly of mothballs. Muff resembles a ripe strawberry in her new pink dress, and Freda, looking more man than woman, is all decked out in a brown polyester suit—complete with vest and tie.

I'm wearing a yellow dress that Granny admired on more than one occasion by saying, "Stole a few yards of sunshine to make that, I reckon."

Frank didn't come, thank God, and Rhonda has a fever. When I told her Granny had died, she curled into a ball, her face the color of stone, her eyes transformed into round black windows—like something evil had sucked her soul through her pupils.

Spirit cried out loud when I phoned him the news. "I can't believe it, I can't believe it," he kept saying, and his sorrow struck a chord so deep I couldn't bring myself to say anything except, "I'll call you after the funeral."

The cemetery is soggy, the sky an immeasurable swatch of gray flannel that stretches from one horizon to the other, threatens to unleash yet another gullywasher. Elijah sobs so hard I expect his heart to snap in two. Drained and shaky, me and the kids join in—our grief so profound, so palpable, the red oak sheds its leaves and the chickadees head south.

Preacher Thompson says, "Earth to earth, dust to dust, and ashes to ashes," and Granny makes a whirring descent into a muddy canyon. Part of me goes with her. My history, my skin, teeth, eyes, hair, my DNA, all that I am, all that I came from goes down with her, joins her inside the velvet-lined box.

When she touches bottom, we toss the wild yellow tansies and the white oxeye daisies Pearl gathered onto the casket. My ears ring, and there, white and still, in the churchyard 'neath a bower of faded roses, I spy Shamir. The second he's gone, I find myself wondering with a trace of amusement if, up in heaven, Granny is still counting her frogs—if the Planet of Headbreakers has caught on that she hasn't checked in for four nights—if they'll overlook this oversight or charge her a late fee.

It is then, without knocking, that a dull-eyed melancholy tiptoes into m'soul. Like an old dog settling in for a cold spell, it huffs and puffs and rummages around, stirring up the covers. Elijah slips his arm in mine, leans against me, and whispers in my ear.

"Soon as I'm able, baby girl," he says, "there's a mess o' things I gotta tell you."

The Wrong Road

In a room where the air is stale, where curtains are limp and shabby, I reassure Rhonda that the service and burial went well—that Granny couldn't have had a better send-off had she been Queen of the Nile. "A fine funeral, in every sense of the word." Satisfied with my report, she takes a brush to her hair, and clips it back off her ears.

Momma just took Pearl and Jessie home with her, but only after I promised to pick them up in an hour so she can go to Big Bucks Bingo with Muff and Freda.

Elijah remains dazed and unsettled. Just minutes ago, I saw him wandering up and down the hallway, hands in his pockets, his eyes bloodshot and downcast—and without a word, he left.

Rhonda's pink cheeks come as a surprise. The nurse informed me she'd eaten a poached egg for breakfast and potato soup for lunch, so maybe the new drugs *are* working. Face shiny as a china plate, she's studying the pyracantha bushes outside the window. They've withered, but not from drought. Lace bugs, small insects with colorless wings, have bled them dry, left behind a sticky yellow foliage and stunted berries. Rhonda shudders. "I should've been there today," she says, wiping her eyes. "For Pearl and Jessie's sake."

"When you're stronger, we'll all go to the cemetery together.

Granny's in a lovely place under an oak tree, and me and Elijah's got a fine headstone picked out." I tell her this knowing cool weather will soon move in, that caladiums will turn listless, elephant ears will wilt, and one night, while we're all asleep, the earth around Granny will freeze.

"You sure the kids are okay?"

"They're fine, honest."

Rhonda toys with her blanket, finds a loose thread in her sheet. "Jessie seems different. There's a brightness in his eyes. Know what I mean?"

"I think I do."

"Saw that in your eyes when you were his age, Darla." She wraps the thread around two fingers and pulls it. Cuts herself, barely bleeds. "Pearl worries me, though. She seems tight, locked up, like she's holding on for dear life."

Her eyes search my face like a searchlight. God forbid she's heard about Mardel. "They've both got a lot to deal with, Rhonda, but they'll be okay. They're stronger than we think."

She relaxes against the pillow. "Poor Granny," she says. "What a life she had. So many things she never saw—never did—never had. Is there one thing you want more than anything else?"

"No *one* thing, no. Leaving Paradise has always been high on my list, though. How about you?"

"I've often wished I could be buried at sea."

My heart turns cold. "At sea? For Christ's sake, Rhonda, this is Oklahoma, not Florida."

"I know, but I've always wanted to see an ocean, to swim in one."

"You never told me that."

"I know, but I've dreamed about it for as long as I can remember—even imagined myself deep sea diving, or laying flat on my back, drifting in and out with the tide."

I take her hand in mine. God, she's cold. I blink back a tear. "We'll go to Galveston when you get well. We'll take the kids, okay?"

"That'd be nice. Frank once promised he'd take me to Galveston, but he never did. Which reminds me—I haven't seen him in a couple of days. I know he came by the other night while I was asleep, though, 'cause he left a Milky Way on the bedside table."

Give Frank a gold star. "He's probably working hard."

"Said he can't find work, bad time of year." She massages her forehead. "Y'know what? If I could mentally let go of this thing in my head, I think it would vanish altogether."

"Worth a try."

She's turning weepy and she's mighty pale. "This is an awful place, Darla. Folks are dying all around me."

"I know, baby."

"I wake up some nights in a cold sweat thinking I've got to get back to the trailer 'cause Frank and the kids are waiting supper on me—I just don't have the strength to get out of the bed."

What a thought. If she ever gets back to the trailer park, she'll hear about Frank and Mardel, and all hell will break out.

I grab my purse and gather up her dirty nightgowns, stuff them in a Wal-Mart bag. "You need some rest and I've gotta go get the kids 'fore Momma gets antsy. Can you believe her? Buries Granny this morning, and plays bingo in the afternoon."

"Yeah, I believe it," Rhonda says. "I really miss Big Bucks Bingo."

Outside in the fresh clean air, I take deep breaths to clear the smell of disinfectant and soiled sheets from my head, and drive down Main Street thinking of Spirit, hundreds of miles away in the boonies of New Mexico. How long, I wonder, before I hold him again? And why didn't he just up and leave whatever he was doing when Granny died? Wouldn't I have done that for him? Wouldn't I? And what if he never comes back? What if he's already fallen in love with someone new, a fair-haired creature with a pure heart and a religious spirit, a demure woman untouched by time and experience? But wasn't it Spirit who said, "Why eat toast when you crave cheesecake?" Yes, it sure as hell was. So why would he be messing around with someone else? And wouldn't I have caught on by now? Wouldn't deception taint his voice?

I turn on the tape player. Pavarotti sings "Celeste Aïda" by Verdi. I reach behind the sun visor—check on the business card Cindy Harker gave me. It's still there. Gerald D'Angelo, New York. Got a nice ring to it.

I look for signs that the world has changed, but it hasn't. Al Finch, the barber, is giving some guy a four-dollar haircut for which he'll receive a fifty-cent tip. Rob's Grocery is advertising GRADE A SIRLOIN, $2.59 A POUND, TWO DAYS ONLY. The ad in Brandy's Beauty Shop window offers four dollars off any perm, good till Labor Day, and at the intersection of Main and Oak, Marjorie Turnbull, her hair in rollers, is on her porch shaking a rug. Seventy-eight years old and she still does her housework in an Esther Williams swimsuit. Today it's the white one with red cabbage roses.

An army of black clouds stomp across the sun and blot it out. A single raindrop hits the windshield, trickles down like a giant tear. And for reasons known only to God, or the Devil himself, I find myself on Maple Street, parked outside Billy Joe Comfort's white frame house.

What Are Old Friends For?

. . . .

There's a storm brewing. Black as pitch to the west.

The minute I get on the porch and ring the bell I think of Momma and that old farmer. I'm about to turn around and hustle back where I came from when Billy Joe answers the door munching on a lettuce-and-bologna sandwich.

"Hell, never thought I'd see you on my step again," he says, crushing me in a one-arm hug. "Come on in 'fore I have a heart attack and die, girl."

I follow his tight butt through the small living room, down the hall into the kitchen—and wonder what the hell I think I'm doing. What's come over me? He's got the same old swinging walk, but he looks taller than when I last saw him at the garage.

Smelling of gasoline, oil, and Brut, his trademark cologne, Billy Joe gestures toward the pine table. "Sit y'self down. I just ran home for a bite. Want some?"

"No thanks, not staying long." I look around, take in the pale lemon paint, the dropped ceiling, the recessed lighting, the designer wallpaper and trim.

"Coffee?"

"Half a cup." The change astounds me. When his parents were

alive the paint was brown, and the smell of boiled cabbage clung to everything, even Billy Joe. And since Mr. Comfort's frail lungs needed humidity twenty-four hours a day, an assortment of simmering pots and kettles steamed up the windows.

"Made a few changes since Mom died."

"I can tell, Billy Joe. You've done a great job—but then, you were born with your sleeves rolled up." His smile reveals strong white teeth. He's still the best-looking guy to graduate from Paradise High. That I know of, anyway.

"New floor. Corfam counters. Garbage disposal," he says, and points at each item. "Built-in microwave. New appliances. Wall-to-wall carpet. Redid the whole house m'self. Everything top o' the line."

"You always were good with your hands."

His grin gives him away. He's remembering the time we ran off for the weekend. Fired up by the Dance Barn's dim lights, by each other's hot young bodies, and Ray Price singing "Lay Your Head Upon My Shoulder," we jumped into his souped-up Delta 88 and didn't stop till we reached the Rail Fence Motel in Tulsa.

"I've improved with time, Darla," Billy Joe says. "Thing is, you won't ever give me the time of day."

"Proving I don't have a lick o' sense, right?"

He leans back, takes a big swig of coffee, and looks me in the eye. "So, what brings you here, sweet stuff?"

"Buried Granny this morning."

"I know. I was there."

"You were?"

"Saw you hustle that woman outside. Couldn't have done better m'self."

"Wish I'd seen you."

"I was in the back row. Couldn't go to the grave. Had a customer coming in."

"Thanks anyway, Billy Joe."

"Granny was a sweetheart. She liked me when nobody else did." He laughs to himself. "Didn't know a damn thing about me, either, which might have had something to do with it."

"I doubt it. Granny didn't know what was going on in the world, but she always was a good judge of character."

"What else is on y'mind?"

"Rhonda's real bad off."

"I know."

"Doctor said she was dying."

"Is she?"

"I thought so. Not so sure now."

"How's her kids?"

"Fair. They'll do better once their momma perks up."

Billy Joe shoves his sandwich aside. "I dropped by to see her the other night, but she was asleep. Left her a Milky Way bar. I know she's partial to 'em."

Cancel Frank's gold star. "Your momma sure knew what she was doing when she married a Comfort."

"I'd be be a happier man if she'd married a Pavarotti."

Eyes wide, he waits for me to swallow the bait. I don't.

"So where's this preacher boyfriend I've been hearing so much about?"

"New Mexico."

"New Mexico?" He lets out a low whistle. "Long ways off at a time like this, I'd say."

Lightning flashes and thunder rolls. Rain spots big as quarters hit the window. Funeral weather. My eyes are so full of tears I can't see my hands. "Hell, for all I know, he might never come back."

"Aw, don't cry, girl. Nothing's ever as bad as it seems."

"I feel like crap, Billy Joe. Worse than crap."

"I can tell."

"Like life's too heavy, like I'm about to snap in two."

He scoots his chair next to mine, lifts my chin and brushes my hair off my forehead. His eyelashes are thick and brown. His sideburns and eyebrows are streaked with gray. "I'm here for you, Darla," he says. "Always was, always will be, and like you said, I'm good with my hands."

You'd think I weighed nothing at all the way he scoops me up in his arms and carries me back down the hall—and as if on cue, Patty Loveless starts singing "Just Been Lonely Too Long."

He puts me on the bed, undresses me the way he might a child, his voice soft and reassuring. How strange. Being held 'neath the covers like this, being kissed by someone who hasn't kissed me in ten years or more, feels like the most natural thing in the world—like me and Billy Joe had a two o'clock appointment.

Buried Secrets

. . . .

A glowing, Cheyenne dawn rises from the purple-and-gray haze as I reach Elijah's—a blaze of breathtaking color. I find Elijah at the kitchen window, facing east, holding Granny's floral apron.

I kiss his cheek, and we watch another morning lick its lips and swallow up the night. What was he thinking when I came in, I wonder? Erasing his last image of Granny, battered and broken, her hair still wet? Or remembering Granny as she is right now, curled on her side, bathed in impenetrable darkness, a Tootsie Roll Pop in her hands? Maybe he was wrestling with his own mortality, pondering on when and how his life might end. I am certain of one thing. Elijah would not call me here at this hour of day for no good reason.

Without so much as a "Hello, how are you?" he switches on his coffeepot and hangs the apron on its hook. "In all my seventy-odd years," he says, "I ain't never seen one sunrise that looked exactly like another, and they all been glorious."

"You ailing?" I ask. "Is that why you phoned?"

His eyes resemble wet ashes, his shoulders are hunched under an old, threadbare work shirt, but, as always, he smells clean as rain. "Same way with women," he adds. "They's all different, they's all beautiful, but Sophie was special. I loved her the first time I set eyes on her and I never stopped—you know that?"

"Yes, I know that," I say, as I collapse into a chair limp and exhausted. Irregular meals, a guilty conscience, and coming to grips with the fact that I'll never see Granny again have taken a toll. "You loved her a lot."

"No, *loved* her, Darla, *loved* her," he says, like I didn't know how to pronounce the word. "I could lose everythin', including m'life, and consider m'self a rich man for having known and loved y'granny."

"Then she was the luckiest woman on earth."

He clears his throat and fiddles with the apron, takes it off the hook again. "Anyways, at two o'clock this morning I got to thinking of things you oughta know in case sump'n happens to me—some things y'momma don't know—and some things she knows but chooses not to tell. C'mon in here."

Prickling with apprehension and curiosity, I follow him into the living room and join him on the couch. He turns on a lamp and withdraws a handful of photos from a dog-eared brown envelope on the coffee table. He cradles them in his hands, gazes with awe and reverence, like a young boy holding his grandpa's pocket watch for the first time, and hands me one.

"That was taken 'fore you came along. It's y'momma and daddy. Hank Stone was a driller, worked in the oil fields when he worked at all. Roxie said they was married, but I never saw no certificate."

I gaze at a stranger's face, at the dark hair down to his shoulders. Broad and handsome, one arm around Momma's waist, he towers over her. Momma leans against him, her head on his chest, smiling. If she saw this picture today, my guess is she'd remember what they did that night, what he said, and how he said it—while the only recollection I have of Hank Stone is laced-up work boots, like the ones he's wearing in the picture.

Elijah takes the photo from me, hands me another. "That there's y'granny and her husband right after they married. Mr. and Mrs. Nathan O'Toole."

"O'Toole? Never heard that name before."

"That's 'cause Roxie and y'granny has gone by the name of Moon for as long as I can remember."

Short and trim, her long hair parted down the middle and braided, Granny wears a long, plain dress. She's standing behind a beefy man in a black suit. He sits erect, grim, cross-legged, a hat on his knee. The backdrop is a realistic painting of the Taj Mahal in India. At first glance, one might think the couple were on vacation, that they'd stopped to catch their breath in the palace's driveway. A moment of harmony frozen in time.

Elijah's eyes mist up. He clears his throat. "Ain't she the purtiest thing?"

"And you met her when?"

"We was fifteen. Me and m'family moved to Bigstick, Arkansas, and m'daddy got hired on at Thomas O'Toole's Chicken Farm. Mr. Thomas was a big-hearted Irishman. He let us stay in a nice little house on the premises. Sophie's folks, the Moons, worked there too. Had a lot of their own tools and an old tractor. Rented a small place down the road."

The coffeepot's percolating. The unmistakable aroma of Maxwell House coffee wafts up my nose. "And you and Granny fell in love?"

"Couldn't stand being apart. Couldn't think of anyone else. We met behind a neighbor's barn every opportunity to kiss and cuddle and make plans—nothin' else. The world was different back then. Young folk had more respect for themselves and each other. When a fella's motor started racing, he turned off the ignition, that simple—'cause if his daddy heard otherwise, he'd make an earnest attempt to beat the brains outa his head. Most of the time, me and Sophie dreamed. Dreamed of the house we'd live in, the kids we'd have, the crops we'd grow—but it was all empty, foolish talk. Deep down, I think we both suspected nothing would ever come of it. The Moons were full-blood Cherokee, at least her daddy was. Proud folk, they were—but they figured a Nigrah farmhand wadn't much better than a thievin' dog, 'specially when the only things my kin laid claim to were the clothes on their back and a coupla cook pots."

"And Nathan?"

"He was Thomas O'Toole's only son. Mean sonovabitch, and God won't mind me saying so, either. Inherited everything when Mr. Thomas died, including coupla hundred acres of prime bottom. Then, outa the blue, Mr. Nathan offers five of them acres and a coupla mules to Mr. and Mrs. Moon in return for a bride—Sophie. The idea of becoming landowners must've staggered 'em, and a deal was struck. Well, Sophie and me thought the world had ended, and in a way it had."

Elijah wanders into the kitchen while I rifle through sepia-toned photos. In one, Granny gazes down at the baby in her arms. She looks overwhelmed and scared. On the back, in Elijah's writing, it says SOPHIE AND BABY ROXIE. There are other photos of an American Indian couple with three small children. On the back of one is written DEACON AND SARAH MOON WITH CHILDREN. RUTH, JAKE AND SOPHIE. BIGSTICK, ARKANSAS, SEPTEMBER 1938. My great-grandparents stare defiantly, not to mention a mite suspiciously, into the camera's cold eye—chins raised, shoulders squared, as if they knew a day would come when kin would examine them through a magnifying glass, searching for flaws. They are beautiful. He's darker than she is.

Another faded photo shows eight young men, a mix of blacks and Indians, gathered outside a barn. On the back, Elijah has written ME, FRONT ROW LEFT. Good-looking, fifteen or sixteen years old, wide-shouldered and muscular, he stands out from the others because he's not smiling. Thought posing for a photograph was beneath his dignity, is my guess. More pictures of Granny with Nathan O'Toole and an older woman. His mother, maybe.

Elijah returns with two cups of steaming coffee. "Soon as y'granny wed, she moved in with Mr. Nathan and his mother. She birthed Roxie nine months later, and right away took sick and turned strange. I'd see her sitting at one window or another staring at the clouds like she was reading a magazine. 'She's either stubborn or crazy,' Mr. Nathan would say. 'Don't talk to no one 'cept herself.' Poor little thing *always* had a mess o' bruises or a black eye, and we all suspected Mr. Nathan beat her when the fancy took him. Some folks thought he had a right, that she only pretended not to recognize him, or anyone else, not even her baby. Next thing I hear, she's in Little Rock getting *treatments*."

"The lobotomy?"

He stares into space, shudders. "Not sure what they did. Someone said they drilled a hole in her brain. I do know she come home worse—a child who recollected only two words of Cherokee. But I think her sickness started long 'fore she had the baby. Could've bin Mr. Nathan threw her up against the wall one too many times. Anyways, I was so crazy worrying about her, my folks threatened to pack up and go north. They'd guessed, y'see, how I felt about Sophie, and they feared Mr. Nathan would find out—that he'd get rid of me, one way or t'other. Then, one hot day as I'm stacking firewood near the O'Tooles' back door, Sophie races outside, screaming at the top of her lungs, and Mr. Nathan's on her heels, yelling and cussing and waving a knife, so I take off after them, right into a cornfield, and—" He stops short, catches his breath, and his eyes tear up as if the incident occurred just yesterday.

I put my arm around his shoulders, squeeze tight. "It's all right, Elijah, it's all right. Don't tell me if you don't want to."

He keeps shaking his head. "No, no, no, you have a right to know these things."

"So tell me. It can't be that bad."

"It is," he says, "it is. Y'see, half a dozen other fieldhands heard the commotion, and when they found us, Sophie was covered in blood, her hands and arms cut from defending herself—and Mr. Nathan was on the ground, a knife buried to the hilt in his belly, dead as they come."

"Oh, no."

"Ever'one understood, o'course, on account of Sophie not being in her right mind. The sheriff, the county prosecutor, even Mr. Nathan's mother didn't hold it against her. Fact is, the old lady raised y'momma till she hooked up with Hank Stone and they headed for Oklahoma—and when Mrs. O'Toole made 'em take Granny along, I followed."

"And Granny never remembered any of this?"

"Not a minute of it. Even back then, them darned frogs were more real to her than any breathing person. You wouldn't believe the times I've showed her these pictures, told her over and over who the folks were, that they're her heritage, that they were fine people, but nothing registered." He slips the photos back inside the envelope. "And why would I expect anythin' else? She never remembered me from one day t'the next for the next sixty-odd years."

"Is that what this is all about, Elijah? The fact that you loved Granny with all your heart and she—"

He throws the envelope across the room, spilling its contents. Tears stream down his face. "What this is all about," he mutters, "is the truth, and the truth is, God help me, when I struggled with Mr. Nathan for the knife, it ended up in his belly."

The room spins. I stare into Elijah's chocolate-brown eyes and see his pain—it sits right up front. How did this precious soul carry such a secret all these years? I pull him to my breast and rock him back and forth as we cry together.

How often, I wonder, has this role been reversed? Countless times, including the time Momma locked me and Rhonda outa the house and Rhonda got stung by hornets—and the time Momma said, "Next time you bust in on me and Uncle Jim, I'll serve you for lunch at the gator farm."

The Midnight Freight

. . . .

I'm still in shock and my head is spinning. I barely remember the drive home. The kids have left a note. "We're at the drugstore. Back soon XOXO."

I call Brandy. "She's not here, and I don't know why," the shampoo girl says. "She called here fifteen minutes ago, bawling."

I phone Brandy at home, but she's sobbing so hard I can't understand her. "A venereal infection," she shouts into the receiver. "A simple checkup, that's all I asked for, and he says I've got a venereal infection. Can you fucking well believe it?"

"I'll be right over."

"Says I should be checked for HIV, can you fucking well believe it?" she asks again. "Can you?"

"No, I can't," I reply, but I can. A woman lets a man rush into her life like a whirlwind—lets him catch her up and spin her around so hard she loses her balance and plunges headlong into Disney World. And if that's not enough, she falls back and opens up her legs like he's the remote and she's the VCR. I know. I've done the same thing myself.

When I arrive at Brandy's duplex, her car's gone. God knows where she's at or what frame of mind she's in.

I spend the rest of the day working on the Lincoln Center Gown.

Trying to, anyway. Elijah's confession and Brandy's problem have turned my brain to mush. I feel as if I'm in a nursery rhyme—like I'm one of the king's men and I'm trying to fit all the broken pieces together in the hopes I can put Humpty Dumpty together again—that I'll see someone I recognize: Granny tending her frogs. Elijah stirring turnip greens, testing the "pot likker" with a wad of corn bread. Rhonda before she married, before she took sick. Brandy dancing her fool head off at the Dance Barn. Spirit on Main Street, waiting for me under the streetlight.

I fix tacos for the kids' supper. Me and Jessie pick at our food, nudge it around the plate. Pearl, on the other hand, eats like a farmhand and asks for seconds—an encouraging sign. She showers at nine. Smelling sweet as a baby, she makes a fuss of Jessie before she climbs in bed with me and cuddles up.

Out of the semidarkness, Jessie's voice comes high and clear. "God bless Mommy, Grandma Roxie, Elijah, Darling Darla, Pearl, and me—and give Granny Moon a nice soft bed and keep everyone we know safe from harm, amen."

"Amen," says Pearl.

I wake from a deep sleep, gasping. Some monster has sucked the last dab of oxygen from my lungs. The phone rings as the midnight freight roars through town.

"Come right away," the nurse says. "Rhonda's disappeared."

Here and There

. . . .

The midnight freight scattered Rhonda's body for close to half a mile.
Why in God's name do I want details?

> You found her where?
> On the tracks.
> On the tracks?
> Between Paradise and Layton, ma'am.
> Exactly where between Paradise and Layton, you ignorant
> sonovabitch?

The uniform shifts from one foot to the other.

> Here and there, ma'am, here and there.
> Where?
> On the tracks.
> On the tracks?
> Between Paradise and Layton, ma'am.
> Exactly where between Paradise and Layton, you ignorant
> sonovabitch?
> Here and there, ma'am, here and there.

Proof? Rhonda's tennis shoes, in pieces.

Like an old black-and-white horror movie, I run the scene through my head over and over again. Rhonda's mouth moves, but it's out of sync with the soundtrack as the midnight freight thunders through Paradise, its shiny, double-edged wheels thick with blood.

Here and there, ma'am. Here and there.

My brain explodes. The world shuts down.

Where the hell is the justice? What'll I tell the kids? And why, God, didn't you wake me when, like a dream I'd already dreamed, my sister slipped from her bed and wandered into the night?

The Ponderosa Motel

. . . .

"Why, why, why?" I ask no one in particular, and Elijah replies, "God sometimes takes the sweetest flower in the garden, baby girl."

"Then He's one selfish sonovabitch."

The air is bitter, too thick and contaminated with suffering and tears to inhale. No purse, no hat, no jewelry, only the unbearable weight of misery pressing down. Spirit emerges from where dreams are born, dark and warm, face damp, his eyes squeezed tight against my pain. His wide shoulders form a barrier between me and those who wail and sob and wring their hands. Elijah, Jessie, Momma, Muff, Freda, Miss Cissy, Cindy Harker. Brandy, pale as flour and oozing Opium, says, "Don't worry, you'll get through this, y'hear?" and Shamir is barely visible in the dark recesses.

"Don't tell them," a woman screams. "Don't tell Pearl and Jessie their momma's gone," and Spirit says, "Hush, Darla, hush. Just tell me what I can do."

I float through door 24. Is that an important number, I wonder? Inside, between cool sheets, I struggle for air and swim against a roaring tide—vaguely aware of the familiar beige lamp shade and the cowboy print on the wall. The name Billy Joe snags in my throat. My God, my God, my God. What did I do, what did I do?

Spirit towers over me, dabs away tears and blots out the light, shuts out all sound, says my name over and over and over again.

"Just love me," I tell him. "Just love me."

Here and there, ma'am. Here and there.

The Truth Shall Set You Free

No one has seen or heard from Frank 'cept Mardel. She met up with Miss Cissy in the grocery store and said Frank stayed drunk, that he couldn't keep his eyes open long enough to find his truck keys, let alone drive, that he got more depressed when his dog died, and he was broke.

Well, he must've found some change, 'cause when I looked down on Main Street this morning, there he stood, staring up at my window, a piss-poor attitude in a wrinkled shirt. He took a long drag on a cigarette, ground it into the pavement, and with a smile, strutted back to his truck. Soon as he drove off, I phoned Elijah.

"When a wolf shows his teeth, he sure ain't laughing," he said, which gave me no consolation whatsoever.

But that which once seemed irreparably torn apart miraculously came together again, melded like warm wax, became recognizable. I can distinguish light from dark, sweet from sour, hot from cold, and I can listen to Pavarotti without crying. Last night, the moon descended in a perfect arc, and when the sun rose like a beacon, I felt the familiar pull of unknown places and people. But it is Pearl and Jessie who get me up and going.

Pearl dunks an Oreo into a full cup of milk, gobbles down the cookie, and looks at me. Barefoot, her hair still wet from the shower, she says, "Momma's probably better off. She's with Granny Sophie, and she's not hurting anymore—isn't that right, Aunt Darla?"

I dry the last dish and put it in the cupboard, hang up a clean tea towel. "Absolutely right. She's not hurting, and Granny Sophie's mind is sharp as a tack. I bet they're having a fine old time."

She smiles, the first time in ages, and takes another cookie from the jar. "And she's bound to be happy—'cause we're with you, right?"

"Right."

"Can I spend the night with Elijah?" Jessie asks.

"Sure."

"And can we eat lunch at the Dead Bolt Cafe instead of here?"

"Thought you'd never ask."

His tummy full of pancakes and bacon, Jessie swings around and around on Elijah's old tire. Feet dragging, he starts and stops, starts and stops, his tennies stirring up dust clouds.

Stretched out on an old quilt, Pearl keeps her eye on him. Thank God they're not in here listening to this news bulletin.

Momma resembles a garage sale on its third and last day. Mismatched and frayed at the edges, she sits on Elijah's couch next to a spotless Miss Cissy.

"You were too young," Momma says, her voice smoky. "Too little to be told anything."

"And now I'm almost thirty I'm old enough?"

"Too young to understand, I mean."

"Understand what?"

"That I didn't do it on purpose, that your daddy was drunk and fell off the steps on the way out—hit his head."

"I'll never know why she called me," Miss Cissy says. "And she didn't either. Claimed her fingers walked straight to my number."

Momma stiffens. "Never said no such thing,"

"If she'd done told me on the phone what was going on," Miss Cissy adds, "I'd have called the police, 'cause that kinda secret fixes you to a place. Leave Paradise with that on y'conscience and it'd drag behind you like a sack o' rotten potatoes the rest of y'life."

"She begged us," Elijah says, nodding in agreement, "and considering what'd happened in Arkansas, I daren't call the authorities 'case they started nosing around and asking questions."

"Wouldn't have called anyone if I could've moved him by myself," Momma says. "He must've weighed two hundred, and there he was, bottom of the porch steps, late Saturday night, where Lamb o' God would see him Sunday morning. It just happened, you know?"

"Just happened," echoes Miss Cissy. "That's what she said when I got here."

Elijah buries his head in his hands. "That's exactly what she said."

I can't believe what I'm hearing. "Just happened? Too much salt in the potatoes just happens. Mustard on a shirt just happens. A man buried twenty years 'neath a goldenrain tree in the front yard is something else altogether."

"Sump'n else altogether," Elijah agrees, "but if a man's to sleep nights he don't dare put a name to it."

Miss Cissy clears her throat. "Amen to that."

Try as I may to absorb what they're telling me, my brain is too full of other things. "Y'know it's strange. I've waited years for an answer, waited and waited to meet up with a daddy I never knew, and now that the truth is out, all that longing's gone outa me. Truth is, I couldn't care less if ten men are buried under that tree. All I can think of is, Granny and Rhonda are gone."

Elijah pats my knee. "I'm as sorry as I can be, Darla."

"For Pearl and Jessie's sake, I've got to get on with my life. Besides, who's to say the man under that tree is m'real father? Could've been any man that came and went through our front door. Could've been one of those men you drove off with, Momma. So what did I miss?

Nothing, that's what I think. Can't put no price on the love me and Rhonda got from Elijah, 'cause it's priceless."

Elijah pats my knee again. "Thank you, baby."

"Know what, though, Momma? I can forgive you for almost everything, 'cept you involved two law-abiding folk in your crime."

"Weren't no crime, the man fell," Momma says.

"That's what you say. But who's to say you didn't have a fight, that you didn't grab that old baseball bat, that a well-aimed blow to the skull didn't kill him?"

Elijah and Miss Cissy look shocked. "What baseball bat?"

"The one I found down by the Rattler that Momma kept in the kitchen behind the trash can, the one that disappeared on Halloween. What happened to that bat, Momma? You never did say."

She narrows her eyes, looks at me like I'm from another planet, and quick as a pulse beat jumps to her feet. One hand on the doorknob, she points a blood-red nail in my direction.

"Before you heat up the tar and feathers, remember one thing," she says. "If I drown, Elijah and Miss Cissy drown with me."

"I know."

She opens the door, stares toward Lamb of God, and starts coughing, a deep chesty bark that turns her face red.

"Truth of the matter is," she says, when she recovers, "you and Rhonda needed more than I had to give. Christ, I know I was a terrible mother, but—"

"Don't dare use His name in this house, Roxie," Elijah snaps. "Hard for me to believe the Christ I know is the same one you're suddenly so crazy about."

"But I kept a roof over y'heads," she goes on, "and if I could do it over I'd do different. I'd make my kids proud."

That's the closest I'll ever get to an admission of guilt or an apology—and for the briefest of moments my heart softens round the edges. "But why?" I ask. "Why that life?"

She clears her throat. "Hell, I don't know. I've straddled the fence somewhere between shit and shit all my life. Told m'self I was m'own boss, obliged to nobody, that it was exciting and glamorous—even as m'customers spit out plugs o' tobacco. Hell, even the best of 'em got on my nerves, 'specially when their false teeth clicked."

In the uncomfortable silence that follows, as the jarring ring of katydids slices the air, Elijah and Miss Cissy sit stone-faced and silent. They're digesting the baseball bat, the plugs of tobacco, and the clicking teeth, I reckon.

"Things happen," Momma adds, with a shrug. "Life's cruel. People come, people go, Darla. But you know what gives a woman the most pain? It's learning to live without the one person who made life worth living in the first place."

I'm tempted to comfort her, and though something tells me I might not see her again, I decide against it.

She closes the door and shuffles across the porch and down the steps in her rubber thongs. I watch her still-shapely legs disappear inside the Pontiac. Windows down, she revs the engine. Her hair blows every which way in the crosswind, and she drives off dabbing her face with a tissue. Tears? Unlikely. My guess is, a speck of dust flew in her eye.

Tit for Tat

. . . .

I'm asleep and dreaming—or am I? The moon dangles from the ceiling by a spider's thread, and night has tucked me into its fuzzy blanket like a worried mother. The smell, however, a mixture of rain and earth, is tainted by another—something dark and unpleasant. A phantomlike shadow blows on my forehead. A southern breeze, I tell myself. North winds are rough and cold and they mess up my hair.

A hand slams against my mouth, smothers me. My eyes spring open to a blinding light. The taste of copper floods my teeth and gums, pools in my left cheek.

"Make one sound," the man says, "and I'll slit y'throat here and now."

It's Frank. My chest explodes with fear, knowing Pearl and Jessie are just feet away—until I remember they're safe at Elijah's.

Frank turns off his flashlight, fumbles in the dark, knocks my alarm clock to the floor, flicks on the bedside lamp. God help me. His eyes are clear and focused. He's sober.

His right fist arcs down, impacts my left cheek. Pain shoots through my face. Gurgling sounds bubble up and out of my throat. My ears ring. The room spins.

"Scream and I'll slice you into little pieces. Do you hear me? Tell me you hear me, bitch."

I nod frantically.

The next blow falls short of my cheek, slams into my jaw. I swallow the blood along with the groans in my throat—hammer a scream so deep in my chest no one can hear it but me.

"I've got a name, bitch. Say 'I hear you, Frank.'"

"I hear you, Frank," I mumble. "Honest to God, I hear you."

"Don't mention God, you no-good whore, 'cause he ain't here. It's just you and me, and when this night's over, it'll just be me."

He flips me over, rams my head into the pillow. Ice-cold steel moves against my spine. Snip, snip. He's got my scissors. He's cutting off my nightgown. I'm naked underneath. I hear his zipper. He's struggling with his pants. He's going to rape me.

"Made a fool of me, you know that, don'tcha? Put a gun to m'head and walked outa jail like all you'd done was spit on dirt."

My brain scrambles around, searching for all those tips on self-preservation I'd learned from Oprah. One thing's for sure, flat on my stomach like this, I can't poke him in the eyes or kick him in the balls.

"Turned m'wife against me, got me so fired up I messed with a kid, can't get welfare, and no one'll give me a job."

I make a futile attempt to roll on my back, but he grabs me by the hair, hits the back of my head with his open hand—hits me again and again before he clambers on top of me and straddles my butt. I'm dizzy. He brushes his penis back and forth against my skin. What if I fall unconscious and never wake up?

"No-good bitch. Sleeps with anything that walks but turns her nose up at me."

He grunts and groans, rubs and rubs, cusses under his breath. Starts cutting again. Cut, cut, snip, snip, like my nightgown's twelve feet long—'cept the sound's different. Clumps of something fall on my cheek and on the bed. Hair, my hair, piles up on the sheet. Frank's penis stirs, stiffens against my backside. Tears roll down my face. He emits a low, animal moan, hisses through his teeth—grabs a handful of hair and pulls so hard I squeal with pain. He drops the scissors and slides his free hand under my belly so's he can jerk up my hips. His stubbled chin feels like sandpaper against my right shoulder. The stink of his foul breath and sour stomach rushes up my nose and slams into my brain.

"I promise you one thing, you ratty-headed whore," Frank hisses. "When you die, when you take your last breath, I'm gonna hold your eyes open so the last thing you see is *me*."

Then, from out of nowhere, a familiar voice whispers in my ear. "Lie here, die here, Darla. Rise up victorious," it says, and I move my right hand down, close to my knee. I find the scissors, grasp the handle, rear up and back with every ounce of strength I can muster, and swing the weapon over my right shoulder. They hit, sink in. I pull them out, jab again and again. Frank falls between me and the wall, screaming. I roll off the bed, grab the lamp cord and pull it from the socket. I'm headed for the front door. I fall over a chair. Frank groans, scrambles in the dark—and I'm on my feet. The overhead light comes on and Frank, wearing a ripped T-shirt, his pants around his ankles, is just four or five feet away, finger on the light switch. Blood pours from the wounds in his shoulder. He's ashen. Behind him, near the bed, is Shamir, wings spread up and out.

My nightgown slips from my shoulders to the floor. Dazed and winded, I slump against the wall, the scissors behind my back. I'm shaky, but I'm alert.

With his eyes locked on mine, Frank backs up to the recliner, reaches inside his jacket, withdraws something small and shiny, and points it at me. It's a gun. One I've seen before, maybe?

"Hell, I'll just shoot you." He's wild-eyed and gasping for air. "Wipe it clean, put your prints on it, and everyone'll say, 'Miserable, no-good whore couldn't take any more. Went and blew her fuckin' brains out.' What d'ya think of that, huh?"

The anger in his voice prompts me to go with my gut feeling.

"Last man had that gun," I say, low and deliberate, "is the man who took it from me in Woody's Bar with half a dozen witnesses looking on, or have you forgotten?"

He blinks, tries to remember.

"You got that from ol' Leroy, didn't you, Frank? Did he sell it to you? Trade it for something? Think he'll keep quiet to save *your* neck?"

He blinks again—his small doggy brain barely clicking over—unable to comprehend if what I'm saying makes sense or not.

My head feels small, light, and cold—like it belongs to someone else. "And my hair, Frank. Think anyone'll believe I chopped it off before I killed myself?"

Still blinking, he takes a step forward.

"And my scissors, Frank. Where the hell are they, huh? Think you can find 'em 'fore folks come running to see where the shot came from? What happens when they find your prints on 'em alongside mine?"

He sways, falters. With lightning speed I'm on the floor, at his feet. I swing the scissors up, knock the gun from his grasp, and with two frenzied jabs, ram the glittering points first into one thigh then the other. Frank's face registers shock. He looks at the blood gushing from his legs onto the carpet. Eyes bulging, mouth hung open in a silent scream, he grabs his wounds, sinks to his knees, and rolls over.

Naked to the world, I throw open the front door, and without even taking a breath, and with no apparent effort, I grab Frank by the T-shirt and drag him outside. One good push sends him tumbling to the bottom of the stairs. Illuminated by a hundred-watt halogen floodlight, his ass shines like a full moon.

"You sonovabitch, you no-good sonovabitch," I screech till every porch light on Elm goes on—then I dial 911 and scream directions at the operator.

No sign of Shamir, God bless him.

Oil and Water

. . . .

Some guys, and God knows I've had my share, are knockouts, kick-in-the-heart gorgeous—but like Granny said, the good-looking ones think they shit chocolate. Watch them, catch them off guard, see if their faces light up whenever they see a good-looking woman, if, as one walks by, their lusting eyes follow her swinging rear end. If that's what they do, say hello to trouble. Such men are full of themselves, and would, if you lived with them twenty-four hours a day, year in, year out, quickly sour one's disposition. Spirit, however, has no idea how gorgeous, inside and out, he is. Or if he does, he's not impressed by the fact.

Room 24, midday, the Ponderosa Motel, and the curtains are open. Cars and trucks streak by on the highway. If someone did happen by and look in the window, all they'd see is a good-looking man and a woman with short hair curling round her ears, sharing a flask of Maxwell House.

All talked out, I head for the bathroom to stare at my reflection. I run my fingers through my hair. Spirit's right. Frank Slater, may he rot away from the inside out along with Leroy Poteet in that miserable penitentiary, did me a favor. Evened out, the short pixie cut makes me look younger, sassier.

"Okay," Spirit says from the other room. "I get it, I really do.

You've been in this room before. You spent an hour or so with Billy Joe What's-His-Name. You drink the occasional beer with Brandy. You drank harder stuff in the past. You've dated a lot—"

"*A whole lot.*"

"Okay, *a whole lot.* You slept with some—"

"I said I slept with a bunch. A dozen, maybe."

"Okay, so you slept with a dozen, maybe more," he comes back. "So what? Don't see wings on my back, do you?"

I turn off the bathroom light, march right back in and sit on the bed—stare him in the eye. "Do you have any idea why I laid my soul bare?"

"None whatsoever."

"Take a guess."

"You thought I'd hear it from someone else? Confession is good for the soul? You want my forgiveness? God's forgiveness? I don't know."

"You thought all those things, didn't you?"

"No, I—"

"Didn't you?"

"Well, it occurred to me that—"

"Got nothing to do with forgiveness, certainly not yours. I just wanted you to know everything about me."

"Nothing wrong with that."

"No, nothing wrong with it, but like I said on our first date, we're oil and water, you and me, and when we hit a rocky place, as most married folk do, you might be tempted to bring up Billy Joe Comfort's name, and the drinking, and the men I've slept with."

"I used to drink, I've slept with other women. I'm not a saint. Besides, I begged you not to tell me all those things. I didn't want to know."

"Wouldn't be right if you didn't."

He throws up his hands in desperation. Paces back and forth

between the two queen-size beds. "Darla, go on this mission to Australia with me. We can work through it. We'll have a great life together, I promise."

"You're a wonderful man, Spirit, the best. I may never find another like you, but—"

"But—?"

"I've got kids to raise."

"We'll raise them together."

"There's gowns and suits dancing round my head, begging for pencil and paper."

"You want a career? I won't stand in your way."

"One foot in New York and the other in Australia, huh?"

"If anyone can do it, you can."

"Remember," I add, feeling my heart break, "when the going got tough, I jumped in bed with an old friend."

"For an hour," he says. "What's an hour? I've had headaches longer than that," and I recall that first night, how handsome he looked in the half-light of Main Street—how we walked side by side, careful not to touch—how till Granny died, he came to mind the minute I awoke each morning, and stayed on my mind till I drifted off to sleep.

My heart leaps as I recall our first kiss, the first time we made love in my apartment—and something Momma said echoes in my head.

You know what gives a woman the most pain? Learning to live without the one person who made life worth living in the first place.

"Please," Spirit says. "We love each other. With God's help we can make it." But I don't answer. Instead, I grab my purse and rush past him. "You'll thank me for this one day, Spirit. God-fearing churchgoers won't tolerate a preacher's wife who swigs beer, wears shorts and halter tops, and cusses. And can you imagine the scandal when her and the local mechanic—? Well, it doesn't bear thinking about, does it?"

He follows me. "You're a three-alarm fire, Darla Moon," he says as I start the car. "You light up my life, you make my bells ring—and no matter what you think, this isn't the end of it by a long shot."

I drive off honking the horn and bawling my eyes out. I catch sight of Spirit in the rearview mirror. He's where I left him, outside room 24, waving.

Too vulnerable for Pavarotti, I switch on the radio, and Barry Manilow sings, "And when will I see you again?"

New York, New York

· ·

It is lovely—the ferocious nip in the air. A body can breathe and think and feel alive on a morning like this. The sky is clear as an ice cube, and a northwest wind slaps my face with its wide hand. Last night, Gary England announced the first major winter storm of the season. He said it had summoned strength and formed a head of steam that stretched across Montana and the Dakotas, and was headed this way. Tonight, snow flurries will dust the panhandle. Tomorrow, an "Arctic Express" will barrel across the plains and bury Paradise in a deep, deep freeze.

A flock of Canadian geese skims the treetops, all of them honking, it seems. Fleeing the peril, they head south in a perfect V formation, the sound of their wings barely audible. Their excitement, their desire to escape, is contagious. The fire that rages in their breasts is the same one raging in mine.

Pearl and Jessie say December is the worst time for me to go—that I should wait till after Christmas. Elijah says it's the best time, seeing as I should have left in September and I'm already late. Me? I'm ready. I've talked with Gerald D'Angelo so many times, I feel like we're old friends. He wants me. I want the job. Besides, soon as I settle in and find us a place to live, which'll be a month or two at the most, Elijah and the kids will join me.

I ease into old Doc Hartley's gravel driveway and park near the newly painted house. Empty paint cans and rolls of plastic sheeting are stacked against the wall behind the lilac bush. I walk round front, climb the porch steps, and peek in the window. The waiting room is now a jumble of sawhorses, paint, varnish cans, and more plastic sheeting. Rolls of wallpaper stacked in the corner—some have flowery patterns, others are covered with lambs and rabbits and birds. Young family moving in.

I think of Spirit—how, if this were our house, we would have picked out the paint and wallpaper together, painted and pasted together, had a picnic in the midst of it all, and made love on the floor afterward. Could still happen—couldn't it?

Last time I came here, nine years ago, the room was filled with hacking, sneezing patients—half of them children. Up on the table, my feet in stirrups, with old Doc Hartley's bald head nodding between my thighs, I learned I was pregnant. I returned that night for "the procedure." I parked round back, rapped on the rear door, and a light came on. Fifteen minutes later, Mandy was gone.

A shutter rattles. A board creaks. The apple tree in the middle of the front yard shivers with cold. I feel Mandy nearby. The tiny phantom skips across the porch and stirs up a flurry of crisp brown lilac leaves, blows on my cheek, kisses it, and giggling with impish delight, she grabs the wind by the tail and flies south.

Everyone shows up for the farewell breakfast at Elijah's. Everyone, that is, 'cept Momma.

The kids are in the kitchen with Elijah. Pearl's slicing a honey-baked ham, Jessie's cutting biscuits with a juice glass, and Elijah's stirring redeye gravy with a wooden spoon. Every now and then, he dips in a finger for a taste. Seeing the three of them together like this—the way he keeps hugging Pearl and tussles Jessie's hair—stirs memories. I see how the kids look at him, their eyes full of love, how he jokes with them. He's calling Pearl "baby girl," so I'm not sure if I've been demoted or promoted. Years ago, that kitchen, and the man who runs it, was me and Rhonda's world. Now it's Pearl and Jessie's world. For a while, anyway.

Muff and Freda show up with scrambled eggs, scones, and home-made strawberry jam. Brandy brings a crock pot of black-eyed peas and a pan of jalapeño corn bread. Miss Cissy totes in her famous pork chops and fried okra, and places her mile-high peach cobbler center stage on the kitchen table. Billy Joe arrives with cinnamon rolls, still hot from the bakery.

Everyone's eating and laughing, stepping around the table to get a little of this and a tad of that, hugging and smiling, and I can't help but wonder if I know what the hell I'm doing. Is it possible that everything I've ever wanted has been here in front of my nose all along—that I just didn't see it? I mean, an outsider looking in might say, "Okay, so things were rough at times and there's rotten apples on every tree, and Paradise is sinking fast, but only a fool would leave folks like this behind," and they could be right. They could be wrong, too. All I know is, I must find out for myself.

Straight up noon, Elijah, the kids, and I squeeze into Elijah's truck. Will Rogers World Airport is close to an hour away. I photograph my entire life through the truck's side window. One click, two clicks, is all it takes. Muff, Freda, Brandy, Miss Cissy, Billy Joe, Elijah's place, Miss Ladybug, and Lamb of God. Beyond the church, the Rattler goes about its business. Land flat as a tabletop. Scrubby pin oaks. These people and this place have shaped my life. Fitted together like so many puzzle pieces, we all made a picture that I'll love and remember for all time.

I try my damnedest not to cry, but I am suddenly humbled by the thought that, despite all the tragedies, despite all of Paradise's faults, this dot on the map gave me a front-row seat to some incredible magic.

No sign of Shamir, but he'll show up when I least expect him at D'Angelo Designs—or onstage at Lincoln Center, alongside Pavarotti.

With my one-way ticket in my purse and my luggage under a tarp in back, me and Rhonda head out. Cremated in the Lincoln Center Gown, she'll travel in a Bolton's top-of-the-line Grecian urn, packed 'neath my undies. Come spring, I'll set her free in the Atlantic Ocean. She'll like that.

As we pull onto the blacktop, I glance at the goldenrain tree—at Momma's place. Elijah reaches across the kids and taps my hand. "Don't ever look back, Darla," he says, but it's too late.

Her blinds are closed. Nothing's stirring. And the Coors beer truck hasn't moved. It's where it was last night, in her driveway. Proving, among other things, that Momma always did have a mighty big thirst.